THE END OF SUNSHINE STREET

A NOVEL BY
JOHANNA CONSTANCE HUNT

Copyright © 2012 Johanna Constance Hunt
All rights reserved.
ISBN: 1466360046
ISBN 13: 9781466360044
Library of Congress Control Number: 2011917395
CreateSpace, North Charleston, SC

To Amos & Andie and in memory of my mother,
June Eleanor Ebbeson Hunt Bailey

PROLOGUE

The train was supposed to leave at 6:00 a.m. and it was now nearly seven. Judy leaned her aching head against the large cold window, stared out at the fog, and sighed. She was usually a cheerful morning person, but this trip was not running according to plan.

She'd come to Peru to hike the Inca Trail to Machu Picchu, a rigorous five-day trip—it was on her life list as a "must do", along with walking the Great Wall of China and hiking across Scotland. Despite her adventurous goals, at forty Judy was still a travel coward. She'd never been out of the country alone, so she had convinced her brother, Frank, and his wife, Mary Lee, to come with her; the three of them had climbed in the Alps and on several sections of the Appalachian Trail and made a pretty good team. They each had a role: Frank managed logistics; Judy was in charge of food, flora, and fauna; and Mary Lee—a beautiful multilingual blonde—was the one they sent for help whenever they got in a jam.

Just three days before, they'd met their guide, four porters, and twelve fellow hikers in Cuzco, the ancient capital of the Incan Empire. It had taken forever to stuff gear and passengers into a tiny bus. Cuzco was at 11,500 feet and Machu Picchu at 8,200 feet; the bus trip involved going farther up into the Andes before winding down to the valley below, where the hiking would start. Everywhere they marveled at the surrounding steep-sided mountains. Judy was in heaven—despite having a fierce headache from the altitude.

Hours later the crowded bus was hot and smelly as it crept down a narrow, twisting, unpaved road to the trailhead in a canyon near Tambobamba. In the rush to get outside, someone pushed into Mary Lee and she slipped on the wet steps, landing with her knee bent at an odd angle. Usually a stoic, Mary Lee's whimpers changed to a piercing screech when Frank tried to straighten her leg. The group finally left without them, and Frank had to pay the bus driver to take them back to town.

The driver dropped them off at a small modern clinic. The doctor gave Mary Lee morphine and was able to straighten her leg and tape it into a brace. He advised them to bypass Lima and go right back to the States for surgery. Mary Lee and Frank flew back to Boston the same day, while Judy stayed in Cuzco. Still determined to see Machu Picchu, she bought day-trip tickets for the train and for the Machu Picchu site.

She shivered. It was cold—fifty or so—and raining, and the train wasn't heated. The clouds were so low, it seemed as if they were settled on the plains, not high in the mountains. It was January and the rainy season; they had to come now because of Frank's schedule.

Judy's car was nearly full, but the seat next to her was still empty. Just as the train pulled out of the station, a man claimed the seat and spent some time digging a guidebook out of his backpack before settling down. They nodded to each other, and Judy returned to staring out the window at the rain.

Lulled by the train's movement, Judy began to relax. She'd been anxious taking the trip alone, but found she was less lonely than when she was with Frank and Mary Lee. With them she was always the odd man out, and she'd become aware of a growing "spinster pity" by them both.

The man next to her smelled nice, a clean, soapy smell. He wore tropical-weight cargo pants, khaki T-shirt, and a worn blue canvas shirt. His hiking boots were similar to hers: brown, lightweight Gor-Tex, though his had seen more miles than hers. She smiled as she realized that his shopping must've been done at L.L.Bean, where she bought all her brothers' Christmas gifts and her own hiking clothes.

She turned to look at him again, and he caught her.

"Hi." His eyes were blue. A light color but intensely blue.

"Hi."

"I'm Sam."

Judy giggled. "Sorry…was thinking 'I'm Sam I am'. I'm Judy."

"Pleased to meet you."

"Me too."

"Are you traveling by yourself?"

"Yes. You?"

"No. With a bunch of guys I knew from college. They haven't changed much—they drank all night. I left them in the rear car to sober up."

"Have you been here before?"

"No. But always wanted to. One of my friends has a travel agency—he called with this reunion plan, and I couldn't pass it up. It wasn't until I got here that I discovered the mountains are under water in January—but I'm still glad I came."

"Yeah. I'm afraid I didn't do any weather research myself. But I'll be happy just to see the site."

Sam opened his backpack and took out a stainless steel vacuum bottle. "Coffee?"

"I'd love some."

"I'm afraid I put a big slug of pisco in it. It's that grape brandy."

"All the better." Judy smiled.

Sam pulled out two plastic cups from his backpack and filled them with the steaming coffee.

Judy sniffed, then sipped. "Yum."

Sam chuckled.

"What's so funny?"

"Your sniffing the coffee. My wife used to call me a dog when I did that."

"My mother makes fun of me too. But I can't help it. It's just the way I eat."

"I only brought coffee. The brochure said there'd be food for sale on the train, but I didn't see anything worth eating back there."

"I checked into that yesterday, so loaded up with food in town this morning. I have some papa rellena and empanada. And some pastries. Want to try them?"

"Sure you have enough?"

"I'm sure. I couldn't make up my mind, so I bought a little of everything." Judy pulled an insulated bag from under her seat.

Sam looked like a man at a jewelry counter, eyes exploring each item. "What's this one?"

"A meat empanada. The papa rellena are these potatoes—they're stuffed with meat, cheese, and olives. I tried one a few days ago and have been eating them ever since. Try one. Oh, and the other things are all pastries, I think. I'm horrible at foreign languages. Feel so stupid. I even had trouble in England."

Sam chose the potato and took a big bite. Bits of it fell down his shirt. "God, this potato is wonderful! Being from Maine, it's one of my favorite foods anyway, but this is extraordinary."

"You're from Maine. Where?"

"Northeast Harbor. It's…"

"Oh, I know. I'm from Bangor, but I've been pretty much everywhere in the state."

"You still live there?"

"No. Moved to Florida quite a while ago. You?"

"I'm still in Maine. Have a small business in Hancock."

Sam bit into an empanada. "Wow. This is good too. We've been staying at hotels that have mostly Euro-American food. I haven't had anything to eat I can't find right at home. Which is a shame. I've tried to get the guys to be more adventuresome, but they're afraid of getting sick."

"You'll have to try cuy."

"What's that?"

"Guinea pig."

"I'm afraid I'll have to pass; they used to be my patients."

"Hunh?"

"I'm a veterinarian. Used to have a private practice. Guinea pigs were steady customers."

"So are you a vegetarian?"

"Nope. I cared for regular family pets…no farm animals. I think I'd still eat meat though—even if I worked at a slaughterhouse."

Sam poured more coffee for them both. "This is all so good. I hope I can find recipes for these things when I get back."

"You cook?" Judy was smitten.

"At first I was just an eater. Then I read cookbooks for years. It wasn't until I got divorced that I really started cooking. Now I guess you could call me a full-blown foodie." Sam shrugged his shoulders, grinning sheepishly.

"I'm the same. I went to France a couple of years ago for a month. A few days after I got back, my boss screamed at me, 'Didn't you do *anything* but eat?'"

Sam laughed. "Some people just don't understand."

Judy daydreamed. Sam seemed like such a nice man. He looked older than she but maybe...? She shook her head. What a useless way to think. Every year or so, she'd meet a man and imagine marrying him. But it never happened. Usually it ended with light banter in a waiting line or doctor's office, not even an invitation for coffee.

When they looked at her, could men detect that something was a bit off? She wasn't sure herself what it was except that somehow she *was* different from women she knew. She was at least as good looking and was smart, friendly. But men locked onto other women, not her. Maybe it was just something she picked up from living with her brothers: she treated men as if they were people just like her—while they seemed to want something else. (And more and more, they didn't seem interested in her, just that damn stopwatch—must jump in bed by first, second, or third date) And now she was getting old.

Judy shivered and leaned back in her seat, closed her eyes, and sighed. Oh, well.

CHAPTER 1

Six years later…

Friday, five-thirty. Judy Haite walked quickly toward the door to the parking lot. A part-time employee at the medical center, she was anxious to get home. She and Sam were having a small dinner party, and she still had some work to do to get ready. The outside door swung open.

Phew! She had lived in Florida twelve years now and was still shocked whenever she went from air conditioning to summer air. Early June, and it was already like walking into a lion's mouth—damp, hot, and smelly. And aggressive—the heat didn't just lie there—it attacked.

At least in summer, there weren't any tourists or seasonal people, so traffic was manageable. Driving across the bridge from West Palm, Judy ducked as a tube of lightning hit the water. Another grand display of Florida weather. It had taken years for the Maine native to get used to the thunderstorms here. Now when she visited Maine, the lightning was like little sparklers—it's hard to believe she and her mother used to cower in their cabin at the lake during storms… lights on, radio blaring.

Judy and Sam owned one of the smallest houses in Palm Beach. Built in 1932, the yellow-frame, two-story house on Sunshine Street was at the north end of the barrier island. Running east-west, their street was shaded by a mixture of fifteen-foot hedges and large old trees. The Haites lived on the west end of the street close to the Lake Trail, a paved path along the Intercoastal Waterway. The east end of the street emptied onto the beach and the Atlantic Ocean.

Along the whole street, only five families lived in Palm Beach year-round. The rest usually came down around Thanksgiving and left in April or May. This was the pattern throughout the town—off-season the population of Palm Beach was around ten thousand, while the population exploded to thirty thousand in season, not counting the extra employees of businesses and homes needed to support the influx. In summer during the day, there was still a lot of activity as grounds people and others worked to keep the houses spotless and grounds groomed. At night, however, it was like living on the moon.

When Sam and Judy first moved to Sunshine Street, Sam—the gregarious one—started a tradition of four families getting together several times during the summer. (The fifth family, William "don't call me Bill" Bean and his wife, asked to be excluded from the group. Bean informed Sam that he "socialized" exclusively for his banking business. Apparently Sam's millions weren't enough to bother with.) At first the families rotated hosting these gatherings, but one of the spouses died, one couple got to be what they thought was "too old" and finally, the youngest couple admitted to having no cooking skills whatsoever. So the group now met only at Sam and Judy's, although the others were generous providers of wines and sweets. They also helped Sam and Judy negotiate life on "The Island". This night was the first of their dinners this season.

Judy didn't mind hosting these parties—in the five years since they'd moved to Palm Beach, she'd made no friends there on her own. She'd never felt the need to have more than one or two close friends anyway, but before Sam she often entertained her friends and co-workers with large dinners, being comfortable keeping busy in the kitchen. Since moving to Palm Beach, however, usually Sam and the five neighbors were the only ones in attendance. Sam liked to dine out at restaurants with his Palm Beach acquaintances, and he didn't like her hospital friends, who talked of nothing but their work and hospital gossip.

Judy would be forty-six in December. She was tall—five foot ten—with a slim athletic build. Her face was long and narrow, with brilliant green eyes and a rather beaky nose. In fact, her nickname through high school and college had been Beak. She was not beautiful. Her face was large and would've been pale, except it was almost entirely freckled from the Florida sun. A mouth breather, her "resting" face made her look almost stupid—and it was this face that she wore most often. Judy's most outstanding feature was her hair—a long, lustrous, wavy auburn with gold highlights.

Twelve years before, an executive for a Hollywood wig firm had seen Judy at LaGuardia and asked to buy her hair. At first Judy thought the man had the weirdest pickup line ever, but he turned out to be serious. He put Judy under contract to sell her hair that was used to lengthen the career of an aging movie star. She received a monthly stipend and had her hair "harvested" every three years. Judy enjoyed the sensation of having her hair shorn in early summer—it reminded her of her brothers getting their annual buzz cuts in the backyard at the end of each school year. The additional income allowed her to take vacations all over the world—all she had to do was stay healthy and not abuse her hair. Her hair paid for the trip to Machu Picchu, where she met Sam.

After their meeting on the train, she and Sam had spent the day roaming the eighty-acre site. The cold drizzle finally drove them to a partially roofed stone building, where they huddled over the last of the coffee and Peruvian pastries. They had been drinking the local coca drink for altitude sickness, but Judy's headache persisted until Sam bought some coca leaves from one of the workers. She chewed these for the rest of the visit, and her headaches stopped.

Instead of returning to Cuzco on the train, Sam booked a room at the Sanctuary Lodge, a five-star, twenty-nine-room hotel owned by the Oriental Express, where they spent two days swapping stories and sampling everything on the hotel's menu—even the guinea pig. They had sex on the third day, Judy's shyness finally worn down not by Sam's obvious eagerness but by his patience. On the fourth day, exhausted, they became tourists again and took advantage of the hotel's location right next to the entrance to Macchu Picchu and had a private tour of the ruins.

After six months of telephone calls and e-mails, Sam moved his business down to West Palm Beach and moved in with Judy. Three months later they married.

⁓⁕⁓

Sam had a miracle life of his own. A veterinarian, he was working at a medical research organization in Maine in charge of keeping the animals healthy when one of the cat colonies developed a genetic anomaly; Sam was ordered to destroy the animals. Unable to do this, he took the cats home. He had intended to sterilize them, but before he got around to do it, one pair of cats had kittens, which were miniscule—they grew to only four inches long as adults. Further breeding experiments resulted in "Sam's Pocket Pets". The animals were extremely popular and sold for thousands each. Sam sterilized each cat sold to avoid others breeding them. In time, he knew, others would clone the animals, but he already had amassed enough money for him and Judy to live comfortably for life.

Living comfortably was foreign to them both: their parents were hardworking, barely middle-class Maine people. (In Maine, the Great Depression lingered well beyond the 1930s…Some say it's still there.) Judy and Sam had each worked to pay for college and stayed in their first jobs for years, afraid to tempt fate with any change.

Judy's family kept a large vegetable garden and canned enough to last the winter. Her father fished and hunted to add variety to the only meats they ever bought at the store—hamburger, pig's liver, and bacon. The bacon wasn't the tidy flat package of meat strips—it was a heaping scrambled package of bacon ends, mostly fat. Judy always loved bacon and still adored her Uncle Hiram, who on her fifth birthday presented her with her very own, beautifully wrapped, pound of lean bacon strips. Judy still remembered when, several years after paying off her college loans, she walked into a grocery store and could buy anything she wanted; until recently that was the richest she'd ever felt.

Sam wasn't home yet. Judy drove to the back of the house and parked. She waited for a break in the storm, then ran for the door. Every year the newspaper had stories of local people killed by lightning, and Judy didn't want to be one of them. The older she got, the better it sounded to die quietly and suddenly in her bed.

Judy loved her little home. She and Sam bought it five years before, after living in her Lake Worth house after they married. They still visited their Lake Worth neighbors, but had fallen in love with their house—finding it on one of their regular walks through

Palm Beach. Solidly built of old southern woods, the original Florida cypress floors, trim, built-in cupboards, and bookcases glowed throughout. The house had a full basement, one of the few on the island; that, thick walls, and high ceilings kept the house fairly cool, even in summer. Throughout the house the walls and ceilings were neutral, but art, curtains, and upholstery were in bright, bold colors. Yellows and reds mostly.

Judy walked through the kitchen to the living room and flicked on the CD player—a loud shuffled mix of Sam Cooke, Leo Kottke, Billy Joel, and a military marching band boomed from several speakers on the first floor. Judy ran upstairs to change. All parties at their house were ultra casual. The Haites seldom used their AC, kept windows open year-round, and lived inside/outside most of the year. Tonight would be a grilling party on the patio.

In minutes Judy came downstairs wearing a one-piece swimsuit and shorts. Barefoot, she pulled vegetables out of the fridge and got them ready for mixed grill. Grilled fish, vegetables, and pineapple were the main menu items. For dessert she'd made her mother's brownies. (Not too gooey; crisp on top and bottom; lots of nuts.) Wines, coffee, and liqueurs would finish the meal.

She heard Sam drive up and washed her hands as he came in.

"Hi, hon. How was your day?" She went over to him for a hug and kiss. Sam smelled of the rain and a little bit of cat.

"Busy. I'm pooped. We got in a lot of orders. I keep expecting demand to drop off, but I think I'll have to increase the breeding stock. Hope you don't mind, but I had to bring a few home tonight. They need some taming before we send them out. I'll put them in the cellar until after the party."

"Oh, let me play with them first." Judy opened the box he was carrying. Four black-and-white tuxedo kittens were rolling around fighting. Each was less than two inches long. "I just can't get enough of these."

"We could always have some here, if you'd get rid of Jack," Sam said. Jack was a full-sized cat—an orange stray Judy had let in a few years ago. There was a large feral cat colony on the island centered not far from their house, and they thought Jack had come from there. The storm over the colony was part of the micropolitics of the island that Judy found amusing, but viewed with a tinge of contempt: two organizations battled for years over the right to feed and care for the animals, piling up fines for unauthorized feeding of the cats and consuming the attention of the local government and the press.

"Any day," Judy answered with a grin. They were both cat lovers and enjoyed Jack's running of their house.

"Need some help?" Sam looked at the pile of marinating vegetables.

"You can slice up a couple of pineapples." Judy sat on the rattan couch and played with the kittens as Sam whacked at the pineapples. The kitchen was large and included several pieces of rattan furniture with bright-flowered cushions, as well as the room's jewel—a large booth Sam rescued from a diner in New Hampshire and had reupholstered in plushy deep red leather.

"Well, I guess I'd better go clean off the furniture." Judy grabbed a dishcloth and a spray bottle of diluted white vinegar and soap.

Sam came out and joined her on the patio. They had a large white table and a dozen dining chairs, plus a collection of chaises and rocking chairs topped with bright yellow and red cushions. Judy set the table and placed candles around the patio while Sam checked the bar and then sprawled on a chaise.

They had modeled their outside patio after the Hotel de Paris in Monte Carlo. It had a retractable roof and upper walls that could enclose the area when they were away or if the weather turned wet or cold. The wall adjoining the main house supported a mini-kitchen with a five-foot grill that was Sam's pride and joy.

"Did you work today?" Sam asked.

"Yup. I was supposed to be out by three, but we were way behind, so I stayed 'til after five." Judy was a physical therapist. She worked throughout the medical center and hospice.

"I wish you'd stop working. There's no reason for you to be tied down like that. Or at least really work part-time."

Judy flinched; this was an old complaint of his. "I'll stop when you do. Don't forget, I did cut my hours way down. No sense having more time to be home alone. And I'd miss the patients—and it's great exercise. Really—why'd you bring it up—your men friends giving you trouble?"

Sam blushed. He'd recently been playing tennis in town. Most of the players were semi-retired executives, and none of the wives worked. "Sorry."

"Accepted. But you should go play golf at Lake Worth and get away from those guys. I'm afraid I'm going to wake up some morning and find a maid in the kitchen."

"You could use some help," Sam tried.

"Oh, go fish. When you stop mowing the lawn, maybe I'll hire a cleaning service again." Judy scowled, picked up the kittens, and took them down to the cellar.

Every married couple has its squabbles. A recurring theme in the Haite household was the level of housekeeping each was comfortable with. Judy thought Sam was compulsive; he wanted every surface to be pristine. Judy preferred a more relaxed, lived-in level of cleanliness. For her, cleaning house was a chore to be saved for a rainy day—those times when she was at loose ends with too much energy and nothing else to do. She kept the laundry up to date and the kitchen spotless, but allowed a little dust to settle in the rest of the house. In the first year of their marriage, she tried harder. Then, two years before, she gave in and hired a cleaning service. But she felt she had to be there when they were. They drove her crazy—she couldn't read or listen to music. And the smells of the cleaning products drove her nuts. So she stopped the service, vowing to try harder—but she didn't. Lately Sam even yelled at her when the house wasn't quite right in his mind. Judy didn't take well to the yelling, but so far fought back with humor. She felt cheated. Sam was backing out of their original agreement: when Sam and Judy moved to Palm Beach, they had sworn they would not "be like them". The town was still full of people with old money and expensive, seasonal homes fully staffed. Recently the average price of a house was $4 million; even condos averaged close to a million—living up to the town's official motto "The Best of Everything".

From time to time, Judy had to pinch herself. She felt she didn't belong, but she still was fascinated by the town—the grand houses, the fancy cars. (She saw more Jaguars in a day in Palm Beach than she'd seen her entire life in Maine.) Thinking of cars, she smiled. When she was in junior high school, her father bought a van. While a big step up from the pickup truck with rusted-out floor boards (you had to lift your feet at every puddle), the van was an old commercial vehicle with narrow bench seats along the sides, side windows in just the front doors, and tiny windows in the back doors. He'd given it a silver undercoating, but never put on the finish coat of paint. It was the first time the whole family could drive anywhere together, although it couldn't go anywhere with a steep hill in the way. Judy and her brothers named it the Silver Streak. Occasionally her father gave her a ride to school. She'd give him a casual "Thanks a lot" when she got out of the van even if no one was around, pretending he was a neighbor or stranger. What an idiot she'd been.

CHAPTER 2

By ten o'clock the party hit its mellow stage. The rain had stopped. The outside room was wide open. Moon and stars were out. Everyone was in a comfortable chair sipping their favorite liqueur and nibbling the last of the brownies. Sam had changed into swim trunks and had been chef and waiter throughout the meal. Judy put the dirty dishes into a couple of plastic tubs on a wheeled cart and parked them in the kitchen.

Margarida Harte, a widow in her eighties, was talking to Sam about some trouble she'd been having with her lawn service. "Every year the cost doubles and the service gets worse. They don't do any real gardening anymore. And the plants are all so common—they look like they've been on sale at Home Depot. Everything looks the same all over town now."

"That's why I do my own work," Sam said. "None of our yards are that big, so it's pretty easy. I hire an expert every now and then to help me pick out stuff and teach me how to take care of it. I just take good notes and do what they tell me." Sam was proud of the work he'd done. Most of the yard was planted in fruit trees, herbs, and spices. The only grass was a little patch out front, and Sam planned to put that into thyme soon.

"It always smells so nice here," Margarida sighed. She was a ballet dancer who had run a successful New York company, retiring just ten years before. She tended to repeat the same celebrity anecdotes, but they were truly funny, and the Haites never tired of hearing them.

"If you'd like, I can come over tomorrow and look at your yard and maybe talk to your man about some changes," Sam said.

"I'd love that. Come at ten, and we can have coffee." This exchange too was often repeated. Margarida was lonely. Sam would go over, have coffee and some pastry, and walk through the yard. At first he'd suggest some changes, and she'd thank him but never follow through with any of them. After a few years of this, he'd started potting up some of his flowers and just bringing them over to her. She was good about watering them. And Sam would swap them out for new ones as things came into season. He'd even started a mini citrus orchard for her.

Judy sat back in her chaise with her eyes almost closed, sipping Irish Mist. Her mind was empty—simply enjoying the sound of others talking.

The Hudsons and Corlisses had grouped their chairs together and were talking real estate.

Bill and June Hudson were a couple in their thirties who owned a small construction business. They had built a large home on Palm Beach on speculation and were afraid to extend themselves further until it sold. When they started construction, they were getting lots of inquiries and some real interest in the property. Unfortunately by the time the house was finished, the market was glutted with homes for sale, and buyers were expecting upgrades and lower prices. They held firm on their price, and after two years, the house remained unsold.

The other couple, Joseph and Eileen Corliss, listened to the Hudsons' woes. They'd heard the lament several times before (preceded by several years of their bragging about the project), but the Corlisses were polite to a fault.

Just after eleven the storm started up again. Sam hit the button for the roof and walls to cover the patio, and they all hurried into the kitchen. Judy passed around towels for them to dry off. They were all used to having their evenings end like this. Once the rainy season began, it rained every morning or every evening—or both—depending on the way the winds blew.

Sam offered to drive Margarida home. She lived just across the street, but it would be safer if there was lightning. After Sam and Margarida left, the Hudsons drove off to their home at the east end of the street. The Corlisses waited a while to see if the storm would ease off. They had walked from their home midway down the street and had refused offers of a ride, determined to walk. Judy wanted them to wait for Sam, but they each borrowed an umbrella and set off briskly for home.

A Jewish couple in their late seventies, Joe and Eileen Corliss walked all over town. They had a car—a ten-year-old Mercedes—but seldom drove it. Eileen had a license, but didn't like to drive, especially "off the island". Joe had severe arthritis; he was able to move his neck less than ten degrees left to right, and his back was extremely stiff and painful. When he backed up his car, he had to depend on mirrors. He had decided the safest way to back out of his driveway was to do it as fast as possible. Neighbors soon learned to check to see if he was in his car before driving past his driveway. Before the neighbors were fully trained, Joe had several minor accidents leaving his home. Eileen was so embarrassed, she seldom drove with him or allowed him to drive.

Judy and Sam put the dishes in the machine, tidied the patio, and climbed the stairs to bed. The second floor had a large master bedroom converted from several tiny rooms, studies for each of them, and a small library, which they also used as a guest room. They'd furnished it with antiques they found in the Bahamas.

They quickly took off their clothes and got into bed. The ceiling fans were on high and all windows opened to the storm. Tonight it was cool enough to use a sheet. Usually they slept naked and uncovered during the hot months May to September.

They both dropped off to sleep in minutes. Neither had talked; both were tired. It was just eleven thirty.

⁂

The alarm seemed to ring within minutes of their falling asleep. Judy struggled to hit the button, but couldn't find it. She turned on the light and realized the button was already in. The telephone was ringing. Her stomach sank. Middle-of-the-night calls were usually trouble—both her and Sam's parents were in their eighties and Judy's brothers, like them, were "getting there."

"Hello." Judy's voice was a quavering croak.

"Hello? Is this Sam?" It was Margarida. Judy sat and brought her knees up to lean on.

"No. I'm Judy—my voice isn't working yet. What's wrong?"

"There are a lot of police or something down the street. I haven't been able to sleep and heard sirens. I can see down the street, and it looks close to the Corliss house. I called them, and no one answered, and now I'm worried. Do you think Sam would mind checking up on them?"

"I'll get him up, and we'll call you back when we know something." Judy hung up and looked over at Sam. His eyes were shut, but she could tell he was awake and just trying to escape. He'd heard it was Margarida, and she'd occasionally call for him to check her house for burglars.

"Sam—that was Margarida. She's worried about Joe and Eileen—there are police down that way, and they're not answering their phone."

"Maybe it's turned off or they can't hear it," Sam grumbled. But he sat up, pulled on shorts, T-shirt, and sandals and after a bathroom stop, went down to investigate.

Judy was wide awake now, so she dressed and followed Sam down the street. It was lovely out—the storm had stopped, it was cool, and the air smelled clean. Several cars with flashing lights were down the street. She could see Margarida's face in her upstairs window and waved.

As they got closer, they could see the activity was just a few houses up from the Corlisses.

There was a short fire truck, two ambulances, and three police cars. A TV vehicle was parked farther down the street. A policeman stopped them.

"Sorry, folks. You can't come any closer."

"What's happened?" Sam asked.

"Lightning toppled a tree. Trapped an old couple."

"Oh, my God! It must be Joe and Eileen!" Judy cried. "They left our house a while ago and were walking home. They live just down there," Judy explained to the officer. "Are they hurt? Alive? Oh, Sam, I should've insisted on driving them home."

Judy turned and reached for Sam, who put his arm around Judy and explained again to the policeman who the couple might be and volunteered to identify them.

The policeman led them closer to the activity. A large Banyan tree had toppled into the street. Several firemen were using chain saws to clear the debris and free the bodies that appeared pinned to the ground. When they got closer, though, they could see that the many support "arms" of tree limbs were keeping the main trunk and the larger limbs from touching the bodies. They could see one of their red umbrellas twisted in the branches.

Coming closer, Judy could make out Eileen's fluorescent green raincoat; Eileen was motionless. Beside her, Joe was beating the ground with his right hand and moaning. A large branch obscured Joe's head as he lay in a growing puddle of blood.

An EMT was starting an IV in Joe's hand. Another EMT was examining Eileen. Firemen were placing pneumatic supports under the heavy limbs threatening the Corlisses.

The policeman led Judy and Sam toward a man in casual clothes. "This is Mr. and Mrs. Haite, sir. They know the victims."

"I'm Lieutenant Mason. Hold on just a sec." He ruffled through a clipboard and produced a form. "It would help if you could provide some information for us." He held his pen at ready, but Judy interrupted him.

"Sure. But first—how are they? We couldn't tell."

"We can't tell a whole lot either," Mason answered politely. "The lady is unconscious and probably has a broken pelvis and internal injuries. Her head isn't injured, so she may have just passed out from pain. The gentleman's head has been badly bashed in, but he's semi-conscious, which is good. We won't know much until we get them to the ER." Palm Beach police are gentle with the residents. If they don't treat each one as their boss, they know they can get into trouble. (A recent book about the island suggested "every Palm Beacher could wear a badge reading 'Do you know who I am?'")

Judy and Sam gave what information they could. Beyond names, ages, and address, they knew they were Jewish and the name of their favorite rabbi. Their family, married sons and daughters, was scattered all over the world. They also knew their attorney (same as theirs), and that he would have family telephone numbers. And their internist was Dr. Helihan at Good Sam.

After the sergeant got their information, he gave them his card and asked that they go back beyond the rescue vehicles. When they came to a streetlight, Sam glanced at Judy and was amazed at her face. Animation was gone; her eyes were flat and her lips lax. She was breathing fast, and her skin was shiny. He led her to the curb and insisted she sit down.

"No, I'm okay," Judy insisted. But she knew she was not. She sat hugging her knees and leaned against Sam. "Or I will be in a minute."

"It's hard to watch someone you know in pain and not be able to help. Boy, I hope they're going to be all right. What a mess! I thought those trees stayed up forever." Sam rubbed his face.

"We've seen them thrown about after hurricanes," Judy reminded Sam. She picked her head up. "I'm feeling better. I'm surprised at my reaction. I've seen so much worse at the hospital."

"But patients are strangers. These are our friends," Sam reminded her.

"Did I turn green?" Judy asked.

"No. Why?"

"Sitting here on the curb reminded me of one day in London—a long time ago—must've been in the eighties. I was there with my brother Frank, and we were walking to a train station. The sidewalks were right up against the traffic. There wasn't a ditch or bicycle lane—the cars went really fast right beside you. And in the wrong direction, of course. A man just a few feet in front of us was walking along when his right hand was nicked by a taxicab. It peeled the thumb right off his hand—his thumb flew maybe sixty feet ahead—

still attached with a thin thread of skin to his hand. The man sank to the ground against a tree. Someone ran ahead and brought back his thumb—that's when we realized what we had seen.

"A lot of people were taking care of him, so we walked on. Frank wasn't very talkative. I looked over at him, and he had turned green—a lime green—almost as bright as Eileen's raincoat. There weren't any businesses open, but a man cleaning in front of a Chinese restaurant let us inside and gave Frank some tea. Frank was shaky all day. He said he kept thinking it could've happened to him. Of course I just thought the whole thing was exciting—especially how far that thumb flew. And seeing Frank turn green, I remember—it happened right in front of that big King Tut exhibit. It was a beautiful day."

Judy struggled to her feet. "I just thought…A better question would be has my hair turned gray?" Although they didn't need the money from selling Judy's hair, she enjoyed treating the money separately—a modern woman's egg money.

Sam punched Judy on the shoulder. "Your hair's fine."

After a half hour or so, one of the ambulances turned on its siren and drove off. They could see a stretcher being loaded into the second ambulance. Judy and Sam waved to the lieutenant and headed for home.

Sam settled Judy on the couch in the kitchen. He then called Margarida and told her what they knew.

"I'll call the Hudsons in the morning," Sam said. He made a pot of Irish breakfast tea and placed the teapot and china cups on the coffee table. "Do you want something to nibble?"

"Do we have any of the lemon nut cookies left?" Judy asked. She loved several of the Pepperidge Farm cookies—especially lemon nut with tea and the little gingerbread men with coffee.

"Ah! You're in luck." Sam found half a package in their treat drawer. To fight the humidity, Sam had built a cabinet with sealed drawers to keep baking ingredients and finished products dry.

They sat and finished off the cookies and then went back up to bed. It was two thirty. They each fell asleep immediately.

CHAPTER 3

At five o'clock the next morning, their cat, Jack, tried to wake Judy and Sam. Judy realized they'd forgotten to feed him the night before. She was surprised to find him inside; usually when they had guests, Jack hid outside in the bushes. Too tired to get up, Judy patted and scratched Jack until he curled up on the bed and fell asleep.

At eight o'clock Jack attacked again, this time walking across their stomachs. That did it. Judy sat up. Sam was faking sleep. "I'll feed him and get us some coffee."

Downstairs she fed Jack and made two cups of filtered coffee. Right now they were drinking "Henry"—a nice strong bean. Plus the package had a cat on it. Judy put some biscuits in the toaster oven, then went to check up on the pocket cats in the cellar. They were in a room with a window, sleeping in a clump with plenty of food and water nearby. She decided to leave them alone and went outside to get the papers—the *Palm Beach Post* and the *Daily News*. She then topped the biscuits with slabs of Irish butter and drowned them in maple syrup.

Back in the bedroom, the coffee enticed Sam into sitting up. "Yum." Maple syrup was one of his favorite foods. "Okay if I turn on the TV?"

"Sure." Judy was busy reading the comics.

Sam jabbed Judy. "Look-it."

She glanced up and saw the scene from the night before. They had caught some close-ups of Joe's face; he looked awful. There was a just a glimpse of her and Sam at a distance. Judy was relieved—she looked a fright when she got home last night. The reporter said that Joe and Eileen were alive, but no details of their injuries were yet available.

"Can we find out how they are?" Sam asked.

"I'll call after nine. It's Saturday, so Peggy will be in this morning, but she won't be in until eight thirty or so. She'll need time to settle in before I can bother her." Peggy was the manager of Judy's department.

"So, what's the day's schedule?" Sam was getting to the last section for him—the *Daily News*—also known as "The Shiny Sheet"—a newspaper with an irregular schedule (depending on the season) that provided Palm Beach news and gossip. It was published by the same business that put out the *Post*.

On weekends neither Sam nor Judy worked. They usually waited until Saturday morning to plan their days.

"We can find out how Joe and Eileen are. Then call 'round to let people know. We can go in to see them, if they can have visitors. After the phoning, though, I'd like a nice long beach walk, then come back here for a swim. I'd be happy to stay home and read the rest of the day, unless you have something you'd like to do."

"Sounds good to me. I'm tired, but I know the walk will get me started." Sam got up and gathered his clothes together. They'd wear yesterday's clothes until after their walk.

Judy called the hospital. Peggy was there and called right back with the clinical details. Both Eileen and Joe were in surgery. Eileen had a chipped bone in her hip and a broken thigh. She had regained consciousness and had some deep lacerations, but no internal bleeding. Joe had three cracked neck bones and a depressed skull fracture. They had elevated the bone fragments of his skull last night. The surgery this morning was to stabilize his neck. He would need further surgery to wire his skull together after they took care of the brain swelling. They were both expected to survive. Peggy said they'd be out of it today, but they could probably have visitors Sunday afternoon.

❧

It was hot—ninety-three degrees—and muggy when they stepped outside. This would be the weather until the end of September. Sam carried a small backpack with bottled water for each of them. They'd put their sandals in it when they got to the beach. There was a nice stiff breeze in their faces as they walked down the street. Crews were working on the fallen Banyan tree—much of it had already been trucked away. They could see traces of blood where Joe had been trapped.

At the Corlisses' house they picked up the newspapers and brought them around to the back stairs. "We'll have to remember to call and cancel the papers," said Judy.

"I wonder what other services they need to change? Or, you know how things happen sometimes, maybe they'll be home soon," said Sam.

"I think they'll be in the hospital quite a while. Eileen will need rehab after the surgery for sure. And Joe—well, maybe he'll be okay, but with a brain injury, he'll need rehab too."

A few people were at the beach—mostly those with dogs. Although against the law, the local custom was to allow morning romps on the beach for the dog people.

They headed south. The tide was low, so they were able to walk in front of the Breakers, one of the area's four-star hotels. They walked past the hotel's beach (empty of guests, but with beach chairs in orderly lines facing the ocean, towels at the ready) to the public beach and found a comfortable place to sit. Sweat dripped from everywhere—their noses, chins, elbows. The heat and humidity made any activity seem much more physical than it was. After a half hour of deadheading flowers in the yard, Sam would come in looking like he'd just completed a marathon.

"Do you know any of the Corliss kids?" Sam asked. "Maybe we should call them."

Judy thought. "I don't know the sons. I met their daughter once last year. I found her kind of icy. I don't know her married name—or even where she lives. We might find out at the hospital tomorrow."

"I hope their kids can come in and visit soon. Having their loved ones there should help them recover."

Judy snorted.

"What was that for?" Sam asked. His face was turning red, and he sounded peeved.

"Oh, sorry. Just the term 'loved ones'. It's a strange term."

"Why is that?" Sam looked confused.

"I don't know, really. I'm just not comfortable with 'loved ones'. I don't even use the word *love* very often—at least when applied to people. I love chocolate sauce and cats, but I grew up not using that word for people. My family was a mixture of taciturn Swedes and New Englanders—maybe that's it."

"You love me, don't you?"

"Sam, of course I do. It's just the words—sounds like something from a funeral scene on TV. I like my family, but I just don't think of them as 'loved ones'. And I'm really not that close to most of them. I mean, really, Sam, before you I think the closest connection to any human being I've ever felt was that kid I shot from the car."

"Whoa! What are you talking about?"

Judy laughed, trying to ease tension. "Sam, simmer down. Didn't I tell you that one? I was driving back from a meeting in Augusta. This was when I worked at that hospital in Bangor. I was supposed to testify against a bill for my boss. I got nervous and really screwed up. Driving home I took the back roads. I like the little towns and needed time to cool off.

"It was one of those miserable Maine spring days—gray, cold drizzle, muddy. Whatever snow there was, was dirty. I came into this town behind a couple of cars. A kid stood on the left side of the road, in the ditch. He had a toy rifle and was shooting at each car that went by.

"I don't know why I did it, but when I came up to him, I used my right hand as a pistol and motioned to 'shoot' the kid.

"It was marvelous. He didn't miss a beat. His feet flipped into the air the second I shot. He threw down his gun, clutched his chest, and fell backwards down a hill of snow and mud. I laughed the rest of the way home. Here it is, more than twenty years later, and I believe that was the best connection I've ever had with anyone. Short, though. Love? No. But…"

"Do you think the kid remembers it?" Sam asked.

"No. Not unless he got into big trouble over his dirty clothes."

"You're just too weird sometimes." Sam threw a handful of sand at the ground. "Let's get back."

They walked back slower than they had come. And both looked at their feet instead of at the beautiful homes or the sparkling ocean.

Judy worried at Sam's reaction. They had married so quickly after they met and had lived together just six years. She felt Sam was afraid of their differences, preferring to have a fairy-tale life.

"Sam, Sam, Sam. Let's stop a minute and talk."

Sam looked at Judy and was softened by her earnest face. He held out his hand and led her to a sea wall, and they sat down against it.

"Sam. I need you to know how deeply I love you. For me it's magical. Do you know how much I look forward to just going to bed every night? Not because I'm tired, or sleepy. Or need to lie down because my back is killing me. And no—not just for our sex. It's so I can lie there in the dark next to you. I shut my eyes, and I see stars. Lying by your side, I feel our souls rise to the stars and merge. I let myself go and float up to sleep. It's so different from all those years I was alone. Dozing off and on and watching TV all night."

Then she chuckled. "But those nights had their rewards too. Waking up for that Jerry Lee Lewis recording session—the one with Willie Nelson. Or…Sorry, I'm off track. You and I happened so late in my life. I never dreamed that this existed. I was never unhappy before; I was quite content—I enjoyed my life. But I just didn't know how much better it could be. I'm no good at lovey-dovey language, but I love you, love you, love you." Judy pushed Sam over and started kissing his face, his neck, his belly.

Sam guffawed and hugged Judy. They rolled around in the sand—which stuck to their sweaty skin and clothes. They lay still for a few minutes, then broke out laughing. They chatted for a while, then walked into the ocean and washed the sand off. Sopping wet, holding hands again, they headed for home. Heads up this time.

Sunday. After breakfast Sam went out to wash off the cars. When they moved in, the house had an open driveway. Sam built a four-car-wide carport so they could come and go without getting wet. He put himself in charge of their two cars—Judy's Accord and his Forrester, each four years old. He tried to rinse the salt off them at least once a week. He no longer changed the oil himself, but faithfully brought the cars in for that and other fluids and grease. He even had all the lightbulbs changed once a year.

Sam kept a logbook with maintenance schedules for the cars, yard, and house. He did the same for their medical tests and appointments. He was convinced this freed his mind for better things. He had inherited this approach from his father, a pilot killed in Korea. His father had set up logs for Joe's mother to make it easier for her to manage during his long absences. Sam still maintained those logs for his mother. Every fall he went up to her home in Maine to make sure everything was in order. Once Judy kidded him about having a compulsive disorder, and he snapped at her. He *was* compulsive, and he did not like to be kidded about anything. Judy hated having to tiptoe around his sensitive ego—in her family teasing and kidding were a way of life.

Sam, now fifty-six, was a handsome man. Judy thought he looked like Steve McQueen. Perhaps a little heftier, but he had the light hair, wide mouth, and the same rueful smile. She had first been attracted to him by his cobalt-blue eyes. She liked his solid body—he moved like a ship, cutting through the air and ground. She discovered later that his smile was mostly his vanity: nearsighted, he wore glasses only when he was sure he wouldn't be seen—his squint drew his mouth into an almost permanent smile. Judy sat in the kitchen watching Sam while playing with the little kittens he'd brought home Friday. They were frolicking on the couch chasing a yarn ball she had tied to a wooden spoon.

She planned to join Sam at church soon. When she moved to Florida, she hadn't had a regular church. Margarida had introduced her and Sam to the one in Palm Beach, and they usually took her with them. The elegant building and professional choir added to their religious experience. Plus, Judy enjoyed waiting for the service to begin—Margarida knew everyone and kept Judy amused pointing out local celebrities and telling their stories.

※

After church they dropped Margarida at her house and drove over the bridge to Good Samaritan, the medical center in West Palm Beach. Judy called registration and found that Joe and Eileen were both in the surgical ICU. Generally only family was allowed to visit patients in the ICU, but as Judy worked throughout the hospital, she was sure they would be able to see the Corlisses. They checked at the nurse's station and discovered that the Corlisses' daughter, Marilyn, had already arrived from Boston and was angry that she was limited to five-minute visits with her parents every hour—a restriction to protect patients from exhaustion.

Judy found the Corlisses' nurse, Helen Eps, in the lounge. Helen was a tiny high-strung fierce defender of her patients. "The Corlisses? She's doing well. We could transfer her to med/surg today if they had enough staff. I don't think she'll be in acute care for more than a week or so. She'll need rehab, but she's strong and healthy. She'll need PT and some nursing care at home for a while, but eventually should be good as new."

"What about Joe?" Judy asked.

"He's conscious but dopey. Slurs his words and doesn't make total sense. It'll be a few days before we know how he'll be mentally. Physically, they left his skull open until the swelling goes down. It was a dirty wound, so we've got him on powerful antibiotics. Infection could be a problem—his body isn't in the greatest shape to begin with. Dr. Munabi thinks he'll live, but he's not making any promises.

"Is it okay for us to visit?" Sam asked.

"Well. I'd better make sure his daughter doesn't see you," Helen answered. "She's pissed at our family visiting policy—she wants to stay in their room all the time. God, she'd kill them. She already has Eileen upset, and I'm not sure if Joe isn't pretending to be asleep when she's in there." She left to see where Marilyn was.

Helen returned in a few minutes. "It's okay. She just visited them and has gone back home to shower. Don't stay more than ten minutes. Eileen asked to see you." Helen smiled and went back to the nurse's station.

Joe and Eileen were in a glass-enclosed room together. Both were hooked to IVs and monitoring equipment. Joe was asleep. Eileen's leg was in traction. She was sitting up, eyes open.

"Sam, Judy. It's so good of you to visit." Her voice was weak but clear.

"Eileen. We've been so worried. How are you?" Judy gently kissed Eileen and Sam touched her hand and smiled.

"I'm okay. Everything hurt so much when it happened, but they've given me something so I don't hurt at all. I'm so worried about Joe, though. Marilyn's here. She's gone home for a bath. And Josh and Steve called. I told them not to, but they both sent flowers." She smiled.

"Oh, you love your boys, don't you?" Judy said.

"They've been good to us. Marilyn tries, but she's wearing me out. She wants to move both of us to a hospital in Boston, and I'm afraid she'll do it some time when I'm asleep."

"She can't do that if you don't want to. Does Joe need some special hospital?" Sam asked.

"I don't know. I know I don't; I can go home soon. Oh, Judy, can you do my PT at home?"

"I'd love to," Judy said. "I think I can even start while you're here. I'll talk to my boss."

"Eileen, I'm sorry, but we have to leave. Your nurse said we should stay just a few minutes. But you relax—we'll be back tomorrow. Is there anything we can do in the meantime?" Sam asked.

"Can you call our attorney, Mark White, and ask him to visit? I want to make sure Marilyn doesn't send us away." Eileen let her head fall back and closed her eyes. "Thank you."

Sam and Judy tiptoed from the room.

Judy drove them home while Sam called Mark White. He got the answering machine and left their telephone number and a brief message.

"Well. I guess that's all we can do today," Sam said.

"Poor Eileen," Judy said. "What a shock this whole thing must be. I hope they get well quickly enough so Marilyn will leave them alone. Times like this I'm glad I don't have kids."

"Don't forget the good sons," Sam reminded her. His marriage to Judy was his second. He had wanted children, but his first wife was unable to conceive and didn't want to adopt.

"Oh, I know." Judy patted Sam's thigh.

That afternoon Sam and Judy lolled in their yard reading. As usual, Sam was reading nonfiction, this time a new biography of

Charles Darwin. Judy was weighed down with *Freddy and Frederika*, Mark Helprin's spoof of the British monarchy; the 553-page book, though a paperback, had been left out in the rain and had swollen to twice its original size.

Sam looked over at Judy. "Hey, I think we could afford another copy of that book."

Judy looked up and grinned. "Waste not, want not." And went back to reading.

When it got dark, Sam fired up the grill, and they had a quick meal. Want instant sundaes?" Sam asked. Usually they ate fruit for dessert.

"You're bad. Have I ever said no?" Judy moved to a chaise. Sam put some hot fudge in the bottom of two bowls and microwaved them until the sauce bubbled. He then scooped vanilla ice cream into the bowls and brought them over.

"This is so good. Too bad you can't patent it." Judy tried not to eat too quickly.

"I think we have enough patents," Sam said, smiling.

CHAPTER 4

Judy wasn't scheduled to work on Monday but dressed in her scrubs and went in to talk to her boss, Peggy. She figured it would be easier to see Eileen and Joe if she was wearing a uniform and ran into their daughter, Marilyn.

"Hey, Judy. I didn't know you were scheduled today." Peggy looked up from her cluttered desk.

"I wanted to drop in on the Corlisses and see how they were doing. Wanted to look professional."

Peggy laughed. "Don't worry. I already know about their daughter. She's so angry, she even challenges the doctors going into the room. What a bitch."

"Eileen is going to need PT when she gets home and wants me to do it. Is there any reason why I can't? I don't want to charge her."

"We can cover your liability through our home-care agency. You might want us to charge an administrative fee to cover our costs. As long as we don't pay you, we won't charge for labor."

"I never thought about the legal stuff," Judy said. "That sounds like a smart way to do it. Can I also treat her in the hospital?"

"Sure. I'll arrange it—as long as you'll come in at least five days a week. We don't have PT orders from the doc yet. He'll probably order it when she's transferred to med/surg today."

"With Marilyn's attitude is it safe for me to visit them today?" Judy asked.

"As long as you check in with her nurse first."

"Thanks, Peggy."

"No prob. I'll call when I get her PT orders." Peggy went back to her pile of papers.

Judy went down to the cafeteria before going over to see Eileen and Joe. She didn't need any food but did need time. She got coffee and a Danish and sat at a table along the wall, facing out. The cafeteria was in the basement and looked it. Drab brown paint on the walls, bright blue on the floor, energy-saving lighting. Garish curtains—parrots and jungle—only emphasized the dreary area. Shallow windows next to the ceiling, though not large, did open to bright blue sky. Judy's eyes were drawn outside, and she let her mind go blank.

The coffee was watery and too hot. The Danish limp and too sweet. Judy put them both down, leaned back in her chair, and closed her eyes. She admonished herself to get a grip. Put on the smile and march over to the patient units. First see Joe, then Eileen. Maybe by then there would be PT orders, and she could be useful. If she ran into Marilyn, she'd be friendly, professional, and…Well, she'd try to avoid any argument.

She put her uneaten food in the washing-up area and walked over to the ICU. Joe was asleep or still unconscious. Reading his chart, Judy found that he'd been babbling and pretty much out of it. The neurosurgeon was unsure of Joe's prognosis. Joe was getting meds to prevent brain swelling and infection. CT and MRI studies showed a large area of damaged brain tissue; on the positive side, there was some circulation to the damaged area, so there was hope of recovery.

With no reason for Judy to linger, she went upstairs to the orthopedic unit. She checked at the desk and found that orders for PT had been written, so she went in to see her patient.

Eileen was sitting up in bed. Her face was purple and swollen, and her leg was in traction, but she was smiling and looking chipper in a bright pink bed jacket. (Judy often wondered if Eileen had some visual problem—she always wore such intense colors.)

"Judy, how good of you to come. I know you're usually out walking on Monday morning."

"Got to get you up and going. How do you feel?" Judy walked up to the bed.

"Battered. But pretty good. Anxious to get home. Do you know how long I'll be here?"

Judy didn't. "It will be a few days before Dr. Munabi will know for sure. And then he might want you to go to rehab for a while."

"I hope not. I just want to get home," Eileen whined a little.

Judy smiled. "And *do* what? Let's go with what the doctor says. He's good at getting people back in shape quickly. Today I'm just going to give you a light massage and move your limbs a bit. Let me know right away if I hurt you."

"You touch her, and I'll sue!" A large woman strode into the room. Her voice was low-pitched and loud. She looked to be in her fifties; she was tall, broad, and wore a dark purple silky dress with long sleeves and a hem close to her ankles. Her hair was a dull flat black, shoulder length, with a wide bald-looking part straight down the middle. Prison matron.

"Marilyn, dear. This is Judy. She's going to be my physical therapist. She's also my friend, so don't talk to her like that." Eileen's lower lip quivered.

"Mother, you're not ready for therapy," stormed Marilyn. "You should rest." Her face was pale, but her nose and chin were turning red.

Judy held her temper. "The doctor has written orders for PT to prevent your mother's joints from stiffening and to avoid muscular atrophy. The orders are standard treatment for injuries of this kind."

Marilyn huffed, "I don't care. I want my parents out of this awful place and up to Boston where they can get real medical care. This hospital is a backwater."

Judy counted all the way to three. "Your mother is my patient, and we're both going to follow the doctor's orders. Now, would you please leave so she'll have privacy." Judy pulled the curtain around Eileen's bed, shutting Marilyn out, and began therapy.

Marilyn slammed the door, leaving the room.

"Oh, dear," Eileen said. "I don't know what's wrong with her. I wish she'd go back up north."

Judy sat and smiled at her friend. "Well, she *will* leave eventually. We can both look forward to that."

Eileen asked about Joe, and Judy told her all she knew. Eileen got teary. "It's so hard being away from him. And him so hurt. I pray all the time for him to be all right, but I'm so worried."

"We all are," said Judy. Patting Eileen on the arm, she got up and left the room.

❦

The days quickly fell into a pattern. Every morning Judy checked in on Joe and then went to treat Eileen. Eileen got stronger, her bones were healing well, and she was ready to be discharged to the rehab unit. She'd be home in a week or two. Unfortunately Joe had not improved. He was still semi-conscious and had recently developed a high fever. The infectious disease specialist tried several antibiotics, but none had worked yet. The neurosurgeon did a brain biopsy, hoping to isolate the organism causing the infection.

Whenever Marilyn met Judy at the hospital, she glared at her but never said a word. Eileen's attorney had met with Marilyn to restrain her from interfering with her parents' care. This meeting had not improved Marilyn's icy demeanor. She still lived at her parents' home and came every day to torment the hospital staff. Judy thought maybe she should invite Marilyn over for a meal, but never dared ask.

Tuesday morning. Judy was already getting tired. She wasn't used to working so often. Plus, she and Sam had played tennis and golf Saturday, then had dinner with friends that night, followed by dancing, and didn't get home until almost four. While they hadn't done so much on Sunday, seeing Joe and Eileen the day before had disturbed her terribly. While she and Sam loafed last night and turned in early, this morning was steamy hot, and she woke feeling like she'd had no sleep at all.

To make it worse, a loud noise like a giant coffee grinder came from below. Groundskeepers.

Judy stretched. The bed had one of those space-age foam mattresses. This indulgence was how she and Sam enjoyed their wealth. They seldom splurged on clothes, jewelry, cars, or vacations. Even their house had been a bargain; just by accident they learned of a family selling off an inherited house more interested in getting money quickly than in getting top dollar. They had offered half of the asking price, and their offer was accepted.

Judy went downstairs, made coffee and brought it up for her and Sam. The TV news was on. It was getting into hurricane season, so they kept watch for storms. Now quite a few waves were coming off Africa, which could develop into something bad for Florida.

Sam groaned. "Tomorrow we'll check our hurricane lists and make sure we have everything."

"I love a man with a list." Judy stretched and lay back in bed while Sam went to shower.

No I don't, she thought. I *like* a man with a list, but…oh, she really didn't want to probe this. She hadn't been truthful on the beach when she told Sam how deeply she loved him. Actually, she often lay in bed wondering if she was next to a stranger. Did other people feel like that? She had fallen hard and fast for Sam in Peru and later in Lake Worth. It seemed when they moved to Palm Beach that Sam had become more distant; she felt like she was one more thing to be managed with his lists and notebooks. Sam was becoming more like a demanding parent than her husband, especially when he'd been drinking too much. He'd scream over the tiniest things—dust behind a toilet, a sticky ring on a side table.

She took a deep breath and shook her head. Maybe she was just still hurt by the birthday present Sam had given her last month. He so proudly presented her with a large gaily wrapped carton of photo albums. She had no idea what they were for. Recipes? Oh, no. He had intended for her to organize the loose photos she kept in a box in her bedroom closet. Every once in a while, she'd pore through them, either looking for a particular one or just roaming through her history on a rainy day. This was the way her parents kept their photographs, and she still enjoyed flipping through them and quizzing them about their past. Of course, without children, any interest in her own photos ended with her.

They seldom fought; most days were pleasant, but she often wondered if Sam regretted marrying her, if his loving bantering was an act. He had wanted a child so badly, had divorced his first wife because she didn't want one. But then he turned around and married Judy when she was already forty-one. They'd tried at first to have a baby, but that hope died early. By then Sam didn't want to adopt, so neither did she. They hadn't really talked about it. They didn't talk about anything important anymore; just food and the house and…

Sam came out of the shower. "Hey girl, you'd better hustle if you're going to work today." He snapped his towel at her feet.

"Ouch! That hurt, you brute!" Judy rolled out of bed and headed for the shower. She turned it on extra hard and hot, hoping to wash off her doubts.

Thirty minutes later Judy was in the ICU. Joe's room had a "No Admittance" sign, so she went looking for Helen Epps, the head nurse.

Joe's infection had become systemic, and no antibiotic combination had worked. The culprit was MRSA, antibiotic-resistant bacteria that had been plaguing hospitals for several years now. MRI scans Sunday night showed large portions of dead and dying brain tissue. The doctors no longer had any hope of Joe's survival. Helen said that Dr. Monroe, the neurosurgeon, was with Eileen now. Joe would either have to go on life support or be transferred to the hospital's hospice unit.

"Do you agree with the doctors?" Judy asked.

"Yes," Helen said. "Joe's brain was pretty much mangled in the accident. He never showed signs of improvement before the infection. Since the infection he's been in a deep coma. Now his hind brain is threatening to shut down, which means his heart and lungs will stop."

"I guess I'd better wait a while before I see Eileen. I don't want to get in the middle of that. How long do you think he'll live?" asked Judy.

"Without life support maybe a day or two. With life support it's hard to say. That always creates a messy situation—as you know. I hope Eileen decides on hospice, but I bet her daughter will give her trouble."

"If he's going to live such a short time, why the transfer to hospice?" Judy asked.

"Dr. Monroe does that so the family gets the message. If the patient stays in ICU, the family thinks there's hope and has a harder time accepting the death. Plus, hospice is a great help for the family after a death.

Judy thanked Helen for her time and went back to see Joe for herself.

Red signs now peppered the glass walls and door, warning those who entered Joe's room to follow strict infection control measures. Judy washed her hands in the anteroom, put on gloves, paper gown, and mask, and entered. There were even more machines and wires than the day before. Neurosurgeons had put a pressure-monitoring sensor in Joe's skull. The large knob attached to his head with wires dangling over to the monitor made him look like a robot—hit a lever, and maybe he'd move. His hospital gown had been left open and pulled up to expose his puny chest with a single, long, white hair springing from a nipple. Judy glanced to see if anyone was looking, then pulled the gown down. She sat next to the bed holding his hand…He made no movement at all. If only she'd given him a ride home.

It was almost noon before she headed toward Eileen's room.

Judy could hear Marilyn's yelling long before she reached the room. Eileen had a roommate now whose bed was curtained off from the action.

"You're going to kill my father!" Marilyn shouted at Eileen. Her nose was right up against Eileen's. Marilyn turned and glared at Judy as she entered the room. "And you, I bet you encouraged her!"

"Eileen, I just heard about Joe this morning. I'm so sorry." Judy pretended to ignore Marilyn and approached Eileen from the other side of the bed.

Marilyn continued to accuse her mother and the hospital, threatening to sue everyone. Finally, getting no response, she said she was leaving and not coming back until the next day. She was going to call her Boston lawyer and "do something". As usual, she managed to bang the door shut on her way out.

Eileen sat in her fluffy purple bed jacket. "Judy, I decided on no life support for Joe. We'd talked about it years ago, and neither of us wanted it. My heart is breaking, but he'd kill me—if he could—if he woke up without a real brain."

"It's the right thing, Eileen," Judy said. "Poor Joe's brain is so damaged, he can never come back. It's just hard you have to put up with Marilyn's tirades."

"The doctors said he'd probably die in a few days. After they move him to hospice, they'll let me visit."

"That's good. Oh, what do they say about you?" Judy asked.

"I'm going over to rehab today—probably for just a week or so, and then I can go home. I was so looking forward to it, but without

Joe…" Eileen stared into space. "When Marilyn comes back, I'll put her to work. Joe will need to be buried right after he dies, and we need to get the family here now." She brightened. "It'll be nice to have the boys with me."

They sat quietly for a while, then Judy got Eileen out of bed and put her through her exercises.

That night Judy and Sam both were home by five. Sam made gin and tonics while Judy put some snacks together. They went out on the patio to talk. They put the TV on a local station to catch the weather.

"Do you really think the hurricane will hit here?" Judy asked.

"We're overdue—nothing's hit here for what—two—three years?" Sam was wolfing down a slab of Stilton. "God, this is good."

"Three, I think. I love Stilton too. I meant to use it to make fancy mac and cheese. I'm still trying to copy that wonderful concoction I had at the Norton last year. That was the best. They haven't had it since; I don't understand why."

"Some people go to the Norton Museum for the art. You go for the food."

"Not just. But…oh…Here comes the weather." Judy turned up the volume.

The forecast track to the now-named Hurricane Darlene showed it headed right for Palm Beach/West Palm Beach. It was three or four days out, and the prediction was for a Category 3 storm, with winds up to 130 miles per hour—capable of blowing down trees, seriously damaging buildings, and destroying mobile homes.

"Oh, wow!" Sam looked worried. He got up and went into the house. In minutes he was back with the red loose-leaf notebook he kept hurricane plans in. He started to sit down, then picked up their glasses and refilled them. "Well, might as well run through the checklists now. Then I'll feel better."

They drank and nibbled while Sam made to-do lists for each of them. As usual, Sam had everything up to date. The house and yard were in good shape, and they needed just a few extra hurricane supplies…fresh batteries and food. The house's shutters were electric, and they could put them down in minutes, as long as they didn't wait too long and the power went out—then it would take an hour to crank them by hand. The cellar had plenty of room to store anything outdoors that might blow away…plants in pots and pool paraphernalia.

Sam would check on Margarida in the morning to make sure she was set. If a hurricane did hit, she'd move in with them. The Haites's house was rated to withstand a Category 4 storm. While their house could take the winds, the barrier island was only seven feet above sea level. The shallow waters off the coast lessened the height of any storm surge, but surges of over fifteen feet had been reported historically. Their plan was for all of them to move over to Sam's business if such a strong storm were forecast. The Pocket Pets building was built to withstand two-hundred-mph winds and was far inland on high ground, so it would avoid floods. Sam kept basic hurricane supplies at the business for the employees and Sam, Judy, and Margarida.

Judy would call Marilyn tomorrow to see if she needed any help getting ready for the storm. Their other neighbors, the Hudsons, would be safe. They usually locked up and went to an inland hotel.

Their hurricane plans set, Sam and Judy made quick work of supper: grilled hot dogs, coleslaw, and grilled fresh peaches with frozen yogurt. They watched a movie on TV. Then, when it got dark and cooled off a bit, they swam for almost an hour. They went up to bed at ten, and both fell asleep almost instantly.

CHAPTER 5

The next day, Wednesday, Judy was at the hospital by eight. She found Joe had already been transferred to hospice and was not expected to live out the week. Eileen was a bit teary but looking forward to visiting Joe later.

When Judy came into the room, Eileen was making a list. "Marilyn is calling family today. We've reserved rooms at the Breakers. I've got to make sure we don't overlook anyone who'd expect to come to the funeral."

"What about the hurricane?" Judy asked.

"Joe's family won't care. They'll come and expect a funeral even if the winds are three hundred miles an hour."

Judy remembered her own "to-dos". "I meant to call Marilyn to see if she needed any help getting the house ready for the storm."

"I've already called our maintenance company. They'll come by and put up the shutters tomorrow and pick up the yard. And I've given Marilyn a list of supplies she'll need, plus where everything else is in the house. I think we're all set."

"Should I call her anyway?"

"Might be a good idea. She thinks you're the devil herself." Eileen chuckled, and then grew serious. "I don't know how I can laugh, I feel so sad."

Judy thought she'd better change the subject. "How many people are coming from away?"

"Our three boys and their families—two wives, eight kids. Joe's two sisters and one husband; his three brothers and two wives; and three of Joe's cousins, no spouses," Eileen read from her list. "We've reserved two suites and eight other rooms. I hope that'll be enough. Of course, any overflow can stay at our house."

"Wow. That'll cost a pretty penny."

"Well, rates are lower in the summer, and they shouldn't be here all that long. I'm happy that we can do it. And the Breakers should make them feel a little better, I think."

———

Judy left Eileen and spent the rest of the day in a fog. She saw several patients and then sat through an interminable department meeting. The meeting was billed as a quality of care session, but was blatantly another cost-cutting presentation by Jack Hewitt, one of the administrators. He mapped out a scheme to substitute therapy aides for many of the more highly trained therapist positions—much as he'd done in nursing, substituting aides for RNs. Normally Judy would've battled him, but she sat dumbly through the presentation. She scowled a couple of times at Peggy, hoping she'd protect her turf, but it seemed she'd already accepted the plan, if not authored it. Judy watched the tall, slim, well-scrubbed man in an expensive gray suit, red power tie, and polished wing tips and felt ashamed of her slouching, pudgy, scrub-suit-clad comrades. Not one of her co-workers made eye contact with Hewitt or with one another. Change was inevitable and she hated it, but unlike most of her co-workers, at least she didn't depend on retiring from the hospital.

On the way home, she frightened herself. When she backed out of her parking space in the garage, Hewitt was walking to his car. His back was toward her, and he was strutting in the middle of the driving lane, blocking her exit. For an instant she accelerated and headed toward him, ready to strike. She pictured him splattered on the ground and began to invent an excuse for hitting the accelerator instead of the brake. At the last moment, she braked. Hewitt didn't even turn around at the squeal, and she had to drive at a crawl until he reached his vehicle.

She got home by four, exhausted. After a shower she lay on the bed wrapped in a towel and flicked on the TV. The phone rang before she found anything to watch.

"Hello."

"Hello."

Judy hated this. It was her mother, Greta, who when she called always had Judy start the conversation.

"Mum. You called me, remember?"

"Hello, dear. I know. I'm not stupid."

"How are you? And Aunt Helen?" Judy's parents were in Miami looking after her father's sister, who'd had a stroke.

"We're all fine."

"Motherrrrr...Any specific reason you called?"

"Well. It's the hurricane."

"I guess it'll be close this time. I just turned on the TV. Has there been any change?"

"Oh, I don't know. I leave that all up to your father."

"Last we heard it's headed right at us—you'll probably be okay down there."

"You never know."

This conversation could go on forever before Greta got to the point.

"Mother. I just got out of the shower, and I've got to get dressed."

"Oh, dear. Well, why I called…" Greta's voice faded.

Finally.

"Well, your father decided we should drive north, just in case. He put Helen in a nursing home, and we're driving out tonight."

"How far north are you going?"

"Oh, he says he'll play it by ear."

"Can you stop here?"

"Oh. That's why we called. We're stopping at that lovely B and B in Lake Worth tonight."

"You *could* stay here, Mother."

"Oh, you know your father. He likes to be waited on."

"I know." Her parents had visited once for over a week when she lived in Lake Worth. They had dropped in unannounced, and her father especially seemed oblivious that Judy had a full-time job in addition to catering to their every whim. Toward the end she telegraphed her impatience, and since then they always stayed in a motel or B and B when they visited her.

"Well. Anyway. We don't know when we'll get in. Your father has a lot of packing to do, and he keeps getting distracted by the TV. But we want to see you for breakfast. We'll be leaving early. Ansel wants to be on the road by six, but he'd love to see you before then."

"All right. But is anything open that early?

"Oh, your father fixed that. They'll leave things out for us, and we'll unlock the door at five."

"Oh, okay. I'll come then and go to work from there."

"That's why I called. I have to go now. Good-bye."

Greta hung up the phone before Judy's "good-bye" left her throat.

Judy hung up the phone, rolled over and smothered her face in the pillows, and growled. Jack jumped up on the bed, curious and concerned…or so it seemed. Judy rolled over and sat up, laughing. "Hi, Jack. Oh, I'm okay. Just a mother-daughter thing." Still laughing she got dressed and went downstairs.

She was peering into the refrigerator looking for a snack when Sam came home.

"Hey, girl. Cold in there?" He tossed his briefcase onto a counter.

"Yes. Want to join me?" Judy stood up and smiled at Sam.

"Hungry?"

"Always."

"I need a drink. Greta just called."

"What's up? Ansel run away?"

"Nope. They're driving north to escape the storm. They'll be at the Cove Inn tonight."

"Want to go over?"

"I've been invited for breakfast at five tomorrow."

"Oooh. Would you mind terribly if I miss it?"

"Actually, your name wasn't mentioned. God, it took forever for Greta to come to the point. I wish I could be more patient with her, but it drives me nuts."

"My mother affects me the same way. But I think I'm reacting to her getting older…And I'm next…So I react like a spoiled little kid."

"She's always driven me nuts. Hmmm…Beer okay? I don't feel like cooking." Judy held up a bottle of Sam Adams and wiggled it at Sam.

"Sure. I'll grab chips, and we can soothe ourselves outside."

Judy opened the beers and followed Sam onto the patio.

Sam stood by the TV. "On or off?"

"Let's keep it off. I'm not ready for hurricane hysteria yet."

Sam took glasses out of a cabinet and swapped one for a beer. They each plopped onto a chaise and poured out the beer.

"I love that sound," Judy mused.

"Nothing like it," Sam agreed.

They sat without talking for several minutes.

Then Sam spoke. "I've been thinking…"

"Uh-oh." Judy smiled. This was the usual preamble to a new planting scheme or a project on the house.

"I'm getting bored at work. Now that I've established the business, it's the same every day."

"Thinking of opening a practice over here?" They'd talked once of offering a Pampered Pets veterinary care service on the island, but decided while it would be profitable and the pets would be okay, the human customers would probably be more than they could stand.

"Oh, no. We killed that idea long ago. And I got over the need to care for other animals by volunteering at the shelter. No. I thought I'd hire someone to run the business and stop work altogether."

"Wouldn't you be more bored not working?"

"Nope. I've decided I'll buy a boat and sail around the world. Just bum around. Never really stop."

"Are you serious? What about me and Jack?"

"Oh, you would come too. I'd need you for crew. I don't want to have hired help on the boat—that'd ruin the whole thing."

"Are you insane?" Judy no longer smiled. She *hated* sailing. It was okay for a few hours, but it was dangerous in bad weather and boring in good.

"I'm perfectly sane, and I'm serious. I know just the boat to buy—you'd love it. We'd take short cruises at first to get used to the boat and then take off." Sam got up and hurried into the kitchen, returning with a large colored pamphlet. "See. This has plenty of cabin space. The galley is modern. The sails are easy to hoist, and it's got two huge engines."

"Sam, you know I don't like sailing. And you haven't done much in years. What put this into your head?"

"I know what you're thinking, so don't give me any male menopause shit!" Sam snapped. "I'm bored and need a change, dammit." Sam grabbed the brochure and stormed into the kitchen.

Judy sipped her beer. It would make Sam happy if she went along with this, but she just couldn't. She'd crossed the Atlantic several times on regular liners and had seen the waves in just minor storms—and would not want to try even that water in anything smaller. But poor Sam. How long had he felt that way? Was it somehow her fault he'd gotten into this state?

Sam came back out, picked up his beer, and began pacing. "I thought I had the solution. But maybe I could do something else."

"Could you start another business?"

"Hell, no. They're really all the same unless there is something you're burning to do. I just don't care anymore about having employees and making money. We have enough. I just want to enjoy it more."

"Instead of your own boat, what about crewing for other people? There's always talk down here about the America's Cup. Maybe you could get involved in that."

"That might be fun. But it was the island-hopping, lazy lifestyle that really called out to me. That America's Cup deal is serious. Probably too serious for me. And I'm probably not fit enough anyway. Damn. Are you sure you wouldn't go?"

"Sam. There's a lot I'd do for you, but I don't like boats. Maybe you could go with someone else. You wouldn't have to stay away forever. And you might be able to get it out of your system. I don't want you to turn into an angry old man who blames me for ruining your life."

"I wanted you and Jack to come with me. Damn. I really thought it was a good idea." Sam grimaced. "Oh, well. What's for supper? Or do you want to go out?"

"I'd be happy with just another beer. I've got to get up early to see the folks, and I'm more tired than hungry right now."

"I'm starved. Mind if I walked into town and got something? The walk will settle me down."

"Go ahead, Sam. See you tomorrow."

Sam quickly gathered his keys and left through the kitchen door without saying good-bye.

Judy sat and patted Jack, who had just wandered in. "Jack, meet the new me—Judy the dream smasher."

Then she laughed ruefully and ruffled Jack's fur. "And I don't care what he says, it *is* male menopause."

CHAPTER 6

Judy lay awake. She wanted to fall asleep fast so she'd be alert at breakfast, but she also was waiting for Sam to get home. He'd left about seven, so she expected him at least by ten. But ten, eleven, twelve passed with no Sam. With each hour she became less sleepy as she bounced between worry, anger and what? Maybe a twinge of guilt for handling the boat issue. She could've been more sensitive. At least she hadn't laughed at him.

Her alarm rang at four, and she silenced it on the first slap. Somehow she'd fallen asleep, and Sam was there, sleeping on his back with a sweet smile on his face. He looked like a ten-year-old boy.

She got to the inn at 5:05 a.m. to find her father standing outside waiting. She parked and hurried up the slate walk.

"You're late." Ansel turned and went inside—barely holding the door open for her as she trailed behind. His face was red, his posture overly erect, his black hair (dyed?) in a buzz cut. Ansel once had the build and still had the demeanor of an army colonel. No one would guess he was the retired owner of a small women's dress shop in Bangor.

"Five minutes," she insisted, defending herself. He didn't respond. She knew better than to force it, and followed him into the building.

The inn was in a historic house—by Florida standards. Built in 1941, the ceilings were low, and all surfaces were of gleaming woods. She shivered from the abundance of Early American furnishings as they passed through three public living rooms to reach the dining room. Her mother sat at a narrow trencher table eating a muffin. She took a big drink of coffee as Judy came into the room.

"Hi, Mum."

A long pause as Greta swallowed. "You're late. We were worried you weren't coming—and after Mrs. Moore was so kind to put out our breakfasts." She took another bite, holding her muffin delicately with long pale fingers. Greta wore thick glasses in big black oblong frames; she aimed them at Judy as if looking for flaws.

"I'm five minutes late. Jesus!"

"Don't swear. You know your father doesn't allow that kind of talk." Greta turned her attention back to the muffin. Ansel sat down, focused on his food. Neither offered Judy anything, so she picked up the cup at the third place setting, found the thermos placed on a counter in the pantry, and poured herself a cup. Back at the table, she sat and took a muffin.

Her parents each had butter on their plates. "Where's the butter?"

"Oh, we figured you weren't coming, so put it back in the fridge," Greta said.

Judy now noticed that both her parents also had juice and fruit salads, but both dishes and food were out of sight. She gave up and nibbled at the large dry muffin. The coffee was good. Strong.

She stared at her parents. They grew a little smaller each time she saw them. They were drying up.

"How's Aunt Helen?"

Her mother stopped eating. It took at least thirty seconds before she spoke—and when she did, she waved her arm as if directing an orchestra, one beat per sentence. "She's better. She can walk quite well as long as she's on a smooth surface. She has trouble in her apartment, though—the carpets trip her up. And her arm still doesn't work. And I can't understand a word she says—Ansel gets some of them, but it's frustrating for all of us." Greta went back to her food.

Ansel banged his knife handle on the table. "You should have gone down and stayed with her as we asked. She gets therapy, but the staff changes every day. You could've helped my sister recover. We are very disappointed in you. Your own family—and you wouldn't help."

"Dad. I couldn't leave Sam and my job. Full recovery from a stroke like hers takes months. She shouldn't have gone home so soon from the hospital—moved to a rehab nursing home like her doctors wanted. And I did suggest several homes near here where I could've added to her therapy and kept an eye on her. I can't help it if she's a stubborn as a mule." Judy had never liked Aunt Helen. She was sharp with kids—nothing pleased her. Judy tried for years, but gave up when she was fifteen or sixteen and Helen had criticized a Christmas gift she'd given her as "ugly as sin". Judy not only stopped trying to please her aunt—she began to enjoy irritating Helen while escaping notice of her parents. Just little things. She'd hear Helen hated the color mauve and then search for gifts for her in that color. She'd pretend to mis-hear orders for drinks and bring her beer instead of sherry, carrot sticks instead of carrot cake. She gave her a kitten for Christmas, knowing Helen hated cats and was allergic. (This trick she regretted—having to watch Helen ignore the animal until finally her housekeeper rescued it.) And she celebrated when Helen finally left Maine and moved to Florida.

Time to change the subject. "I don't know if you heard—it was on TV up here—but two of our friends were badly injured walking home from dinner with us. A storm tipped a tree onto them. One is probably going to die—Joe Corliss—I don't know if you ever met him."

Ansel looked up, interested. "That reminds me. Frank just got a big promotion—moving to Colorado to head up one of the companies."

"That's great. Bet you'll miss the kids, though." Did they ever hear her?

"Not so much." Greta daintily dabbed her mouth with a napkin. "Mary Lee has been involved in a charity and drops the children off for us to mind. It's hard on your father with all their ruckus."

"Does this happen often?"

"Almost every month. And she just shows up with them, so we can't very well refuse." Greta held her nose in the air, one of her most disapproving poses.

"That doesn't sound like her." Mary Lee was scared to death of Greta and Ansel and was always polite to a fault.

"Well, we may have agreed in principle to do it for her meeting," Ansel fumed. "But she should call and remind us."

Judy withdrew into her coffee cup. How many times when she was a child had she hoped what she heard was true: as the only redhead in the family, she must've been adopted or dropped on the doorstep. Whenever she saw a family of redheads, she'd wonder if they were hers. Her dreams were dashed in the ninth grade science class when she learned that the gene for red hair was recessive, and you needn't have a mother with red hair to have it yourself.

And what had happened between her and her father? Her mother had always been cool and distant, and now was just more so. And Judy could understand that. But she had been close to her father. Since she was three or four, they had gardened together, and fished. She was the one to jump into the car to go on errands with him. He'd been the one to read to Judy and her brothers when they were children. Every night, hanging on his armchair, vying to get closest to him and the book. Later, when she was in high school and college, she'd shared her new literary finds with him, and he had read poetry to her whenever they were at the cabin together. What had happened? Did he feel unsuccessful? His business never really took off as he had dreamed. Maybe he just got worn away living with Greta. Maybe it was television. He used to make fun of people who he stopped visiting because they wouldn't "turn the damn thing off". But now he was one of them. For years now, whenever she visited her parents, the TV was always on and their attention to the screen—even during the ads—was greater to it than to her. And she never saw him read anymore—except to scan the local newspaper. She'd find books she'd given him for Christmas or birthdays sitting unread in a pile behind his La-Z-Boy chair. She missed her old father.

Judy dramatically lifted her arm to look at her watch. "Hey, it's almost six. You've got to go and so do I." She stood up and backed toward the exit as her parents gathered their dishes and disappeared into the pantry.

⊂₰⊃

On Thursday Judy intended to visit Joe in hospice. He'd been put in a room at the far end of a corridor that had special air-handling equipment to prevent spread of infection. The room was entered through two doors; Judy opened the first one, but stood and leaned against the wall, not even looking into the room. She was overcome with sadness over her good old neighbor. After five minutes a nurse came into the foyer.

"Can I help you?"

"No. No. It's just so sad."

"Are you family?" The nurse stopped and put her hand on Judy's shoulder.

"Friend. Neighbor."

"Are you going in?"

"I think I'll wait and come back tomorrow." Judy gave a weak smile to the nurse and fled the unit. So much for being a health-care professional, she thought, as she hurried down the stairs to visit Eileen.

<hr />

On Friday night Hurricane Darlene was predicted to hit Palm Beach at three the next afternoon. It was still expected to be a Category 3 storm.

Judy and Sam were ready. While there was an evacuation order for the town, they were staying home. Margarida was coming over at ten the next morning. They had already secured her house and brought her things over. Sam had moved the patio furniture to the cellar, where they would spend the night. He'd primed the generator; iced the coolers, and stocked the cellar's refrigerators. Sam had five large battery-powered lanterns ready to go. They had radios, a battery-powered TV/DVD player, magazines, books, bedding, towels, and toiletries.

Joe was still alive in the hospice unit. Eileen would be discharged as soon as the storm was over. Her relatives were all at the Breakers. At the last minute, Marilyn had also moved to the Breakers. The Hudsons had left the island.

At work, Judy noted a wide divide between homeowners and renters. The renters were more like little kids, excited by the approaching storm, while homeowners were tired from putting up shutters, doing last-minute yardwork, and shopping for supplies in crowded stores with mostly empty shelves. The media hype didn't help—few homeowners had truly hurricane-safe houses, and after a few days of watching the storm approach, they walked around in a state of sustained panic. Often the renters weren't so giddy after a storm, as many carried no insurance for the contents of their damaged homes and apartments.

Before they moved in, Sam had hired an engineering firm to study their house. Then he had a construction firm make the changes suggested by the engineers to strengthen the roof and windows of the already sturdy home. So Friday night Sam and Judy felt safe and a little excited about the days ahead. They would stay home until the hurricane's mess had been cleared—usually a week or so. Sam had three employees staying at his business during the storm. At the hospital, PT staff were staying there and would sub for Judy.

Celebrating the end of a busy week, Judy served for dinner two Maine lobsters, melted Irish butter, green salad, and a cold muscadet. They sat sucking on shells and praising the tender meat as it grew dark outside. After coffee and cookies, they went outside shaking a bag of catnip-flavored treats and captured Jack. Once inside they went to check the cellar to make sure everything was set. At ten they went up, had some sleepy sex, then watched TV in bed until they dropped off.

<hr>

The TV was still on when Jack batted at Judy's eyelids. He would be trying to get outside all day—until the storm came. Then he'd be happy in a cellar closet.

"Hi, Jack. Want breakfast?"

Jack jumped off the bed and started down the stairs. Judy stretched and then followed. She fed the cat, popped some crumpets into the toaster oven, and put on water for coffee. Twenty minutes later Judy had a full tray and hummed upstairs. Sam was awake and getting dressed.

"I thought we'd eat in bed."

"Oh. Okay." Half dressed, Sam sat back on the bed. "Bad news on TV. The storm has strengthened, and it could even be a Cat Four when it hits here. I'm waiting for the next weather report—then we have to review our options."

Judy's mood plummeted. Happy, secure one instant changed to the falling stomach and dimmed vision that comes with fear. She grabbed an old newspaper hurricane guide from the nightstand: Category 4 storms had wind speeds of 131 to 155 mph, with extreme, almost total destruction of doors and windows, with many roofs lost.

"Can our house stand a Cat Four?"

"It's supposed to. And our trees are small and safe. Danger could come from one of Bean's trees toppling over onto our house. I'll go outside and double-check. I don't know enough about floods—

storm surge and all that. I'll call Jim at the engineering firm. If he says we're okay, we'll stay."

The next weather report came on. Prediction was now for a Category 4 storm to hit about five o'clock that evening. As part of the forecast, the local TV station showed photos of the hurricane in 1928, which killed 2,500 people.

"Well, I'm convinced," Sam said. "Let's pack up and move out now for the office. You call Margarida and get Jack in the carrier. I'll pack the cars. There's room in the garage over there for both of them. I've paid the employees to use cabs."

For two hours Judy and Sam packed cats, entertainment, food, and clothing into the two vehicles. By nine o'clock they were ready, and Margarida was sitting in Sam's front seat.

The phone rang inside the house, and Judy ran to answer it. She came outside where Sam was double—checking the supplies against his lists. "It's Eileen. The Breakers has closed. They're sending everyone off the island. The hotel found space in a motel out west for most of the family, but Marilyn needs someplace to go…She wasn't a registered guest, and the family is already going to be crammed in with cots at the motel. Eileen thought we'd be staying here and could put Marilyn up."

Sam rolled his eyes. "I'll probably regret this, but tell her that Marilyn's welcome at Pocket Pets. Tell her to take a taxi in a couple of hours. And pack for three days and bring whatever drinks and snacks she uses. We'll have plenty of real food unless she's on some weird diet."

Judy relayed the message. Then she and Sam went back inside to get additional supplies for Marilyn, in case she came.

"Do you think Marilyn will come?" asked Judy.

"She will if she saw the same TV program we did." Sam grinned and swept his eyes over the vehicles to see if they'd forgotten anything. "This'll be a tight squeeze over there. We can use my office. Margarida and Marilyn can have the one next to mine. The staff can have the rest of the offices, and we can all share the reception area."

Half an hour later, the two vehicles were packed, and they moved out. The roads were fairly busy with those leaving the island. Few cars were coming the other way. It was breezy out, but the sun was shining and the sky bright blue. No sign of any danger.

As Judy drove alone, she was beginning to feel better. Pocket Pets was a building built for hurricane safety and was on high ground. They would be safe, and the storm would be over by morning. They'd just have to stay a day or two camping out. They had plenty of food and things to do. And she could play with the little cats.

Just at noon they drove into Pocket Pets, a one-story complex painted a cheery rose. Sam was upset to find Hank and Roberto's cars in the garage. He sent those employees home to return later by cab if they wished. Judy, Sam, and Dave, the "good" employee, unloaded the vehicles and set up the cots and supplies.

Dave knew of a neighborhood restaurant that was staying open until late afternoon, so they all walked over and had a lively lunch. Southern cooking was the specialty, so they attacked a pile of ribs, greens, sweet potato fries, and corn bread served family style.

"This is great. I'm so full, I'll probably sleep all afternoon." Sam wiped his face with a frayed paper napkin and yawned.

They strolled back to Pocket Pets. Sam and Dave went to work caring for the animals. Judy lay down for a nap. Margarida settled in a comfortable chair. She was "redoing" the classics and had brought

Pickwick Papers from "my Dickens". Margarida had a large library, which included first editions of Dickens, Hawthorne, and Poe.

It was about three when a cab drove up. Sam could see Marilyn arguing with the driver. She finally handed him some bills, and he got out and pulled some bags from the trunk. He got back in the cab and sped off.

Sam and Dave retreated to the breeding room as Marilyn stomped into the building.

"Helloo! Helloo! Anybody here?" Marilyn yelled.

Judy woke, heard Marilyn, but stayed silent.

"Shhh! Judy's sleeping," Margarida warned as Marilyn came into the reception area.

"Oh. Hello. I think we've met. Can someone bring in my bags?" Marilyn demanded.

"Sorry. This is a shelter, not a hotel," said Margarida with the courage of age.

Marilyn stood stunned. Then she turned and went to get her luggage. It took her three trips.

Judy smiled at Margarida's pluck then got up to support her.

CHAPTER 7

Marilyn stood in the middle of the common room with her matched red leather luggage piled around her. She cleared her throat, a deep rumble.

"Oh." Margarida looked up from her book. "I'm Margarida, Marilyn, we met last year at your parents' house—we're going to be roommates. Your cot is in the room over there." Pointing, she smiled, then returned to her book.

Marilyn dragged her luggage into the office and took up most of the available floor space with it. She unpacked some things and then returned to the room with a laptop and some files. She made herself comfortable in a large leather chair in the corner opposite Margarida and settled down to review some documents for the insurance company she worked for.

Sam and the men came back from working and turned on the TV. Judy slept until five. When she came into the common area, a weatherman was promising Darlene's landfall within an hour. Everyone was silent watching the screen.

Judy didn't nap well. Her face was wrinkled from the pillow, her eyes were swollen, and she felt slow and stupid. She took a Mountain Dew out of the fridge and sat next to Sam on the couch.

She picked up the book she'd been reading earlier—*Monet's Table*—the cooking journals of Claude Monet. She'd leafed through the book ages ago, fascinated mostly by the photos of Monet's dining room. She'd even copied the yellows and blues as trim colors in their kitchen. Now she was reading for recipes and techniques. She and Sam had signed up for some lessons at the cooking school in West Palm, and Judy had been reading all their food books to get ready.

Marilyn was sitting in a chair in the corner, sitting erect with her eyes glued to the TV.

With effort, Judy put on a welcoming smile. "Oh, Marilyn. I just noticed you. I'm glad you came."

"Thanks for having me," Marilyn murmured without moving her eyes from the TV.

Outside the wind had picked up quite a bit. Judy watched the window instead of the TV. She'd never been in a hurricane in the daylight. It was less scary somehow, being able to watch. Right now, the rain was being blown horizontal to the ground, with leaves, paper, and other small objects being carried along with the rain. This hurricane "confetti" went as high into the sky as she could see.

A large, old, red brick building sat across the street. Suddenly the wind got stronger, and the windows in the building started popping out. Red curtains on one of the upper floors flapped against the building. Judy was fascinated. In just a minute or so, about half the windows had blown in. The large windows at street level were all still intact. She wondered how long they would last.

She started as Sam shook her shoulder. "Hey, wake up. I've called your name three times, and you're totally spaced out."

"It's the storm—it's been popping the windows out across the street," Judy said, stretching herself to try to wake up. "It was almost fun watching."

"Poor Bob Ranier," Sam said. "He's been trying to sell that building for two years now. I hope his insurance is up to date."

"Sorry to be so callous, Sam, but it brought me back to my childhood." Judy smiled.

"Your criminal childhood?" Sam asked.

"Oh, come on. Compared to my father's generation, we were hothouse plants. He and his brothers used to bend willows and send their youngest brother flying—he was only four. And their Halloween pranks—they'd tip over outhouses and throw the town's wooden sidewalks into the river. When I was growing up, I had the feeling I disappointed my parents by being too *good*. It's just that people weren't so quick to turn in kids doing mischief back then as they are now."

"Mischief! You guys were little vandals, from what you tell me. What's the connection to this storm?" Sam was laughing.

Judy felt the gulf between their childhoods. She and her brothers were left pretty much on their own during the day—they had chores to do, but otherwise were expected to stay outside except for meals. Sam, on the other hand, was a "city boy", growing up in an apartment in Portland under his mother's constant scrutiny—she made sure everything he did was correct, polite, and legal. She wouldn't even let him walk on the lawn. When he was about eight, he found a dead bird in the yard and was curious to see what was inside it. He mother caught him mid-operation and was incensed. For the next year, she made him join her every Saturday morning at the local Audubon Society. While meant as a penance, it provided him the basis for a life's interest in animals of all kinds.

She smiled and leaned back. "On the street behind our home was an older man, Mr. Hilton. We kids were all afraid of him—I don't know why. He was tall and thin, never smiled. But he only yelled a bit if we did something bad. But, anyway, for some reason we were always trying to get back at him. One time a group of us—five or six kids—gathered beside his barn. It was next to a vacant lot we used for a baseball field. It was late fall, and crabapple trees were all around. Made the prettiest jelly. Anyway, we made up this game. We took turns throwing apples at the little panes of glass in the windows of the upper story of the barn. You lost your turn if you missed or if you broke a window out of order. We broke every window on that side of the barn. He ran us off waving a rifle. He never shot it. Better yet, he knew who we were, but he never told our parents. Only years later did I realize that. Then I felt guilty, and he was already dead. I guess we were a bit awful back then."

"I just hope you got it all out of your system," said Sam. "Uh-oh—here we go!"

Just then the lights flickered as the power went out and the generator kicked in.

"Let's all go turn off lights we don't need. The generator can keep the A/C going if we're careful. Don't use the microwave. And ask me if you plan to use any other electric appliance," Sam ordered. He got up to go back to the animal area. Judy and Margarida checked lights everywhere else.

"How long will the storm last?" asked Margarida.

"I haven't been listening too well, but the whole thing is one hundred miles wide. Earlier it was going eight miles an hour. So—it should be over in the morning unless it stalls out," Judy guessed. Then she added, "Margarida, Marilyn—are you hungry at all? We'll put something together later, maybe tacos. Chopping up the vegetables will give us something to do."

"Yummy," from Margarida.

Marilyn looked up from the TV and nodded, saying nothing.

"Wow! There go the big windows over there," Judy was back storm watching. "Anything on TV about local damages?"

"They've pulled in all their crews," Margarida reported. "And national TV is the same as always—swaying palm trees and ocean waves and men in rain suits. No one is out where the storm is. Power is out in the whole county, and they're getting reports from people who've lost roofs. Trees are down all over. But the ocean is staying put so far. It's strange being in this building; it's like there's hardly any storm at all."

The men came back from the animal area. Sam offered to make cocktails, and they all applauded.

"We need vitamins...I think Bloody Marys are called for now. Just what the doctor ordered." Sam busied himself in the kitchenette and eventually appeared with a tray of drinks and a platter of celery and carrot sticks and blue cheese dressing.

As they drank, they chatted about their families and earlier storms. Sam checked the telephone to see if it was still working. Often they lost cell phone coverage, but the landline usually held. "If anyone wants to make a call, this might be a good time. I know my cell is out, and probably yours too."

Marilyn got up. "I'd better call my mother and let her know I'm here and safe." It took a while for her to get through, and then the conversation was short. "Mother is fine, just worried about the house," she reported. "Dad's no worse."

The employees also called their families. So far their houses were okay.

"After the storm, can we go right back to Palm Beach?" Marilyn asked.

"Probably not. They usually block the bridges until the roads are cleared and the water on the roads goes down. It could take a couple of days. On the mainland it depends where you live. Usually the main roads get cleared pretty quickly. It takes longer to clear out the neighborhoods. And there's the power issue—we've been without electricity for two, three weeks," Sam said, adding, "We've got a generator at home, but most of the houses in our neighborhood don't.

By seven o'clock the storm was impressive—lightning coming in bursts of four or five strikes every few seconds. The rain was in sheets, not drops. The wind was hard and steady. They could feel the whole building shift now, with the wind hitting its broad side.

In the kitchen Judy heated taco meat from home, and she and Margarida cut up tomatoes, lettuce, and onions. Hank came in, tested the meat, and declared it "passable" but needing more cumin. Roberto joined them and agreed with Hank and rummaged around the cabinets for seasoning. He and Hank busied themselves over the pot until Judy gave them tortillas to fry.

The little kitchen had no windows, and for a while Judy forgot the storm. It was fun cooking, and their finished product was tasty. Soon they were all eating, fat dripping from the tacos, drinking beer and babbling about everything but the storm. Slightly tipsy and tired, Judy and Hank cleaned the kitchen, while Sam, Dave, and Roberto worked. Then everyone gathered to watch TV.

Steady winds of 155 and gusts of 170 were reported from the city. Roads were impassable. Damage to buildings and trees was widespread. The news, however scary, soon became repetitive, so Sam got up and put in a video of *Waking Ned Devine*. With lights dimmed they sat flinching at the lightning outside and laughing at the movie.

When the movie was over, they split up to get ready for bed. Sam and Judy were already in their cots when the A/C went off.

"Damn!" Sam fumbled for a flashlight and went out into the common area. Marilyn was coming out of the kitchen holding a steaming cup. She stared at Sam. "The power went off."

"No kidding. What happened?" Sam grumbled.

"I don't know. I was making tea, and it just went off." Marilyn walked toward her "bedroom".

"How did you heat the water?" asked Sam.

"The microwave," Marilyn answered as she shut the door.

"Goddamn it! I told everyone not to use it for this very reason!" Sam shouted. Sam went back to Judy. "That woman used the microwave."

"I heard. We'll have to tape it shut tomorrow. Can you restart the generator?"

"Yeah. But it'll take a while. I have to go around and turn absolutely everything off. Then fiddle with the generator and then make sure everything the cats need is turned back on. It'll work, but it's fussy. Oh, I'm just so tired."

"Can I help?" Judy asked.

"No. I'll do it. But I could wring that woman's neck. Her whole superior attitude. Not a hint of apology."

Sam busied himself with the generator. An hour later when he finished and the power was back on, the noise outside suddenly stopped. He went and shook Judy awake.

"C'mon outside. The eye must be overhead."

Sam and Judy walked outside. It was eerily quiet. There wasn't much debris just outside the door, but when they went farther into the yard, they were amazed by the amount of damage. Windows, roof pieces, siding, signs, and tree limbs piled on the road and around the building. Wary of live wires, they retreated to the door.

"It's so quiet. How long will this last?" asked Judy.

"I don't know. But isn't this wonderful. Look at the stars—the eye must be directly overhead." Sam hugged Judy and sighed. "I guess we have Marilyn to thank for this. We'd be sound asleep if not for her."

"What's the saying? It's an ill wind that blows no good?" Judy smiled. They hugged, then returned to the building and bed.

As they slept, the storm came back full force. By morning, however, the lightning was sporadic as bands of clouds, wind, and rain swept through.

When Judy woke up, everyone else was in the common room having breakfast and watching the weather on TV. She got coffee and joined them.

Sam looked up. "Phones are still out. Palm Beach has at least a foot of water on the roads. The streets are full of trees and stuff. The county has declared an emergency: no one on the roads except police and utility crews. So we're here for today at least." Sam turned to the group and added, "Oh, and please remember—don't use any electric appliance without asking me first. It's okay to use the TV, radio, VCR, and lights. Anything else, ask me first. The generator can't do much more than AC. If you need to use something, I can always turn off the AC for a while. Everyone got that?"

There were murmurs of assent. Then Judy and Sam went outside.

"Oh, I miss our bed! I hurt all over." Judy stretched, then looked around. "Where did all this stuff come from?" The grounds around Pocket Pets were hip high in tree limbs and trash.

"From the sky, I guess." Sam chuckled. "I hope it looks worse than it is. This is going to be a long day. I woke up still seething about Marilyn. This whole thing feels like a murder mystery—you know—a bunch of strangers all locked up together—and she'd be the *perfect* victim." Sam leered, crossed his eyes, and pretended to strangle someone.

"Sam." Judy shook her head.

"I can dream, can't I? Oh, well, maybe she just forgot about the generator."

"I bet she remembered, but didn't believe you," Judy reasoned.

"You're probably right," Sam agreed.

"What's the plan of the day?" Judy asked.

"The electricity is off, so it'll be safe to clear up this debris. We can start. The guys can take care of the cats, then they can come out and help. By the time we're done, we'll be honestly hungry. We can haul the grill out and cook out here. Maybe Margarida and Marilyn can pull stuff together for that."

"Sounds good. Let's get started. I think I brought my gloves," said Judy as she walked inside.

The men were already taking care of the cats. Margarida was cleaning up from breakfast. Judy peeked into Marilyn's room and told her of the morning's plans. Marilyn was sitting on her cot reading a document. She was drinking from a large, full glass; a bottle of scotch stood on the floor by her elbow.

"I don't know where anything is," Marilyn stated. "And I don't cook. I can't do any of that."

"Then come outside and work with us. Later I'll come in and help Margarida." Judy tried to be calm.

"I don't have any clothes for that," Marilyn countered.

"You can use some of Sam's. He always keeps extra work clothes here for everyone." Judy still thought she could get Marilyn off the cot.

"I just can't do that," Marilyn snapped and then turned her back to Judy.

"Jesus!" Then Judy caught herself and went into the kitchen to talk with Margarida. "Later can you pick out some stuff for us for lunch? Sam'll get the grill going."

"Sure. That'll be fun." Margarida smiled and started looking through the boxes Sam and Judy had brought with them.

Judy got her gloves, found the trash bags, and went outside fuming and muttering to herself. "That bitch! If it weren't for her father dying, I'd smack her a good one!"

※

By two o'clock the weather had cleared and most of the yard was picked up, with trash and vegetation in separate huge piles by the road.

Sam started the grill, and Judy helped Margarida bring out the food. Hugo and Roberto got the picnic table and benches from the garage.

Margarida had made a beautiful salad and cut up a watermelon. She made crab salad rolls and marinated chicken wings and vegetables for grilling. Everyone came out and had a good time, except Marilyn, who stayed in her room.

By the time they'd eaten and cleared up, it was almost four. The men went in to care for the animals. Judy went in back and brought Jack into the common room. Jack didn't do laps, but sat beside Judy and leaned against her, purring.

Margarida brought in coffee for them, and they sat quietly for a while.

"Did Marilyn eat anything for lunch?" Judy asked. She didn't know why, but her whole life, she'd had an interest in food and in feeding people.

"I think she's been snacking on stuff she brought. She hasn't been out of our room since breakfast. She's been drinking quite a bit—she brought a half gallon of scotch, and it's more than half gone."

"Has she talked to you?"

"Not really. She might be upset about Joe. But she seems more angry than sad. I know she hated Sam's yelling at her."

"She probably blames Sam and me for Joe. It was our party that night, and I'm associated with the hospital she thinks is killing him. And now she's stuck here with us instead of being with her family." Judy thought she may have been too hard on Marilyn and decided to try to make Marilyn feel more comfortable.

※

Around five Marilyn came into the room and sat in a corner to read. Sam was in the kitchen making cocktails…Manhattans this time. As Sam brought the drinks out, he saw Marilyn, so warned everyone again about the electricity. "Ask me before turning anything electric on. The generator is making funny noises, and we sure don't want to lose the air—most of the cat areas don't have windows that open."

Judy brought out a basket of small bags of chips and other nibbles. She, Sam, Margarida, and Dave started a game of whist while Roberto and Jim played a video game. Dave put some Oscar

Peterson CDs on. Every once in a while, one of them would try the telephones, but landline and cell phones were still out. It was sunny and quiet outside.

After more rounds of whist, Judy decided they should have a proper supper, so she put two small chickens on to roast. Margarida joined her, and they prepared the meal together.

Sam came out from the animal area and settled on the couch next to Judy and Jack. "Oh. Anyone who wants can have a shower. We've got plenty of hot water, and Dave put out towels, soaps, and stuff. It's the room to the right when you go into the lab area."

Marilyn put down her drink. "I'll take one now." And she went into her room, came out with a large bag, and went into the lab.

Roberto and Jim finished their game and turned on the TV. They'd all been busy (except for Marilyn), so hadn't monitored the news during the day. The national news was on and focused on the Palm Beach area. A disaster was building. For years erosion had been a problem along the coast. Several parks and homes had been closed, and their beachfronts reinforced as the ocean threatened to reclaim them. During the hurricane heavy seas had again attacked the coastal buildings. At three o'clock, two large older condos in Palm Beach lost their foundations and toppled into the ocean. While the island was still closed to traffic, it was feared that several residents of the building had stayed during the hurricane and were dead or injured. Roads were a mess, so the first rescue workers arrived on foot, bicycle, and golf cart.

"Any idea where those condos are? They haven't mentioned any address." Judy sat on the edge of the couch and held onto Sam's knee.

Sam covered her hand with his. "I can't make it out—we'll probably have to wait for the local news. Jesus. Never imagined a building could just collapse like that. They can't be that old." A reporter was standing nearby. Behind him waves fifteen feet high pounded the beach, but he was too far away from the condos for them to see the wreckage. Weather reports were for high seas for several more days. There would be no chance to strengthen any endangered structure for several days.

Then the TV went off.

CHAPTER 8

"Dammit!" Sam growled. He took a flashlight and hurried into the lab. He came right back out. "Marilyn used a hair dryer. What is it with her? I feel like picking her up and putting her in a tent out back." Sam walked around the room to cool off, took a deep breath, then asked Dave and Hank to pull out all the electric plugs from the wall. When they had finished, he'd go out and start the generator again."

Sam plopped on the couch next to Judy. "She's pathologic."

"Probably." Judy put her arm around him. "It's some kind of test. You get through this, and something really nice is going to happen."

"Sure. Or we're on some kind of reality show. Well, if the prize is never seeing that woman again, I'm game."

"Maybe tomorrow we can all go home."

The men came back into the common area and said all plugs were pulled, so Sam got up to start the generator. Half an hour later, the AC and lights came on, and Sam came back.

Judy and Margarida had finished cooking dinner using the gas stove and lanterns. As soon as Sam came back, they sat down to eat.

"Where's Marilyn?" Judy asked.

No one had seen her.

"Is she still in the bathroom? Maybe someone should check. I can't. I'd kill her," Sam grumbled. "Dave, would you please check on her."

Dave first checked the bedroom and reported that Marilyn was in there, but didn't want to eat.

"All the more for us," Sam said. "C'mon, eat up."

They were hungry and made short work of the meal. Later they sat back on the more comfortable chairs and had coffee and cookies.

"Aha!" Sam tried his phone and got a dial tone. "We're back in business."

Dave went into the office, but found the landline was still out.

For the next hour they made calls. Sam called his engineer and asked him to check out the Palm Beach houses and find out when they could return to the island. The employees called their families; all three would be able to go home as soon as roads opened.

Later Margarida brought the phone in to Marilyn so she could call the hospital. Joe was still alive, and her mother was eager to get home. Marilyn also talked with her relatives at the motel out west. They had been told that the Breakers wouldn't open for weeks. The hotel itself hadn't much wind damage, but erosion had eaten away a huge section of the grounds. They were closing to reinforce the foundation on the ocean side of the buildings. The motel couldn't keep the family more than two days, as other guests with reservations were arriving.

Marilyn stayed on her cot the rest of the night. Everyone else watched TV a while, but there were no new reports of the condo catastrophe, so they put on music.

Dave and Hank brought six tiny kittens out and put them in a corral. They brought out boxes of toys and put up a miniature town, with streets, hills, and trees. Then they took out two small radio-controlled cars and raced them through the city. The little cats chased the cars, and the men had a grand time. They'd obviously invented a game with elaborate scoring, but no one else could figure it out. Jack went over to the corral and sat, tail swishing, watching the action intently as if he knew the rules.

The cheerful noises from the game made Judy smile. It reminded her of her family on Christmas morning. Which then reminded her of eggnog. She went to the kitchen and came back with a tray of mugs with eggnog and bourbon and a loaf of her fruitcake. She, Sam, and Margarida sat sipping and watching the men and cats at play.

Later they each showered, Judy and Sam going last. Judy was asleep on her cot when Sam came into the office. He banged around, waking her.

"Judy. You awake?"

"No."

"Hey, c'mon. Let me in." Sam sat on her cot and pulled on the blanket.

"Sam, you'll kill us both. This cot barely holds me." Judy hung onto the blanket and smacked Sam's hand. "We could do it on the floor." Sam grabbed Judy and rolled her off the cot, knocking her head on the floor. "Ouch! Jesus Sam, go away!" Her head had hit so hard on the floor that her teeth hurt. Stunned, she struggled to stand, grabbed a blanket and stormed into the darkened common room.

Sam didn't follow her. She stood a while fuming then pushed two chairs together (the couch was too short) and made an uncomfortable bed for the night.

Sam's sexual appetite was beginning to irritate Judy. He could be a pest about sex. Every night wasn't enough for him—and when he wanted sex, he could get rough. Usually just verbally, but he'd pretty much forced himself on her a few times. Maybe she'd just lived alone too long. She'd dated some. And every few years a romance developed…but she'd not had much sex in her life before Sam. But she'd had partners who were better at giving her pleasure than Sam. Lately Sam just wanted to please himself. She seldom was aroused and more and more felt used by him. Occasionally he'd get silly, and they'd play around, but it was happening less and less.

Judy would have said she'd stayed awake most of the night but awoke at dawn feeling rested. Her forehead felt tight and hurt when she touched the large lump over her right eye. She was surprised not to have a headache. She pulled her hair over the bump before gathering her blanket and going to get dressed.

Sam was snuggled on his cot, snoring softly, holding Jack in his arms with his head resting on both of their pillows.

Later, they had a quick breakfast while watching TV. Most of the major roads were open, although none of the traffic lights were working. Police were directing traffic at a few intersections; at most, however, the four-way stop rule was in effect.

Right after breakfast Sam called for taxis and sent his employees home. He would care for the cats, and the men would resume their regular schedule the next day.

Marilyn hadn't said a word since her shower. At nine thirty she appeared in the common room with her bags packed. Just as she came into the room, Sam's engineer called. Sam and Judy's house was fine. Their generator had kicked in and was still working. There was a little debris around the yard, but no real damage. Margarida's electricity was out, but the house wasn't damaged. Joe and Eileen's house, however, was badly damaged. A large tree had squashed the roof, and another section of roof had been torn away. His men were putting up tarps, but there was water damage throughout the house. Until repairs were done, the house would be unlivable. Palm Beach was allowing residents back to the island at three thirty that afternoon. He had no idea when power would come back. Florida Power & Light was still evaluating its system; fortunately the city had just buried electric cables in much of the island, so few lines would need repair.

Marilyn stood and stared at Sam as he made his report.

Margarida smiled. "I'm so relieved my house is all right. I can live without power—done that many times. Right now I'm anxious to get home and clean out the refrigerator—it'll be real smelly by now."

"Oh, I'm relieved about our house too. It's a strong building, but I always worry. I'll drive over around four. Margarida, you do your cleaning, then come over for supper. You can have a nice hot bath too." Judy smiled and went toward the office to start packing, but came right back out. "Oh, I'll do lunch here. We've still got some stuff to work with."

She'd avoided talking to Sam all morning but now beckoned for him to come into the office. "What'll we do about Marilyn? She can't go to her mother's house. No hotel will be open yet. I think we should invite her home with us, but I didn't dare offer until I spoke with you."

"Dammit. I'd rather take in a few bums off the street."

"That's not the choice."

"I know. I know. Okay. But it'd better not be for long, or there will be a murder…or suicide. And Judy…about last night…"

Judy waved Sam away, went back to the common area and took a deep breath. "Marilyn. You're welcome to come home with us for a few days until you can find something else. That way you can work on your parents' house, dry out the art, and get valuables into a safe place. The paper publishes a guide for cleaning up after hurricanes; you can have ours."

Marilyn looked at the floor and mumbled, "Thank you."

During the day Judy and Margarida packed, cleaned and made a simple lunch. Marilyn sat in a corner and read, getting up from time to time to refresh her scotch. They kept the TV on: two more condos had crumbled into the ocean. Several houses along the beach had also been lost to erosion. So far eighteen bodies had been found, but no survivors. It was feared many more were dead.

Sam finished the work in the laboratory and began loading the vehicles. He had to leave a load behind for the next day to make room for Marilyn's luggage.

At four Judy left for Palm Beach with Margarida and Marilyn. Sam would bring Jack in his cage and most of the baggage later. With no working traffic lights, it took an hour for them just to reach the bridge; traffic stopped at each intersection, and one car at a time crept through. The roads were narrowed by piles of debris higher than their car. Only one bridge was open for non-emergency vehicles, and that bridge was crammed with cars trying to get onto the island. Police were checking IDs at the Palm Beach side.

Judy turned into the driveway well after six. "Whew. That took longer than I ever thought." She sat back and closed her eyes for a few seconds, then got out of the car. They all helped unload the luggage, and Judy opened the house for Marilyn to go in.

"Just make yourself at home. I'm going to help Margarida with her stuff, but I'll be right back."

Judy went into Margarida's with the elderly woman. They went upstairs to check for leaks, then walked back outside and walked around the house to survey the damage. Several limbs were down, and a few shingles were ripped off the gardening shed, but everything else seemed all right. They went back inside, and Margarida opened the refrigerator.

"Oh, this smells bad. I'm glad I don't have much in here. I think I'll wait for morning to clean this out, though—those things are so much easier in the morning. Want tea, Judy?"

"Better not. I just dumped Marilyn. I should go back and settle her in. I'll have Sam come over around eight to walk you over for supper."

"I can walk over alone."

"Oh, no. Let's play it safe. He can check the path on the way over to make sure it's clear. I know you can't see too well at night."

"Oh, all right, dear." Margarida put water on and brought down a clay teapot and bone china teacup and saucer from a cupboard. "It's lovely to be home."

Margarida sat at the kitchen table. Judy saw how tired and worn Margarida had become from the storm. "You sit right there. I'll make the tea, and yes, I'd love some too."

After the water boiled, she added some to warm the teapot, then made tea.

After tea Judy stood and stretched. "Well, I'd better go. Oh, do you have a working flashlight?"

Margarida smiled and pointed behind her to a multicolored row of nine-volt lanterns standing against the wall. "Don't worry about me. And take it easy—we'll all be tired tonight and won't need much for supper."

When Judy got home, she found Marilyn sitting in the TV room drinking scotch. She brought her guest upstairs to her room, then took a long hot bath. She was dying to walk down to the beach to see the fallen condos, but they had been warned by the police at the bridge to stay away until crews had declared the area safe.

Sam got home at eight, and Judy sent him over to get Margarida. The hurricane had sucked all the water from the air, so the evening was clear and crisp. They ate on the patio. Sam had a little fire going. Judy baked potatoes and found steaks and oriental veggies in the freezer. They had a peaceful meal. Marilyn ate with them; she didn't offer any conversation, but answered their questions. Her parents' house was a mess. She'd taken down some art that would need restoration and bagged the damp linens. Marilyn didn't know what else she could do without power. She seemed truly grateful when Sam told her of his plan to contact restoration experts and contractors the next day.

After coffee Sam walked Margarida home and came right back. Judy and Marilyn sat drinking Irish Mist. Sam added a log to the fire.

"It's such a treat to be back. I'm so sad about your parents' home. Sam will talk to Eileen tomorrow. Poor Eileen…She's almost ready to come home, and now she can't."

"Hmmm." With that, Marilyn got up and left the room.

Sam came over and sat next to Judy on the chaise, hugging her. "This thing's too narrow for sex, we'd hurt ourselves—let's go upstairs."

"Not yet, but this is nice." Judy took a deep breath, fingering the bump on her forehead. "Tomorrow we need to find out more about the condos and houses that collapsed. I can't imagine being in a condo that just slips over into the ocean. I wonder how long it took? I don't think there's even been a disaster movie about that."

"If it happened to me, I'd hope I was sound asleep."

"This happened here in broad daylight. There will probably be stories about it in the papers tomorrow—so far there's been nothing more on TV."

They sat watching the fire and fell asleep.

The next morning Jack woke Judy and Sam. Judy was stiff from sleeping on the narrow chaise with Sam—he had taken most of it, while she hung over the side. But she was happy too. She was home. Home was safe. She heard noises in the kitchen. She'd forgotten about Marilyn. Oh, well. She went in and found Marilyn looking through the cabinets.

"Morning, Marilyn."

"Morning."

"Can I help you find something?"

"I was looking for instant coffee."

"I have a little instant espresso I use for cooking. It's in the spice cabinet over there."

"Yuck. No thanks."

"If you can hold on, I'll make some real coffee—it only takes a couple minutes."

Judy busied about getting breakfast and brought it out to the patio. The three ate in silence. Marilyn's presence took the air out of Judy. So many subjects could be hurtful to her—Joe, her parents' house, her situation living here. Whenever Judy thought of something to say, she'd anticipate Marilyn's response and then stay quiet.

Soon Marilyn finished and left the table without a word.

"Whew. I don't know why she makes me so tense. I just can't think of anything to say when she's around." Judy sat back, sipping on her third cup of coffee.

"I know. I was sitting here like a little kid trying to think of something to say to the grownups." Sam shook his head. "Well, I'm going up to shower and change."

Sam had just left the patio when the phone rang. A few minutes later he was back. "That was Eileen. Joe's still alive. She's being discharged this afternoon. She tried to find a hotel room, but everything's full. I invited her here. We can put her in the TV room. That couch pulls out to a pretty comfortable bed. Don't you think?"

"I feel bad—I should've thought to invite her after we got home yesterday. Did she have to ask, or did you..."

"I invited her. She called about the house and only mentioned being discharged today when I asked her."

"What time?"

"About three. We can drive over and pick her up. We'd better leave about two—it'll be slow going for days without traffic lights."

"I just had a bad thought."

"Huh?"

"What about the rest of the family? I forget how many are here, but they're being kicked out of that motel soon—I forget which day."

"We can talk about it with Eileen. Let's not worry about it right now. I'm going out and clean up the yard as soon as I change. Wanna come?" Sam headed upstairs.

"Sure, in a few minutes. First I need to think of something for supper." As she worked in the kitchen, Judy thought about Eileen's family and what they could do for them. She and Sam still had the one bedroom in the cellar, and they could set up some cots in other areas. Margarida might be willing to take some in, although she didn't have a generator and who knew when power would be come back. She didn't know if the other Sunshine family, the Hudsons, would be back yet. They might take in one or two people, but Judy and Sam would probably have to feed them...The Hudsons never cooked. The few times they'd had the Sunshine group over, they'd had takeout and didn't even know how to heat it up properly. Oh, well, maybe Joe would die today, they'd have the funeral in a day or so, and everyone could leave before there was a problem.

In just a few hours, Sam and Judy had the yard almost back to normal. The pool had been a mess; the neighbor's bamboo forest left a solid mat of little leaves on the surface and thousands more on the pool floor. It was weirdly quiet—not another soul was outside.

"Remember Lake Worth after a hurricane?" Judy stopped raking.

"Some of my best memories of the place." Sam leaned on his rake. "We men went up and down the street putting up shutters and plywood. Then someone would bring out the cold beer…and after the hurricane we'd take everything down. and someone would bring out the warm beer…What were you women doing anyway?"

"I worried a lot. And bought junk food. And went back and bought healthy food. And cleaned trash cans to hold water to flush the toilets. And worried some more. The best part was afterward. when we'd all get together and cook what was going to spoil first."

"I keep hoping to get more neighborhood things going over here, but in the season we never see the rest of the folks. I hardly know the people right next door. Oh, well, back to work."

Both Judy and Sam went to pick up Eileen from the rehab unit at the hospital. While Sam was taking Eileen's things to the car, Judy wheeled her over to the hospice unit to see Joe. Eileen was wearing a bright pink flowered silk scarf as a turban—wisps of gray hair with reddish tips poked out everywhere. Eileen was pale and her attempts at makeup accentuated it. Sitting in the wheelchair, she looked like a startled, sad, little Michelin Man. Short and stubby, she was wearing a turquoise tracksuit several sizes too large. Judy wondered at her getup—maybe it was Marilyn's. Eileen usually wore bright colors, but her clothes were usually impeccably designed of expensive fabrics. No tracksuits for sure. Judy laughed; Palm Beach had infected her vocabulary—she was saying "track suit" in her mind, but it was actually a plain old sweatsuit, aka "fitness fleece" in the Bean catalogue. Joe's room was eerily silent after the hubbub of the rehab unit. Joe's chest moved slowly and barely perceptibly as he took in shallow breaths. Other than his breathing and the slow drip of the IV, nothing else moved in the room.

Eileen held Joe's hand and laid her other hand on his chest. "His heart feels strong."

"Your Joe is a tough one." Judy felt stupid. She couldn't think of anything to say.

"These are his favorite pajamas. I'm glad he doesn't have to wear johnnies anymore."

"Are those silk?" Again stupid, Judy thought.

"Oh, yes. He likes silk or Sea Island cotton for PJs. Nothing else will do. He shops for all his clothes by feel—if it doesn't feel right, he won't wear it. I love one of his outfits—that red plaid shirt and tweed jacket—they look so rough and tough, but they're both cashmere and light as a feather."

Judy couldn't think of anything to say. She was afraid she'd use the past tense talking about Joe, so she rubbed Eileen's shoulders.

"I hate to leave him, but I'm sure Sam's anxious to get going."

"There's no rush, Eileen. Take your time."

"That's sweet, dear. But we should go." She caressed Joe's cheeks and looked up at Judy, eyes tearing. "I wish I didn't have to wear these stupid gloves."

Judy wheeled Eileen out to the car, and Sam helped get her settled. Judy sat in back as Sam and Eileen chatted easily all the way home. Sam told her all about the damage to her own home and others in the neighborhood.

When they got to Sunshine Street, Sam parked in front of Eileen's house.

"Oh my. It's so much worse than I pictured. Poor old thing…It looks so broken. I'm glad Joe won't see this." Eileen sniffed, then blew her nose and sat back erect.

When they got home, Judy was surprised that Marilyn came right out and helped Eileen navigate into the house and get settled in the TV room. Eileen said she was tired and went straight to bed.

Sam and Judy took coffee out onto the patio.

"How's Joe?" Sam asked.

"Oh, Sam. He's so near death—but there's been no real change from a week ago. I don't know what keeps him going. His breathing is so shallow, he must be getting oxygen through his skin! He had—I mean *has*—a living will that states he wants hydration, but no extreme measures—so they're giving him some nutrients via the IV—but they expected him to die a day or two after he got to hospice. If he were a dog, what would you do?"

"Normally I'd euthanize an animal only if it had no hope of survival and if it was in pain—which Joe seems not to be. But yes, if an animal had as severe a brain injury as Joe and had been in a coma, I'd put it down. I never enjoy doing it, but if an animal can't enjoy any part of life, it seems the best thing to do. When I was in training, the part I hated was having to euthanize an animal for economic reasons—we could've made the animal better, but the owner couldn't or wouldn't afford it. That's why I ended up working at the research lab. I bet back in the old days, the doctors would've eased Joe on his way by now, but everything's so regulated…I guess they can't do it anymore."

CHAPTER 9

Over breakfast the next day, Judy and Eileen discussed what to do with Joe's family—they'd be homeless soon.

"You've seen our cellar, Eileen. It'd be comfortable for one or two people or a bunch of kids camping out—but that doesn't do much toward putting up all twenty-four. Is everyone still trying to stay down here?"

"I'll call later this morning to get a better sense of it. Yesterday it sounded to me as if some of the spouses and kids would like to head back home. They were pretty upset by the storm and, I think, discouraged they couldn't use my house." Eileen sipped her coffee.

"We can have Margarida over later for coffee and sound her out. She never uses her second floor—maybe some could stay there. She has a gas stove, but no refrigerator with the power out. With coolers we could set it up so they could do for themselves at breakfast and lunch, then come over here at night for supper."

"What about the Hudsons?"

"I'm not sure they'd take anyone. They certainly wouldn't want them to use the kitchen. You know how they are—they don't cook, and they hate getting their house dirty. Can you think of anyone else who could help?"

"I'll get Marilyn to go over to the house and get my address book. I can't think of anyone right off who's down here now. I hope she can recover some of my clothes today too. This pantsuit of Marilyn's makes me feel like a refugee." Eileen shrugged and added, "Which I am, I guess. At the hospital I called my shopper for some things to wear in bed. I think I'll call her today to get me a couple outfits—something that'll hide this cast without making me look like an elephant."

Around ten Eileen got through to the family at the motel. They'd arranged a caravan to bring the children and spouses back home. Joe's brothers and sisters and Joe's sons still needed space for ten or eleven people somewhere. They'd been phoning hotels, motels, and B and Bs for miles around, but were getting nowhere—many were closed from storm damage, and the rest were packed.

"How should we approach the Hudsons?" Judy didn't know them as well as she knew Margarida and the Corlisses. Bill and June Hudson lived farther down the street, so there was less day-to-day contact.

"I'll call June now. He's never home during the day, but she sometimes is."

Judy brought the phone over to her friend—who had to leave a message for June to call or drop by. Eileen then called Margarida and invited her for coffee in an hour or so.

Judy baked some cinnamon rolls from a tube and made fresh coffee. Margarida rapped on the door just as the rolls were done.

"Oh, Eileen. It's so good to see you." Margarida hugged her old friend and stood back to look at her. "You look pretty good—I thought you'd be all banged up."

"I'm fine—glad to be up and about. Lying in bed all day can really fog your brain."

"Oh, I know." Margarida joined them at the table. "What's up?"

"We feel a little guilty—we've asked you over to…" Judy started.

There was a knock at the door. June Hudson. Judy let her in and settled her at the table with coffee and a roll. June was in her forties and looked her age, but reminded Judy of her college sorority sisters years ago—blond hair short, waved and every hair in place like an old Clairol ad, makeup just so, and dressed in preppy clothes that looked brand new: yellow cotton trousers, penny loafers, white cotton buttoned-down shirt, and a navy blazer with gold buttons. Her jewelry was plain onyx with gold—ring and choker.

Judy began the sale attempt: "Eileen and Joe's family has to leave the motel in Wellington tomorrow. Hotels and such are jammed—we can't find them rooms anywhere. We're looking for space for maybe ten of them for a few days until…um, until…"

"Joe's funeral," Eileen broke in. "Judy and Sam already have me and my daughter and are making their basement available for more. I'm trying to find space for the other eight or so."

June took a bite of her roll. "You really couldn't find hotel space. That's hard to believe."

Margarida brightened. "Oh, my. I'm so relieved. I thought you had some bad news. You can use my second floor—three bedrooms and one bath. It can fit six in a squeeze—the beds are just full-size, and I know most people are used to the big mattresses now. What about you, June?"

June looked at the bottom of her cup. "Errr…I'm not sure what we can do; I really have to talk to Bill. I suppose someone could use the bunkhouse. There are two single beds and a bathroom. They couldn't come into the house—or use the pool—Bill would die. There's no kitchen, or refrigerator, if that's a problem."

Judy was surprised that June offered anything. "Has it been used lately?"

"We've never used it. Bill's going to convert it to a greenhouse sometime."

"Maybe we could go look at it? To see how many it could hold." Judy wanted to be sure the place was livable.

"Of course. Why don't you come back with me, and we can do it now. Then I've got to meet Bill in town." June stood and led Judy and Margarida down the street.

The Hudson's house was a large two-story home with mild Victorian features that would be right at home in New England. Bright white clapboards clad both the house and the little building at the back of the lot. Landscaping was mostly lawn and ficus hedges. There were no flowers on the property. Everything looked just-washed—house, paving, lawn.

The bunkhouse was larger than Judy expected. From outside it looked shipshape—four large windows faced the street, and each had a window box with some kind of evergreen bush with red berries cascading down the wall. The door was large and had shiny brass fixtures. When they got closer to the building, she could see that it was almost as wide as her home and it looked like it would have high ceilings.

June opened the creaking door and they filed in. Hot. Stuffy. Moldy rodent smell. June found the light switch and turned it on. There was one light fixture in the ceiling and no lamps. The room was rectangular, maybe forty by thirty feet. There were two twin beds at the far end, a scarred wooden table with four chairs in the middle, and a couch and two easy chairs at the other end. Judy could see no bathroom. The room was an example of what Florida's heat and humidity could do to man's creations. The walls were painted, but the paint was peeling off in large wafers—some still stuck to the wall, the rest littering the floor, covered by trails of rat "raisins". Judy leaned on one of the wooden chairs, and it wobbled. The stuffed furniture was damp, dirty, and moldy. Stacks of old magazines and cardboard boxes littered the floor. The beds were more like cots and were heaped with clothes on hangers. She thought it would take a week just to clean this place up—and there wasn't any AC or even ceiling fans. God.

"I don't think they could use this." Judy said. "But thanks for the offer."

June smiled. "Oh, you're welcome. I sure do hope you'll find something else for them."

They said their good-byes, and Judy and Margarida walked back up the street.

When they were back inside, Judy exploded. "That place wasn't fit for roaches, for God's sake. And there wasn't even a toilet or a sink. We've been friends for years—she knows you, Eileen, and Joe. Why would she offer that shack? What is she afraid of? Criminals? Germs? Jeez."

"No. It's really okay, Judy. Not everyone would take in a stranger." Eileen patted Judy's hand. "And we just need space for eleven at most, and we have seven or eight already, so we're close. Let's take a break. When Marilyn comes home, I'll go through my book and see if I can find room somewhere. Maybe someone has an RV or boat we could rent. Oh, and Margarida, thank you so much for your offer. Don't worry about food—we'll take care of that. And let me know of any expense they create."

"I'm happy to help. I get lonely sometimes, so having a few people around will be nice. And I'll be glad to see them go too. But then I'd be relieved instead of lonely. Isn't that nice? Let me know when they're coming—I've got to get linens and things out, and get to the store for a few things. Bye."

Watching her walk down the driveway, Judy thought Margarida was too good for this world. "Well. I guess I should go down and get the cellar tidied up. Who would you want here?"

Eileen held her hands nervously at her chest. "It's a huge favor, but my son, Ted. He can be difficult sometimes. I can't foist him off on Margarida. If he's here, I can keep him in line."

"What does he do?"

"Work, you mean?"

Judy smiled. "No. When he goes outside the line."

"He drinks too much. Smokes. Swears. Is selfish. Doesn't wash often. He doesn't work. Nobody likes him. I don't like him much myself. I've learned that it's not my fault—we didn't spoil him or anything, he was just born that way."

"Wow. But sure, we can give him the cellar. Is there anyone else who could bunk in with him?"

"Better not. The gang out at the motel is ready to feed him to the mosquitoes."

"Okay. So we've got seven spaces and need three or four more. I guess in the short run, we could put cots in the living room and in Marilyn's room."

"You don't know this crowd. They'd kill each other, Judy. And no one would share a room with Marilyn. The family's great for a short visit, but they've already been together too long. But don't worry, we'll find something." Eileen stood up and reached for her walker.

"Eileen. Do you want to go over and see Joe today? I haven't gone back to work yet, so we could go anytime." Judy stood and picked up the dishes.

Eileen hung her head. "I don't know if I could stand it. I feel guilty not wanting to go, but it's such torture watching him."

"Your energy is low, that's all. Why don't we wait until tomorrow." Judy put the dishes down and hugged Eileen.

Just then they heard Marilyn bang into the house. She came onto the patio waving a ragged brown book. "Here's your address book. It got damp, and some of the ink has splotched out, so you can't read most of it."

"Oh, good. You're home, dear. Thanks for the book—at least it'll jog my memory. I hate to ask for anything else, but I wonder if you could go back over to the house and maybe find me something to wear?"

"I bagged up everything to send to the cleaners. As soon as one opens, you'll have your clothes. Right now I want to take you over to see Father."

"Honey, I just can't today. I'll go tomorrow. Kiss him for me."

"They won't let me. That infection thing. If you'd only trusted me and let me fly him to Boston." She flung the address book at Eileen and ran from the room.

Eileen collapsed back in a chair and began to weep.

Judy rubbed her shoulders and tried to think of something to say. "Eileen. She's just lashing out at you from sadness and helplessness."

Eileen sat up, choking back sobs. "What if she's right? What if it is my fault? And what kind of wife am I? Worried about looking funny or being sad while letting my husband lie over there all by himself?"

Judy didn't even try an answer. She picked up the dishes and went into the kitchen.

Eileen soon came through the kitchen to go to her room to make some calls, so Judy went to the cellar to get ready for Ted. They'd often had guests stay in the cellar—usually just her brothers' kids, though. Judy was not surprised to find that Sam had returned everything from the hurricane and had taken the lawn furniture back outside. They'd built half walls in one corner, making a fairly private extra bedroom: single bed with a good mattress, leather reading chair, good lamps, TV, closet, and attached bathroom. Sam had even added a tub with spa features after he'd installed a full array of exercise machines for them to use on rainy days.

Judy found some linen in the closet and made the bed, then stopped busying about and plopped into the chair. She'd done it again—promised to do something she wasn't built for. Already she wished Eileen's family would go back home to wait for Joe to die. Eileen was okay, but she really didn't want strangers in the house, nor did she want to take care of the others scattered in the neighborhood. What had she been thinking?

CHAPTER 10

Eileen was on the phone all afternoon trying to find housing for the family. So far she'd had no luck. Most people were up north, and those who were in Palm Beach had come down just to check on their residences and were heading right back.

Judy came up from the cellar still simmering. At first she'd been angry, but she really was more hurt from June's lukewarm offer of the bunkhouse. She thought of the Sunshine Street group as a bunch of real friends. Of outsiders like herself, maybe. She expected more of an all-for-one, one-for-all enthusiasm to help Eileen. She realized this was unrealistic. Naive maybe.

She was puttering around the kitchen, cleaning out cabinets and checking their larder and making grocery lists, when Sam got home right after six. Just as he came through the door, Ted drove up to the house. "Hi, hon. I'm sorry, but we've another guest. Eileen's son Ted—I think that's him now. They all have to be out of the motel by tomorrow."

"Hey. I guess that's okay. Did you find room for the others?"

"Not yet. Margarida was sweet—she'll take six. I think we need room for three or four more."

"I thought there were more people than that."

"Most are heading home tomorrow. Some will fly back for the funeral, but I think the storm wore them out."

"How about a drink?"

"Love one. How about margaritas? If you make a pitcher, I'll whip up some guacamole."

"Deal." Sam slapped Judy on her butt and started gathering ingredients.

The door opened and Ted walked in. Judy thought, make yourself at home, why don't you?

Ted was large—maybe six foot six. And covered in sloppy loose fat. His face was jowly, his hair a bit like Donald Trump's—but greasy. He wore a torn T-shirt, frayed shorts tight in the crotch, and large once-white leather sneakers. No socks. Sweat beaded all over his body. And hairy…His T-shirt stood out a good inch away from his chest. He didn't smile.

"I'm Ted. I guess I'm living here. Damn, it's as hot in here as outside. Think you could turn on the AC?"

Judy couldn't speak. Her "gracious hostess" act just wouldn't kick in. Sam rescued her. "I'm Sam Haite. This is my wife, Judy. The AC *is* on. We usually don't use it, but we have turned in on for your mother and sister. Some of us have arthritis and don't like it cold, so we keep it at eighty. And we're lucky to have it—we happen to have a large generator. If that's too hot for you, I suggest you go somewhere else."

Ted glared at Sam but didn't say anything. He picked up his bags and raised his eyebrows, gesturing "where to?'

Sam led him to the cellar door. "Follow me."

Ted muttered, "Fucking basement."

Sam stopped. "Pardon me?"

Ted almost plowed into Sam. "Damn. Watch where you're going, bud."

Judy couldn't hear the rest of what they were saying, but Sam was back quickly. "Wow. What a sweet fellow. That apple fell into another orchard! Where's Eileen?"

"Probably in her room. She's been calling everyone she knows trying to find extra space. Let's hope she finds it, or we'll end up with a few more."

"Let us pray, you mean. Well, let's forget all that and do our cooking!"

In a few minutes, Sam had a large pitcher of margaritas ready, with iced glasses from the freezer. Judy made guacamole using eight avocados, fearing Ted would scarf up anything less all by himself. They carried their offerings onto the patio. Judy got Eileen, and Marilyn and Ted wandered in later. After the cocktails Judy, Sam, and Eileen fixed dinner while "the kids"—as Eileen called Ted and Marilyn—watched TV in the living room.

After dinner Eileen stayed with Judy and Sam on the patio drinking coffee. "The kids" were back in the living room drinking scotch and watching a video.

It was getting dark out. They each sat with their private thoughts, none talking for some time. They didn't hear Bill Hudson until he rapped on the inside wall of the patio.

"Hi, guys." Bill stepped into the room. Bill would've been called a geek in high school. Thin, slightly stooped, glasses. Dressed in his suit, he looked as if he hadn't a muscle on his body. A general contractor, he was one of those spry wiry men who could go all day climbing over construction, then come home, play golf, and go out dancing.

"Want coffee, Bill?" offered Sam, standing up.

"Something stronger would be nice."

"Hard day?"

"Hard night. June told me about the bunkhouse. Lord—I don't know why she offered that old dump anyway—I wouldn't put my pet rock in there overnight. I've kept it looking good on the outside so I can convert it to a greenhouse. If I tore it down, I'd have trouble getting a permit in this town to rebuild."

Sam gave Bill an inch of Jameson's in a large stubby Waterford glass. "Here you go, Bill. Sit down and take a load off."

Bill smiled nervously at Eileen. "Hey. June's agreed to have some of Joe's family stay with us. I still don't know what she's afraid of—but we have a twenty-three-room house and a big generator, so we'll take as many as you need us to. There's a four-bedroom wing that's fairly separate from the rest of the house. Each room has its own bath. And it has a sitting room that opens right onto the pool deck. I thought that might be best. We can put up as many beds as you need. We can bring some TVs down so there's one in every room. The sitting room has a CD player, and I think there's a game console somewhere.

Eileen got up and hugged Bill. "Bill, you're so sweet."

"When are they coming?" asked Bill.

"They have to be out of the motel by eleven tomorrow morning. So about noon? I'm not sure how many—three or four, I think."

"Well, I'd better drink up and get back to make sure everything's shipshape. I'll drop by the house at noon and be there with June to settle them in." Bill put his glass down and left.

"Whew! That was a big switch. Hope June is really okay with this." Judy realized she wasn't at all ready to feed the hoard that would be descending on the neighborhood. "I'll go call Margarida to let her know the schedule. In the morning we can make grocery lists—Margarida will need her larder topped off, and if we're offering dinner every night, I'll need menus for the next few days before we go shopping. We're lucky a few stores have good generators and have opened already."

She grinned at Sam. "I'm glad you bought that humongous grill I've given you so much grief for. This time we'll really need it."

※

By dinner the next day, Judy was beginning to lose what little enthusiasm she had. Ted was a rude, crude man. Plus, he stomped all over her personal space. He stood so close, his bulging belly touched her thin one when he spoke to her. And his dog breath, with whiskey overtones! He'd talk, and she just couldn't listen as she back-pedaled to get away. She and Eileen were busy all day delivering food to Margarida and the Hudsons, then cooking dinner for the Sunshine Street group and the newcomers. Judy couldn't even count how many to cook for—somewhere close to twenty, she figured. She made a huge dish of seafood Newburg, rice, English peas (what the Florida stores call regular peas in pods you don't eat), and a large salad. She made two loaves of garlic bread and bought a chocolate truffle cake from the French bakery in town.

People arrived all at once at eight o'clock. Sam played host and fetched drinks while Margarida and Judy set the table and carried food to the patio. The patio looked festive with large candles all around and the dishes and serving bowls in primary colors.

Judy wasn't able to put one name to a new face. She'd never been good at names anyway—her mother liked to tell of when Judy was four and focused on getting to be five so she could start school. She'd come in from playing and relate how "Six" did this and "Five" did that. She knew the ages, not the names, of her playmates. And she hadn't improved much since then.

Judy stayed busy fetching food and drinks. Usually she liked to have people in for dinner—she'd rather cook and serve than visit—but this night she felt like a servant in her own home.

By nine all the food was eaten, and Ted and another man were rifling through the refrigerator looking for something more. They finally settled on popcorn and popped four bags of microwave popcorn and melted half a pound of butter before settling in front of the TV with bottles of beer. The others trickled out to their quarters, until by eleven the house was down to those sleeping there.

Sam and Judy were alone on the patio stretched out on the chaises.

"Oh, God. What have we let ourselves in for?" Sam looked at Judy.

"Quite a crowd. And, except for Marilyn and Ted, they're all so tiny. And they ate so much! I'm going to have to change my shopping lists."

"They've been out at that motel, maybe they haven't had a real meal in a long time."

"I hope you're right. Well, maybe it won't be so bad. God, I'm tired. And I have to go back to work tomorrow, so I need to get things in order early."

"I'm glad Bill and June came tonight. They seemed really friendly with their group. And Margarida, of course, is tight with hers."

"Things are working out. Well, I'm going up, you coming?"

"In a bit. Going to savor the silence for a bit." Sam went outside.

On her way through the living room, Judy found Ted and the other man asleep on the couches. Greasy popcorn was scattered everywhere.

"This will make me stronger," Judy muttered as she climbed the stairs.

CHAPTER 11

A week later Eileen was settled in the TV room at Judy and Sam's and had traded her walker for crutches. Marilyn was still in the upstairs library, and her brother Ted was camping out in the basement. Margarida had taken in six of the family, and four more were living down the street with the Hudsons. The family tried every day to find hotel rooms, but the hurricane and condo disasters had filled every hotel, motel and B and B in the county.

Eileen had estimates for fixing her house, and she and Sam were trying to expedite the process, but area contractors were swamped. Every night they all met for dinner at Judy and Sam's to commiserate.

This morning Marilyn stayed in bed until Sam and Judy left for work. She showered, dressed, and came downstairs. Ted was in the living room reading the newspaper and drinking coffee. He didn't look up when Marilyn clomped through the room. Marilyn could hear her mother humming in the kitchen.

"Good morning, Mother."

"Hi, Marilyn. I've made fresh coffee. Can I get you breakfast?" Eileen was dressed in a frilly fuchsia dressing gown—her clothes finally back from the cleaners. Leaning against her crutches, she was cutting cornbread just out of the oven.

"Mother. Every morning I've told you: No. I don't eat breakfast." Marilyn poured herself coffee and stood staring out the window. "Oh damn, here comes that busybody from across the street."

Eileen looked out and saw Margarida stepping delicately up the driveway. Margarida walked bending her knees and pointing her toes ahead, almost like a dancing horse. She'd just had her hair done, a gray/black Persian-lamb do. Her eyebrows were tweezed into an exaggerated arch, her bright lipstick was a bit outside the line, and she had a bright pink circle of rouge on her cheekbones. Margarida was tall for her age (eighty-three)—about five eight—and dressed in a brown knit pantsuit from the seventies…(narrow pants flared at the ankle and belted jacket with exaggerated pointed collar). She carried a large flowered carpetbag looped over her elbow, holding her hand up toward her face. She came close to looking like a clown, but was so distinctive and sure of herself that most people assumed she was an eccentric billionaire and treated her well.

"What an awful thing to say, Marilyn. That's Margarida, and she's a lovely woman."

"She's dumb as a rock."

"She's no intellectual, but then, neither am I."

"I've already heard her stories a million times; she drives me insane. I've got to get out of here. I'll go visit Father—no one else does." Marilyn put her coffee cup on the window ledge and headed back toward her room.

Eileen watched her go. Marilyn was a large solid woman. In her forties, she looked older yet somehow also ageless. She was dressed in a suit that accentuated her bulk—it was of a bubbly pink fabric and had big shoulder pads. She walked through the living room, pushing her size-twelve shoes through the floor as if snowshoeing.

Eileen shook her head and looked out the window just as Margarida reached the door.

Margarida gave one rap at the door, smiled through the glass at Eileen, and came in. "Morning, Eileen. You should go outside—it's still a bit cool."

"What a good idea. Let's have coffee on the patio; it's already opened." She poured two cups. "Here's cream and sugar if you want. Cornbread? Just made it."

"Oh, I shouldn't. I just stopped by to see if you needed anything. I'm going up to shop."

"Irish butter. Homemade marmalade. Cornbread's nice and warm." Eileen was fixing herself a big slab of cornbread.

"Well…If it's not too much trouble."

The two women fixed their snacks, and Margarida carried them onto the patio on a tray. They made themselves comfortable on two chaises in the shade.

"This is tasty, Eileen. I've never thought to make it in the morning. Usually only when I make bake beans."

"Do you make the beans from scratch?"

"Not too often now. Just doctor up the canned unless I have company. Oh, I'd love to have some real beans," Margarida said. "Haven't had them in ages. Suppose we make them for supper tonight? I know Judy's getting tired of preparing these huge meals. Maybe we can do something this afternoon. I've got a big old bean pot somewhere. I can do that. Then all we need is coleslaw and hot dogs. I can pick up everything we need right now. Maybe you could make a cake or something."

"Wonderful," said Eileen. "Oh, dear me, I forgot about Marilyn. She abhors baked beans. I don't suppose it matters much—she hasn't seemed happy about anything we've served. And she won't cook for herself. I visited her once: her fridge is full of yogurt and boxes of Lean Cuisine. I told her we could stock them here, but she barked at me. I wish I knew why she's so prickly. I suggested the other day that she return to New York and come back when Joe dies. She took my head off.

"Was she always like that?"

"I suppose. When she was two...I'll never forget it. I loved to take the kids up to bed, read to them, and tuck them in. One evening she said good night at the bottom of the stairs, turned around and climbed the stairs, went into her room and slammed the door. She was maybe two and a half. I could never hold her or hug her after that. She has no friends. She works for an HMO in New York...is a big executive, has a beautiful office. She does some work from here. I think she's one of those people who say no."

"I bet she's good at that!" Then Margarida blushed. "Oh, I'm sorry."

"Don't be. Oh, I hate to say this, but I wish Joe would die and all these people would go home. The doctors don't know how he can still live; his brain isn't there at all, but he doesn't need any machines to keep him alive. I won't let them starve him to death." Eileen stared into space.

Margarida drank her coffee. She was so thin the skeletal orbits were visible, and her eyes stared out from a depth. She blinked several times and sighed. "I'll be happy to die and meet up with my Connor."

⁂

Sam got home at five thirty and Judy at six. They met in the bedroom. They both showered, then lay on the bed watching the news.

"At least we can still hide out here," said Sam. "For a while I thought we'd have to put in cots. We're lucky the Hudsons took so many. How can Joe's family afford to be away from work so long anyway?"

"They're rich. And Marilyn does a lot of work with e-mail. But have you noticed—they've all managed to rent cars; they go all over the place during the day, but every night they show up here empty-handed expecting to be fed? Last night I almost lost it—I was tempted to serve canned soup, saltines, and canned fruit."

"They're drinking up my wine. And Ted sits down there all day in *my* chair and is draining our bar. Damn. One thing, I'm not buying another drop of liquor until he leaves. Or if I do, I'm storing it under my pillow!" Sam punched his pillow and sat back.

"Maybe since his mother is here, he's just making himself at home."

"Maybe. But when's it going to end? It's been almost two weeks. I'm tired. You're tired. The Hudsons are overwhelmed; they usually can't manage to host a simple dinner. The only one who seems to be thriving is Margarida; she gets peppier every day, and she has six people to take care of."

"Margarida's been awfully lonely since Connor died. It's been over two years, but she was so close to him. Hey, something smells good."

"Eileen and Margarida are cooking tonight. Baked beans from scratch."

"I love Margarida's beans—hope it's her recipe. I feel better already. I suppose I could scrounge up some snacks and drinks. First, though, let's swim." Judy snapped up a red tank suit, jumped into it, and headed toward the door.

"Right behind you."

When they bought their house, there was no pool, and at first there didn't seem room for one if they also wanted gardens. Sam, however, managed to fit an L-shaped racing lane at the southeast corner of the lot. Eighty feet long, it was the site of many late-night competitions.

Judy admired Sam's ability to do anything. He was more of her father's generation in that respect. Her other men friends didn't know how do anything—construction, hunting/fishing, fixing cars. If they didn't have the money for something, it didn't get done.

When they came back in from swimming, they found Eileen and Margarida in the kitchen, and the smell of baking rolls had been added to the bean aroma. Church supper night. Sam mixed Bloody Marys. Judy put together a cheese tray and bowls of carrots and zucchini with a curry dip. People drifted in. Soon the atmosphere was merrier than it had ever been—a regular cocktail party, rather than post-hurricane deathwatch.

They were on their third round of drinks when Marilyn came home. She stood in the doorway to the living room and glared at them. "Have you no respect? My father is over there dying, and you're all having a party. No one visits him. No one cares. I don't know why anyone's here anyway. You should all go home." Marilyn swept through the room and pounded up the stairs.

Judy yelled after her, "I visit him almost every day, and you know your mother can't get into a car yet with her leg." Judy knew this was untrue. Eileen could easily visit Joe, but every day refused offers of a ride. Judy had finally stopped offering. Ted, slouched in Sam's leather chair, added, "Sis, Dad's dead already. I've been over there once, but he's gone."

The mood ruined, they finished their drinks and attempted conversation as they ate dinner. They ate quickly, though, and people dispersed to their Sunshine Street houses.

The beans were delicious, and there were no leftovers.

In bed later, Judy was tired. Usually these evenings gave her a boost. Even if they were often gloomy, they usually ended with people telling great stories about Joe. Tonight she was discouraged. Everything had been going so well until Marilyn got there. How could one person bring so many people down so fast?

"I wish Marilyn would just go back to New York," Judy said. "She's so negative. She sucks the air out of everyone."

Someone pounded on the door. Marilyn barged into the room. She stood shaking, a short, pink chenille bathrobe showing her stumpy calves, her hair in curlers and her face smothered in cream. "I heard that, you bitch!"

"You shouldn't have. Why were you at this end of the house?" Marilyn's room had its own bathroom and was separated by the stairway from theirs.

"Get out of this room right now!" Sam jumped down from the bed, brandished the remote, and stepped toward Marilyn.

Sam's face was red, Judy's white. Marilyn glowered at them, turned, and left, slamming their door, then two seconds later, hers.

"I'm embarrassed," said Judy. "My mother always told me not to say anything about anybody I wouldn't want to see printed in the newspaper. But why was she down here—listening at the door?"

"Maybe she just needed something," offered Sam. "Or maybe just drunk and lost her way."

"What should we do? Maybe I should go talk to her?"

"Oh, forget it. She's probably heard the truth before. Jesus. I wish poor old Joe would die so we could have our lives back." Sam got back into bed.

They watched TV for several hours before calming down enough to sleep.

"Judy, this is just too much for you." Eileen sipped her coffee as she and Judy sat on the patio. At ten o'clock they had just cleaned up after breakfast. For some unknown reason, instead of just Marilyn and Ted, all the other relatives had ended up at the Haites for breakfast. So at eight o'clock, Judy played short-order cook, as no one could agree on what to have. If Judy hadn't been so tired, she would've put her foot down and put dry cereal, milk, juice, and coffee on the table. But, no—instead she made, in addition, omelets, waffles, poached eggs, bagels, French toast, and a huge bowl of mixed fresh fruit with yogurt and nuts.

"I was thinking too slow this morning. I should've sent them all out to eat."

"They're embarrassing me. I see them take, take, take! Has anyone brought anything to dinner? Or offered to pay any of you?"

"No. Not yet. I have been surprised. But the way I've explained it to myself is that they're treating my house as yours, since you're here too."

"You're probably right," Eileen said. "When they've visited us in the past, they've never contributed anything, no matter how long they stayed. Oh, well. But the way they were complaining this morning about not having air-conditioning at Margarida's. Don't they know what a disaster that storm was?"

"It has been hot, and they're not used to it. I'm just surprised they haven't given up and gone home."

"That won't happen. But it's strange. They're here because of Joe and only a few have gone to the hospital to see him. It's the dead Joe they want."

CHAPTER 12

Two mornings later, Judy shuffled down the stairs. Her eyes were dry, and they hurt. She was tired; a full night's sleep hadn't done any good. Walking through the living room, she was repelled by the smell of smoke and beer. Ted wasn't there, but she smelled him—his feet always reeked of rancid movie popcorn. Glasses and bottles were piled on the side tables. Newspapers were scattered everywhere.

In the kitchen Judy started the large coffee percolator; she'd learned to make twenty cups first thing, or she'd never get a second cup. Waiting for coffee she gathered up glasses and plates and put them in the dishwasher. Why can't these people pick up after themselves?

Sam had gone into work early, and Judy had the day off. Maybe she could escape somewhere later. Eileen's bell rang, and Judy went to see what she needed. Usually Eileen would be up by now.

"Judy, I'm so sorry to ring this silly thing, but my leg is screaming—it bothered me all night. I don't think I slept more than an hour. It's so silly—I've run out of water and really need some to take my pain pills. Would you get me some?"

"Sure. Eileen, I've told you before...If you run into any trouble at night, call me on my cell—don't wait until morning."

"You need your sleep, dear."

Judy shook her head and left to get the water. Coming back she handed the water and pills to Eileen. "There you go. Now snuggle down and get some sleep."

Coming back to the kitchen, she met Ted, wearing too-tight silk boxers, pouring himself coffee. "Judy, Judy, Judy…What's for breakfast?"

Judy felt her blood pressure rise. "Oh, I don't know. Why don't you just rummage around and fix yourself something."

Ted stood in the middle of the floor while Judy poured her coffee, walked around him, and went onto the patio. Ted followed her out there, so Judy went into the yard. She wanted her house back! And she *hated* Ted's "Judy, Judy, Judy." Not only was his Cary Grant impersonation terrible, but also she just wasn't that keen on her name. Her mother had named her after her first bicycle, a used one with a bold "JUDY" stenciled on the rear fender. Judy's mother, Greta—like all her family—had Scandinavian names, and Greta had hated hers. When her father gave Greta the "Judy" bike, she discovered that kids who didn't know her thought that was her real name. And she loved it. Now Judy, with her short American name, wished she had a more exotic one.

After finishing her coffee, Judy was hungry, so she had to go back into the house. At least Ted wasn't in the kitchen. Judy made herself a poached egg, toast, poured juice and more coffee, and took a tray up to her bedroom. She took her time eating and watched TV.

Around ten Judy dressed and went downstairs. Ted and Marilyn were eating cake and coffee in the living room. Apparently neither would cook. Judy ignored them and brought her own dishes into the kitchen. She picked up her book and went onto the patio. Soon Ted joined her.

"Shouldn't you get my mother her breakfast?"

"She's sleeping."

"Marilyn and I are going shopping for a few hours. Then we're lunching with friends.

Judy wanted to howl. "Oh, no, you don't. Someone has to stay with Eileen. Her leg acted up last night, and she may need help today."

"Aren't you going to be here?" Ted assumed a stunned little kid look.

"Look, you two have to work out a schedule to care for Eileen. Most days she's okay by herself, but when she isn't, you have to step in. You can't keep assuming I'm going to do everything for her and all of you." Judy slammed her book down and went outside.

She sat by the pool for a few minutes, then Ted called out to her.

"You're wanted on the phone. Should they call back later?"

"No. I'll take it. Thanks, Ted."

It was Peggy. She needed someone to come in from four to ten—there was a rash of patients with hip and knee surgery needing therapy. This wasn't the escape Judy had hoped for, but it would do.

This morning on TV the town had given permission for people to go onto the beaches at the north end, so Judy went to the patio, picked up her book, water, and a portable chair, and went down Sunshine to the beach. She didn't tell anyone where she'd be. Groundskeepers and city crews were busy picking up the last of the debris and hauling it off. The neighborhood was looking surprisingly tidy. Joe and Eileen's house seemed to be the only one on the street to have major damage.

She was shocked when she went through the gate and down the path through tall grasses to the beach: usually the beach stretched out 150 feet at low tide. Today there was at most twenty feet of beach that ended in an abrupt fifteen-foot drop to a sandstone slab below. The little remaining beach was heaped with trees, lumber, furniture, clothing, large sections of roofing, boats…Judy couldn't gather it all in. This beach, like all the beaches in the area, was usually plowed daily to remove trash and seaweed. A few people were picking through the mountains of trash looking for treasure.

Looking down the beach, she could see the area houses were spared any major damage from the storm; the ruined condos and houses were further south.

She found a relatively private space close to the Breakers hotel to read. Every few minutes she'd stop reading and gaze out at the ocean. The sky and water were the same shade of gray-blue—she couldn't tell where the ocean ended and the sky began. Judy had grown up used to the other Atlantic coast—in northeast Maine—rocky (she knew of only one small sandy beach) with hundreds of islands scattered offshore. The view from Palm Beach this day was, quite frankly, boring—no boats, no birds, no islands. And here there was no salty ocean smell. It could be beautiful during a storm, when the ocean ruled, or early morning, when sunrise often came with colors of red that seemed unnatural—but this day only the pile of trash, which stretched forever down the beach, gave the beach distinction. Judy stayed on the beach until three, then went home to change and go to work.

Eileen was up and Ted and Marilyn had gone out.

"Feeling better?" asked Judy.

"Sleep and pain pills did the trick. Where've you been?"

"Just on the beach. My favorite reading place. I have to be at work at four."

"Was that scheduled?" Eileen looked concerned.

"No. But I don't mind going in. I'll look in on Joe before I leave. Can I pick you up anything in town?"

"No. I'm okay. I think I'll sit out by the pool and read. Later I can scare up supper."

"Sure it's not too much for you? You could make your spaghetti sauce—I know Sam loves it, and there's fresh ground meat in the fridge."

"That'll be fun. I miss cooking."

Judy felt a bit guilty for her "poor pitiful me" mindset earlier in the day and went up to shower and change.

Later, Judy worked through the evening, taking time to put each of her patients at ease. Often a few kind words before beginning therapy reduced the patient's fear of pain and allowed longer therapy and quicker recovery.

One of her last patients was Mrs. Elroy, whose lower leg had been amputated just the day before. Expecting a patient overwhelmed by the surgery, mourning the missing body part, in pain and depressed—Judy found her sitting upright wearing a bright pink bed jacket, her hair in tight white wooly curls, chuckling softly to herself.

Judy stood in the doorway. "Mrs. Elroy?"

"Yes, dear. Can I help you?"

"I'm Judy from physical therapy. Just came by today to introduce myself and see when you'd be ready to practice on crutches."

"I'm a little woozy today. But should be okay by tomorrow. I'm feeling so good—my leg hurt so—felt like an alligator had it—and poof, pain's gone. Oh, and I just heard the cutest thing from one of the nurses."

"What?"

"Maybe you've heard. About the man who was in a bad car accident yesterday in Wellington. Came in to the ER late last night?"

"No. What happened?"

"He had to have surgery on his head and when he woke up in the ICU, Dr. Munabi and Dr.... Oh, I can't remember his name, sounds like *pickachoo*. Well, anyway, they were standing over him asking questions like they do on TV to see if you're all there. You know. What day is it, who are you. So Dr. Munabi asked the fellow if he knew where he was. The man looked from one to the other and guessed 'Pakistan?'" Mrs. Elroy giggled girlishly.

"That's a good story."

"I bet you hear a lot of them here."

"Yeah. But I'm afraid I usually can't remember them afterwards."

"Can you remember any? I love stories."

Mrs. Elroy looked so eager to hear a story that Judy came over and sat at the end of the bed. "We have a classic one in rehab, but there's a really bad word in it."

"That's no problem, tell me."

"You sure?"

"My husband uses awful language sometimes. I'm used to it."

"Well, just in case, I apologize in advance. This happened last year. A kid from Lantana drove his motorcycle off an overpass. Broke every bone in his body, cracked his skull into pieces. He was in a coma for months. Almost a year. His bones healed, but the doctors didn't think he was going to wake up. We have a rehab nurse, Cynthia, who is a bear. Determined to fix everyone and get them up and out of the hospital. She doesn't listen to the whines and moans. Anyway, she was his nurse five days a week. We could hear her in his room every day yelling for him to "wake the hell up" as she was putting his body through a routine of exercises. Finally one day in the middle of a treatment, he woke up, looked up at her, and said, 'Good-bye, you fucking cunt!'"

"Oh, my." Mrs. Elroy brought her hands to her face.

"You see, after a head injury, swearing is the first language that comes back. That poor kid woke up just to get her to stop yelling at him. We went around laughing for days. She performed a miracle."

"Is he okay now?"

"Pretty much. Drives. Is married. Works. His IQ might be down a few points, but we were amazed he even woke up."

"Thank you."

"What for?"

"The story. And I've heard those words before."

"Oh, you're welcome, Mrs. Elroy. Well, I'd better get going. Tomorrow we'll start putting you to work."

Judy slipped off the bed, smiled and waved, and left the room.

Judy was a good therapist and enjoyed her work, although it wasn't her first choice of profession. She'd enrolled in pre-med at the University of Maine, but flunked the required organic chemistry course twice, forcing a change in major. She switched to nursing and enjoyed the academic work, but when she went into the hospitals for practical training, she found she disliked the hands-on personal care of sick people. The smells especially bothered her. She thought she'd like nursing the way it was practiced now—aides did much of the personal care, while nurses were much more involved in the planning, management, and technical functions—and regretted she hadn't given it a chance. But back then she'd noticed the physical therapists seemed happier than the nurses, had more freedom to move around the hospital, and cared for healthier patients. So she switched majors again.

Ten o'clock came quickly, and Judy went down to the staff room for her things and walked toward the garage. Oops. Forgot her promise to look in on Joe. Reversing her course, she walked to the end of the complex and up the three flights to the hospice unit.

The unit was decorated in a seaside cottage theme. Furniture was of white, lacquered wood. Fabrics had light, breezy patterns. Each patient room was private and had a sofa and two chairs with bright throw pillows. Photographs of the beach and ocean hung on the walls. The unit had been renovated from an old surgical area; the ceiling was high, windows large. It was a pleasant, positive place.

When Judy reached the unit, lights were dimmed and the unit was quiet. One nurse was on duty at night; Judy could see her sitting with a patient. On this unit there was no high-tech equipment. Patients were given needed pain medication and some needed respiratory care, but—unlike in the acute care units—patients were made comfortable, tucked in for the night, and left alone to sleep. No temperature checks and other nursing visits that make hospital sleeping a struggle.

Judy walked softly on the carpet into Joe's room, not bothering to put on the required mask, gown, and gloves. Joe was illuminated as if on stage by tiny lights on the wall above his hospital bed. The rest of the room was visible but indistinct. A bedside table held just a few nursing items and a small silver-framed photograph of Joe and Eileen in their backyard. She picked up the photograph. Joe and Eileen were standing proudly next to a miniature lemon tree loaded with ripe fruit. It was taken years before Judy knew them—at a time well before they became old—probably her age, just when you discover your parent staring back at you in the mirror.

Joe lay with mouth agape. She had to get right next to the bed to detect his slow, shallow breaths. She felt his hot sunken cheek.

He was so near death…but he'd been like this for weeks now. Poor old Joe. What was the value of his lying here? He wasn't suffering. He just wasn't Joe anymore.

Judy sat next to the bed and thought of the good times they'd had with Joe and Eileen on Sunshine Street. The day they moved in, Joe had come right over with coffee and coffee cake. Eileen followed in a few hours with a pitcher of lemonade (from scratch) and shortbread cookies. They'd introduced Judy and Sam to the neighbors and were always eager to play whist or bridge at the drop of the hat. And for money: Joe liked to gamble in little amounts.

Judy smiled. And now we're all just waiting for you to die. If a dog was this sick, Sam would euthanize it. She got up and kissed Joe's forehead. Joe smelled bad; his partial plate was out, so his upper lip sagged into his open mouth, and his scrawny chin was covered in long white bristles. And he had been such a dapper man, always standing straight and proud. It's awful he's lying there for anyone to stare at. Almost like in an open casket. Judy shivered.

She wondered how hard it would be to end this misery. And in a way it wouldn't be detected. Death in a hospice is expected, planned for. Judy had read enough murder mysteries to know that common ways to murder people in hospitals (such as injecting huge amounts of air) might be detected by hospital or mortuary staff. Even smothering Joe with a pillow might bruise his fragile skin. Maybe she could just pinch his nose and lips—but he might thrash around, or the pinching might itself cause bruising. The more she considered the methods, the more reasonable it seemed for Judy to end Joe's pitiful life.

Experimenting, Judy leaned with her forearms against Joe's chest. His chest moved sideways, and his belly expanded to maintain his slow breathing. She needed more force. She closed the curtain to block the corridor, and leaned across Joe again—this time lifting her feet off the floor to put her whole body's weight on Joe's chest. She heard a light wheeze as his lungs deflated. His mouth opened and closed a few times like a fish out of water. She put her hand on Joe's neck and felt his heartbeat as it slowed, then stopped. She continued to lie across Joe a few minutes as a gray tint moved over his face. Hearing someone talking in the corridor, Judy stood up, pushed the curtains open, and went back to the chair. When she looked at Joe, she was startled to see his eyes wide open. She got up and closed them and sat back down. It had been almost too easy.

Should she let the nurse know Joe was dead?

Judy stepped into the corridor. Dim and quiet. She could hear the nurse talking to a family in the lounge. Turning in the opposite direction, Judy walked as normally as she could on rubbery legs to the exit and walked down the stairs to the ground floor, hanging tightly to the railing.

※

Sam was asleep when Judy got home. She undressed quietly and lay awake beside him, her heart still pounding. After an hour or so, she relaxed and fell into a deep sleep.

The next morning, Wednesday, Judy woke up before Sam. She was surprised to find the lights on and coffee already made in the kitchen. She went out for the papers and took them with her coffee out to the patio. Jack was chasing a green anole up the screen. He'd bring them inside to "play". If Judy couldn't catch them when they were still alive, they'd find a safe place to hide from Jack and die. The smell of a rotting anole was horrible, and Judy would hunt for days to find it—all the while putting up with Sam's housekeeping "hints".

"Oh, Jack, stop that! I'm tired of getting these screens replaced!" Of course Jack ignored her. The anole he was chasing still had its tail, which was unusual—Jack had bitten most of them off. Jack wasn't quite as aggressive with the giant iguanas that were steadily replacing the local reptile population of lizards and anoles. Native to South America, the iguanas were introduced to Florida by people letting their pets go when they got too large. The florescent-green iguanas grew to be several feet long, and while plant eaters, would snap with their sharp teeth if harassed. Judy liked them; they made the yard look exotic.

She heard Eileen's crutches clipping along the floor.

"Hi. How are you this morning?"

"Joe died last night. They called from the hospital about one."

"Oh, Eileen. I'm so sorry." Judy got up and hugged her friend.

"I'll be all right. But I am surprised what a shock the call was."

"Have you told Marilyn and Ted?"

"No. I let them sleep. I remember when my mother died, they called from the nursing home in the middle of the night. You know how dopey you can be…and the woman used so many euphemisms for death, I didn't even understand at first why she was calling. And then I sat, alone, in the middle of the night. So very sad. But there was nothing I could do for her—she was dead. And no one could help me. Joe happened to be out of town, and I wasn't going to wake the kids…Oh, here I go, babbling on. So, anyway, after that I swore I'd never wake anyone up in the middle of the night with bad news they didn't have to act on right away—like getting out of a burning house or something."

"Can I get you anything for breakfast?" Oh, I'm so dumb, Judy thought. She wished she had something to say to help Eileen.

"I've already eaten, thanks. I got up early and called the burial society."

"I'm so ignorant of Jewish customs—does the funeral have to be today?"

"No, thank God. I'll have it tomorrow. We're allowed reasonable time for the family to gather. I do need to ask your permission to use your home tomorrow."

"Sure, but what about today?"

"We've a nice custom—people will leave us alone today. I thought I could have the Sunshine Street group for lunch as well as dinner…Then tomorrow I'll have the traditional meal here after the burial."

"Can I cook anything for that?"

"Thanks, but some people who come will expect kosher, so I've arranged to have it catered. Joe and I didn't keep kosher—but even those who don't sometimes expect kosher at the funeral meal."

"Is it okay for us to come to the funeral?"

"Of course! It'll be a simple ceremony; Joe didn't want a eulogy. You can come to the burial too, if you want. Wear something on your head. It's not all that different from a Christian funeral. Just follow the crowd, do what they do. Oh…except when they sit bobbing back and forth—don't do that."

"And there's nothing I can help with?"

"No. Really. I've known this was coming for a long time. All I had to do was call the burial society and two friends. My friends will call everyone to let them know…Oh, I hear the kids. I'd better go tell them." Eileen got up and went back into the house just as Sam was coming out.

"Morning, Eileen," said Sam, pausing, expecting to chat.

"Morning, Sam." Eileen kept going.

"Hey, what's up with Eileen?" Sam sat with his coffee.

"Joe died last night."

Sam's coffee cup banged on the table. He looked at Judy, eyes tearing, then sat with his head in his hands. Finally he sat up. "Poor Joe. Damn. Why didn't I force him into the car that night? He had some pretty good years left. Now Eileen with that mess of a house. Oh. Damn. How's Eileen taking it?"

"Sad. But she's focused on the funeral right now. She was just on her way to tell the kids when you came in."

"What can we do?"

"She needs the house tomorrow for the meal after the burial. And today she wants the family today for both lunch and dinner."

"And that's it? Should we stay out of the way?"

"You go to work. I'll get together with Eileen later to see what she'll need for food today and help however I can. Maybe tonight we can go out for dinner and let them be alone."

"Okay. Do you have to work tomorrow?"

"Supposed to, but I think I'll call Peggy and beg off for a few days. First, though, I'm going to sit here and wake up."

"Want coffee? A drink?" Sam stood up.

"Coffee. And something sweet."

Sam went in, and Judy sat thinking about what to feed this crowd.

Sam came back with the coffee pot and some cinnamon rolls.

"Thanks, honey." Judy sat back in her chaise and closed her eyes. No energy. Tonight was going to be a long one.

But it turned out to be not so bad. Eileen and Marilyn went out and brought home deli food for lunch. At dinner Sam and Judy stayed home after all, and Sam grilled the beef tenderloin and garlic bread. Judy made chocolate cake from a mix. And they all happily set about making a huge salad. Everyone was so hungry, they fell upon the food as soon as it was set out. After coffee everyone left, except for those sleeping at the house.

Eileen joined Judy in the kitchen to clean up. "Judy. I don't know how to thank you. I'm so grateful for all you've done."

Judy thought, "If you only knew!" She hugged Eileen and didn't say anything.

Sam and Judy went up to bed early and left Eileen with her children in the living room going over funeral plans. After cursory sex, Judy fell asleep before the news came on at eleven. She stirred once during the night when Jack visited, but fell right back asleep. The alarm woke her at six.

She and Sam sat up in bed and turned on the news. Much of the local news was still about the ruined condos. Nothing much was happening nationally.

"Do we really have to get up?" Judy asked.

"You don't. I've got to go in to work soon. Want me to bring up coffee?"

"Will you marry me?" Judy smiled and hugged Sam.

Sam came back with coffee and cake. "I know this isn't a proper breakfast, but…"

"Oh, good. I didn't get any last night. I was in a rush to escape up here."

Sam showered, dressed, and left for work. Judy stayed in bed watching TV until ten. Then she grabbed her book and went downstairs and out to the pool. The house was empty. Funeral errands, she supposed.

Ah…The sun felt good. But her mind was reeling. She'd pushed aside what she'd done too easily. She was working so hard to appear normal, she hadn't allowed herself to think about Joe. Was it murder? From what she'd learned from watching *Law & Order,* it would probably be second-degree murder. Or manslaughter. She'd obviously killed Joe, but she hadn't *planned* to. In the ethics of her old neighborhood—"do unto others"—it was the right thing for her to have done. But it was illegal, and most people would think her a criminal.

    She couldn't make herself feel remorseful—but she'd never be able to tell anyone. Especially Sam. He was so straitlaced, it would be the end of their marriage. He might not turn her over to the police, but he would never be able to accept what she'd done. He might try to stay with her, but she knew that his love for her would be over.

CHAPTER 13

Sam came home at noon to change for the funeral. Judy had just finished her shower and was sitting on the bed filing her nails.

"Hey, girlfriend." Sam stripped his clothes off as he headed to the bathroom.

"Hey, yourself."

He was back in a minute, drying his hair with a towel.

"What should I wear?"

"The suit."

"Oh, no, not the suit!" Sam squealed in mock horror.

Judy watched Sam dress. He sat on the bed in his shorts and pulled on socks. Then flicked his trousers out of the closet and stepped into a leg and a shoe in one fluid motion. Then the other leg and shoe. The sexy part was when he pulled on a tight white tank top.

"I'll wait and put on my shirt and jacket when we leave. I'm still a little damp. Hey, what're you staring at?"

"You. You sexy 'thaing.'"

"What time do we leave?"

"One. We're taking Margarida."

"Well, you'd better get dressed then."

"I've got time. I was just drying off from my shower." Judy got up, slipped on pantyhose, and put on a short-sleeved black linen suit and black flats. She put a deep cherry scarf in her pocket. Her only jewelry was her plain gold wedding ring. She seldom wore jewelry. When they got engaged, Sam wanted to buy her a diamond, but she'd never liked them. He finally convinced her to accept a jade necklace he'd seen her admire in a store window for an engagement gift.

Judy watched her husband; he didn't even think to tidy up his tousled hair. She was never attracted to vain men. Or even a man with a comb.

When they got downstairs, the others had already left. The caterers were busy getting the dining room ready for lunch.

"It really looks nice." Judy peered in. "We should use this room more often."

Sam got his shirt on, and carrying tie and jacket, ushered Judy out to the car. Judy got in back so Margarida could sit in front with Sam. Margarida loved Sam.

When they pulled into Margarida's driveway, she came out of the house with a flourish. She was dressed in a quaint costume—a heavy silk embroidered dress with a mandarin collar and flared sleeves—bright red dress with yellow and black embroidery. She wore a black silk woven shawl, which dimmed the outfit a small bit.

"She always looks so special." Sam smiled.

"She does, doesn't she?" agreed Judy.

Margarida got settled in the car and started right off talking about fruit trees with Sam—the new leaves looked wrinkled.

Judy tuned them out as they drove toward the synagogue. All day she was dreading the funeral. She was expecting to feel deep dark guilt, but as she probed her mind, she found only scattered curiosity. Would the casket be there? Would Sam wear a yarmulke?… He hated hats. Would there be music? Would anyone sob and carry on? Any number of thoughts were bubbling about, but none particularly gloomy. Well, after all, Joe *was* in a hospice and he *was* going to die soon anyway. So there wasn't going to be any problem after all. She was relieved and sat back and enjoyed the ride.

The funeral sped by. Joe's body was in a simple pine box. There were just a few prayers and then people rose to leave, catching Judy by surprise—she hadn't even finished examining the room and the people, all strangers to her except for Joe's family. A quick, smooth drive to the cemetery. Another prayer. Everyone put dirt over the coffin, and that was that. When they reached home, it seemed they'd just left.

Just as they started to serve lunch, someone pounded on the front door. Sam went to investigate. William "Don't call me Bill" Bean was on the doorstep.

"Hey, Bill, what's up? Doorbell not working?"

Bean bristled. "I don't know what your gathering is for, Haite. But I've got strange cars parked in front of my house. One is almost blocking the driveway. Extremely unsafe. My driver will have difficulty backing into the street."

Bill Bean was the president of one of those little banks in Palm Beach that catered to the wealthy. Sam had stopped trying to be neighborly when Bean informed him that he had no interest in social engagement with non-clients. This day he was clad in gray suit, white shirt, and blue tie. This was his bank uniform; his only others were for tennis and golf. He and his wife were never seen outside their house except going to and from their chauffeured automobile. Sam joked that Bean's wife was really a hologram. She'd appear on his arm heading out for charity affairs during the season, but was otherwise invisible to the neighbors.

"Bill, we're hosting a funeral lunch for our neighbors. Joe Corliss died this week. You're welcome to join us. Sorry about the cars, but your driver is a professional, and I'm certain he can navigate without accident."

Mr. Bean's face reddened. He glared at Sam but said nothing. Judy came up behind Sam and hugged him around the waist. "Hi, Bill. Want to join us? Haven't seen you in ages."

Mr. Bean mumbled, "Never you mind" and walked away.

"What was that all about?" Judy squeezed Sam.

"Beany didn't like the cars parked in front of his house."

"Poor Bill. What an ass!"

"I think he had the decency to be embarrassed when he found out it was for a funeral."

Sam closed the door, and they walked back to the dining room.

❦

Sam, Judy, and Margarida had lunch with the other mourners and then withdrew to the patio.

"When is everyone leaving?" asked Margarida.

"I don't think this will run very late, do you, Sam?"

"Judy, I think she meant when is the family going to leave Sunshine Street."

"Oh, sorry. I don't know. As soon as they can get flights, I suppose. Probably tomorrow. How has your group been, Margarida? I see you every night at dinner, but we haven't had a chance to really talk."

"You've been busy, dear. They've been good. At first the heat got to them, but they learned not to complain to me. Whenever they did, I'd sit them down and make them put their feet in buckets of ice water. Chilled 'em right down, that did. It's so nice now that the power is back on today."

"Oh!" said Judy. "I hadn't noticed. I guess I got used to the noise from the generator after all."

"That gas generator worked a lot better than I thought it would," Sam added. "I'm going to replace the one at work with the same make, bigger model, though."

Judy's mind drifted off. She and Sam would have their house back soon, and life would return to normal. Eileen wouldn't be much trouble—she'd probably leave in a month or so—and needed little care.

Later Eileen came out and joined them. "Everyone's gone, and the caterers are cleaning up. They'll send someone in the morning to pick up the crates."

"How are you holding up?" Sam asked.

"Tired. But okay. We did everything Joe wanted—he hated fancy funerals. This was just right—I was able to visit with people I haven't seen in ages."

"Can I get you something?" Sam stood up, ready to butler.

"A cordial would be nice. I haven't touched a drop all day; I was afraid I'd get maudlin."

"Anyone else?" Sam headed for the kitchen.

"Irish Mist for me." Judy smiled.

"Same for me, please," Margarida chimed in.

Sam was back with four glasses and the bottle.

"The main reason I came back here was to let you know that everyone is leaving tomorrow. Just Marilyn and I will stay a few more days."

"Your house will be ready so soon?" asked Sam.

"No. But I met an old friend of Joe's at the funeral. He owns a furnished condo that hasn't sold, and is letting me use it as long as I'd like. Marilyn and I are moving over there as soon as we get it stocked. Marilyn's going over there tomorrow and look it over. So we'll probably move the next day or the day after."

"So soon? I'll really miss you." It was a polite lie—she was *so* ready for her and Sam to be alone in the house.

"We've leaned on you long enough, Judy…and Sam. Oh, that drink hit the spot, but I think I'll go to bed now. It's been a long day." Eileen got up and maneuvered toward the kitchen.

Margarida stayed for another drink, and then Sam walked her home. He was back in minutes.

"She's glad to have her house back too. They've been quite a strain."

"What'll we do with our empty house?" Judy wondered.

"First we'll run naked upstairs and down. Then we'll hire a cleaning service to get rid of the smoke and smells. Then we'll go back to our lazy ways, I guess." Sam hugged Judy, then began picking up the glasses. "Let's go up. I'm bushed."

As they walked through the kitchen, they heard loud voices from Eileen's room. She and Marilyn were arguing, but they couldn't quite catch what was being said. Just then Marilyn stormed out of the room, leaving the door open, and marched upstairs. They could hear Eileen sobbing.

Sam looked at Judy. "Should we go in?"

Judy hesitated. What more could be wrong? Then she took Sam's elbow, and they crossed the corridor and stood in the doorway.

Eileen heard them and stopped crying, but couldn't control the twitchy breathing that followed. She looked like a little broken child sitting in her bed. "Marilyn had an autopsy done."

Judy's stomach lurched. "On Joe? Without your knowing?"

"She forged my signature. I could wring her neck!"

"When was it done?"

"She arranged it over a week ago. They did it right after he died. Marilyn is determined to find something to sue the hospital for."

Judy sat down on the edge of the bed and hugged Eileen.

Eileen shook herself and reached for a handful of tissues. "Damn, my nose is running." She dabbed her eyes and tried to smile. "I'll be all right, Judy. You two go to bed."

Sam walked into the room and leaned down to kiss Eileen on the cheek. "Sure you're okay?"

"Go to bed. I'll just punch my pillow for a while. She did it. It's done. It's over. There's really nothing I can do about it."

As she climbed the stairs, Judy worried. *What if they find something on the autopsy? Who ever did an autopsy on a hospice patient? Did anyone know I was in his room that night?*

Sam came up behind her, taking two steps at a time, and grabbed her around the waist. "Speed up, girlie."

Judy forced a laugh and let Sam push her up the stairs and onto their bed.

CHAPTER 14

Peace began to settle on Sunshine Street. By noon the next day, all the guests at Margarida's and the Hudsons' had headed home. Eileen, Marilyn, and Ted were still at Sam and Judy's, but Ted was scheduled to leave in the early evening.

After lunch Judy went over to Margarida's to help clean. Margarida stayed by the laundry room, while Judy stripped and changed the beds, cleaned the bathrooms, vacuumed, and put everything in order. At five o'clock she was crossing the street just as Sam drove into the driveway. They reached the door at the same time. Sam was still tidy, crisp shirt and creased trousers, while Judy's purple scrub suit had dark sweat stains, her hair was in a tight ponytail, and her face was smudged.

"You been working out?" Sam smiled and put his arm on her shoulder.

"Nope. Just working—helping Margarida clean up after the crowd. What a mess! They never emptied their trash or anything. And they left piles of towels all over the floors up there." Judy opened the door. "And you. You look like you haven't done a bit of work, judging from your clothes."

"Paperwork all day. I hate it. Accountant comes tomorrow, and I had to get stuff in order for the quarterly taxes and stuff. I'll be happy when I find someone to be office manager, and I can just play with kittens." He went to the refrigerator and pulled out two beers and opened them, handing one to Judy.

"Oh, God, that tastes good." Judy plopped on the couch.

"So what's next? You going to clean house for the Hudsons?"

"Don't have to. They have a housekeeper."

"So you're doing our house next?" Sam smiled, but made sure he wasn't within striking distance.

"Actually, smart guy, I am. Tomorrow. Right now, though, I'm pooped. And I'm not cooking tonight—it's pizza and beer. But first I need to finish this beer and go for a swim."

Just then Ted walked up from the cellar with his bags and piled them against the refrigerator. Judy watched in amazement.

"So what's for supper? I have to leave in an hour." Ted looked at Sam and Judy, or rather at their beers, realized he wanted one, saw his bags in the way, and stood helplessly.

"I guess you'll have to fend for yourself or pick up something at the airport. We're having pizza later, but right now we're going out for a swim." Judy put her beer on the counter and headed upstairs to get her swimsuit. She heard Sam right behind her.

Sam closed the door as he went into the bedroom. "That's another thing I'm looking forward to—not having to keep this damn door closed."

Judy grabbed a bright red tank and was in it in seconds. "Me too. But just think—no more Ted, ever! I'm really excited." She ran barefoot down the stairs, grabbed her beer, and twirled outside and jumped into the pool. She floated on her back until Sam joined her.

They stayed in the water until the taxi came for Ted. Half an hour later, Eileen hobbled over to the pool. "Well, Ted's gone. Did he say good-bye to you folks?"

"In a way, I guess. He was upset we weren't having an early supper." Judy smiled.

Eileen shrugged her shoulders. "Can I fix something for supper?"

"We thought pizza and beer," Sam said.

"Want me to order it?" Eileen offered.

"I don't know what kind I want yet. Why don't you check on Marilyn's order, and then we'll call when we get in. I'm just going to do one more lap, and I'll be in. I'm starving." Judy pushed away from the edge of the pool and started a lazy backstroke.

Eileen nodded and headed back to the house.

※

By the time the pizzas came, Judy was so hungry, she was afraid the three pies weren't going to be enough. Sam made a salad and brought it and a bucket of beers onto the patio. Judy followed with the pizzas, and Eileen went to fetch Marilyn.

Sam, Judy, and Eileen were on their third slices before Marilyn finally came out onto the patio. She put a few lettuce leaves onto a plate, examined the pizzas, peered into the beer bucket, and shuffled back into the kitchen without a word.

"Don't mind her." Eileen shook her head and shrugged.

"Oh, we don't. Used to her by now," Judy offered.

They finally gave up when just two slices were left. By then all three were too full even for Jell-O. Eileen gathered up the dishes and went inside. Judy heard her scuffle off toward her room.

"Whew. I feel like the earth's stopped spinning." Judy lay back in her chaise. "The moon's out, why don't you cut the lights."

They sat admiring the moon. The air was still and lightly scented by the rosemary hedge along the back wall of the yard. Jack came through the cat door, took a chair, and began grooming.

Sam stretched. "I'll be glad when Marilyn's gone and the house is back in order. God, Ted's feet reeked. I hope we can get the stink out."

"Tomorrow I plan to put on a scrub suit and play maid—even if it takes all day."

"I'll be with the accountant most of tomorrow. He always finds something we have to research."

Judy turned in her chaise, putting her feet on the floor. "I don't know about you, but this is going to be an early night for me. I think I'll take a little American Honey upstairs and watch TV. Expect to be asleep in minutes."

"Don't rush the sleep bit, sweetie." Sam stayed in his chaise.

"Well, better come up with me now, I can't promise I'll wait long." Judy jiggled Sam's chaise and went into the kitchen.

The two closed up the patio and took their drinks upstairs. Sex, drinks, TV—within thirty minutes Judy was sound asleep, snoring.

⸎

Sam was up before five the next day and left for work before Judy got up. When he went downstairs, she thought of going down to make breakfast, but it was just that, a thought. She fell back asleep and didn't wake again until after nine, when she awoke rested. Clear head, clear eyes. She showered and went downstairs. Eileen had made coffee and was sitting at the red leather booth wearing a blue and yellow Chinese silk robe.

"Wow! Your colors would wake the dead!" Out of her mouth before she thought.

"I love colors. Most clothes are so drab." Eileen didn't seem bothered by the "dead" remark.

"I know. I used to wear just tan and white. I've come a little beyond that, but could never reach your level." Judy poured a cup of coffee and joined Eileen in the booth. "Whenever I sit here, I feel we should have one of those coin boxes for a jukebox. Where's Marilyn?"

"She had something to do for her job. She went to a printer, then is meeting some local people from her company. She told me what it was about, but I don't understand most of what she does."

"What are you up to today?"

"An old friend is picking me up at ten. Having a day at the spa."

"Should be fun." Judy went to a spa once. She was uncomfortable the whole time and felt she'd choke to death on the fumes—perfume and incense were everywhere.

"And you?"

"I'm playing maid today. House has gotten a bit grubby through all this. Then I'll do a backyard loaf—swim, read."

"I wish I could help with the cleaning—but at least we'll be out from underfoot today."

"I'll crank up the music and have some fun." Judy was looking forward to it—not to the doing of it, but to the having done it. And it would keep the thing about Joe further back in her mind.

Eileen went to her room to dress. Judy made breakfast—French toast, maple syrup, grapefruit sections, coffee—and took the tray upstairs.

※

She turned on the TV to watch while she ate. The independent film channel was on, and a movie had just started. It was the Gérard

Depardieu film, *Mon Oncle d'Amerique*. Judy had never seen it, but loved Depardieu—he had such a big oafish head but could play anyone. By the time she finished eating, she was hooked. She had to finish it. Otherwise she'd have to go out and rent it later—none of their TVs could record. So she settled back.

The movie was more than a little strange. There was a conventional story line: wife, husband, mistress. But interspersed was a scientist lecturing on animal behavior. He demonstrated several experiments with a rat subjected to electric jolt to the cage floor just after a buzzer rang; this went on several times a day for many days. The cage was divided in half, with a door between. In the first experiment, the rat could avoid the shock by going through the door to the other side. Even after several days, the rat was fine. In the second experiment, the door was closed. The buzzer rang, and the rat had to submit to the mild shocks. In this series, the rat fell apart—lost hair, weight, and mental stability. The third series was the same as the second, but two rats were in the cage together. The buzzer rang, the shocks came, and the rats fought. At the end of this series, the rats were just as healthy as the rats with the open door. Judy wasn't sure what the message was—was any action better than none, or did it have to be violent action? The key human action in the movie was the wife lying to the mistress that she was dying and asking for her husband back for a short while to help with the children. The mistress agreed, and the husband stayed permanently with the wife.

Before she knew, it was after noon and she was watching another Depardieu movie. At one o'clock she realized she was in the middle of a Depardieu festival: *Jean de Florette, The Stranger, 1900, The Last Metro*. There were only minutes between films, no advertising—so she'd dash downstairs, grab cookies, chips, banana, ham sandwich, or beer—and run back upstairs.

Judy loved movies but until recently probably saw just one or two a year. When she was little, one of her aunts took her to the Disney classics. Later her birthdays consisted of a movie with one friend, followed by cake and ice cream. Her best movie experience so far was during the summer she worked as a chambermaid in Northeast Harbor. One afternoon she went to see *The Naked Maja*—the life of the painter Goya—and was the only person in the theater. She didn't get cable until Sam came to live with her, and had never rented a movie. With cable she was hooked—there was a lifetime of movies to see.

She sat on the bed resting against four pillows. She was on her third beer. The bedside table was covered with empties—plates, bottles, boxes, and bags. She was still wearing the short robe she put on when she got up. Pure enjoyment.

Then Sam was in the room. She hadn't heard him come home. He stripped out of his clothes and put on swim trunks. He sat on the edge of the bed to put on sandals, then turned around and looked at her. "God, it's hot out there. I've got to buy more tropical-weight clothes. I'm in air-conditioning most of the day, and it just kills me to go outside. Oh, Eileen and Marilyn are downstairs wandering around. I think they're looking for food. What's for dinner?"

Judy saw him looking at the detritus on the nightstand and realized she'd forgotten all about her cleaning plans. She felt a pang of guilt, then angry that she'd have to provide an "excuse" for her enjoyable day. "Oh, I don't know, Sam. I'm all dinnered out, I guess."

"Too much cleaning today, eh?" Sam eyed the nightstand.

"Well, not really. Not too much. I came up here for breakfast and got stuck in a Depardieu film festival—they've been running all day."

"All day. You didn't do anything else?"

"No. It was so quiet and peaceful. Each movie just pulled me in." Judy was getting angry. She hated when Sam became the parent and she the bad child.

Sam got up and strolled to the other side of the room. He drew a line in the dust on a bureau and rolled his eyes.

"I saw that you…you…you…" Judy searched for a word, gave up, strode across the room, and punched Sam in the upper arm.

"Ouch! You don't have to get violent."

"You know I hate cleaning talk. I had really good intentions today, and I don't want a super guilt trip laid on me just because I decided to enjoy myself. Actually, I didn't decide anything, it just happened."

"What'll we do for dinner?" Sam was leaving the room, heading for a swim.

"I don't care. I'm stuffed—I've been munching all day. Why don't we ask Marilyn to fix something for all of us?"

She hit the spot. Sam bent over in a fit of giggles, came back into the room, and collapsed on the bed. Judy lay down and laughed with him.

Sam recovered first. "I don't know why that was so funny."

"We were just overdue for a good laugh, I think. Plus, celebrating Marilyn's last day. She and Eileen are making their last trip over to the condo after supper. So I guess I'd better go dig up something special for dinner to celebrate. I'll shower, then be down in a jiffy."

Judy got up and went into the bathroom. Crisis averted. But she'd better do the cleaning soon. Damn.

CHAPTER 15

Three nights after the funeral, Judy woke with a start. Heart pounding, sheets sweat-soaked. Was someone breaking into the house? Everything seemed quiet. Sam lay there gently snoring while Jack sprawled across the foot of their bed. Judy got up, put on a long robe, and crept downstairs. Everything seemed all right. She poured herself a glass of water and went onto the patio. The night was still; a full moon lit up the backyard.

"Maybe I could sleep out here," she thought aloud. So she lay on a chaise and tried to relax. After fifteen minutes she got up and turned on the TV. What time was it? Only two. She found a public station showing a family in Turkey that walked on all fours. Settling down to that, she quickly fell asleep.

Instantly she was back in Joe's hospice room. He lay asleep, smiling. He looked better; were his teeth back in? She walked closer to the bed. He had some color in his cheeks, and he'd been shaved. Then he opened his eyelids, and vacant, pale blue eyes stared out at her. Still smiling, he screamed! Judy sat up. A nightmare. Joe. Oh, God, where did that come from?

Judy got up. Only two thirty. She'd be damned if she'd try sleep again tonight. That must've been what woke her up before. She tried to calm herself. It was only a nightmare. Her own brain was making the movie up. Joe wasn't there; he was safely buried, and all those people had left Sunshine Street. And everything was back as it should be. It would be all right. Somewhere deep inside she must feel guilty, although she really didn't think she was. Maybe technically, but…

Judy turned the TV off and went into the house to get a book. (She was rereading *Setting Free the Bears*.) She made cocoa and sat through the night on the patio reading. At first she had trouble concentrating, but was deep into it when Sam came out on the patio.

"Oh, there you are. Want coffee?"

"Yeah, thanks."

Sam came out with coffee and sat beside her. "Couldn't sleep?"

"Not long. For some reason I woke right up. It's been so quiet these last few days, I guess I caught up with all the sleep I need. It's so nice having the house back to ourselves."

"Yes. I feel I have my energy back. Speaking of which, I'm off. Going to play tennis with Marvin, then we're having breakfast in town. Want to join us there?"

"No. I think I'll laze about today. No plans. No meals. Just a lot of wonderful nothing," Judy said, trying to appear cheerful.

"Okay. I'm off then." Sam leaned down and kissed Judy on the nose.

Judy spent the morning reading, skipped breakfast, and had just a tuna sandwich for lunch. She was surprised she was so hungry. She didn't bother to make it fancy, just took most of the small can, mixed it with mayo, and called it done. She gave the rest of the tuna to Jack.

Later Sam called and said he was going to stay in town and play poker that afternoon. Judy was relieved not to have to talk with him. She was getting tired and was afraid to take a nap. It was silly, she thought, but she was afraid Joe would come back. His scream…Did she hear it? Or just think it? But it was awful. A mixture of a gargle and a squeal. Not loud, very breathy. She shuddered. She had to leave the house. Maybe a walk.

She turned left out of the yard and headed toward the Intracoastal Waterway. She figured she'd walk north on the Lake Trail a while, cut across the island to the ocean, and walk back along the beach. It was hot but windy. It felt good to be moving; she should've done this earlier. No one was out walking. A few employees of the houses on the island came by on their bikes.

This day was too creepy. Why did Joe scream in her dream? He hadn't made a sound when she…when she did it. He had opened his eyes, though. Did he recognize her? No. No—his brain was gone.

Judy stopped and rested when she got to the beach. Most of the trash from the storm was gone, although the sandy area was still narrow and there was a steep drop-off to the ocean. She had forgotten to bring water and was thirsty and hot. She lay back in the shade and watched the waves. No one was at this end of the beach. The beach bordered a road; the houses on the other side of the road had cabanas on the beach, but no one ever seemed to use them. A few sailboats were out. Little ones.

So tired. Each time she blinked, her eyes wanted to stay shut. I must stay awake. She got up and walked down the beach to Sunshine Street.

She needed more exercise. Once home she went upstairs and changed into a modest plaid bikini. Grabbing a bottle of water, she jogged to the pool and jumped in. The racing lane was shaded, and the water was cooler than the air. She did her best Australian crawl as fast as she could. Back and forth, back and forth. Exhausted, Judy turned to float on her back. Orchids attached to the trees draped down toward the water. Sam has made this place so beautiful. Every bit of space was planned to the last plant.

After a few minutes' rest, Judy resumed swimming, but slower now. Each stroke—what can I do?—what can I do? She'd have to turn her mind off somehow, or she wouldn't make it through the day.

The phone rang inside. She let the machine pick up, but got out of the pool to check the message. It was Peggy apologizing for calling on Sunday, but one of the therapists had called in sick, and they were shorthanded. Could Judy come in and help out for a few hours?

Work, the great anodyne. Yes. This would help. She'd go into work, get really tired, and tonight she'd sleep and everything would be all right.

❦

A loud horn startled her. She'd stopped at a red light waiting to go across the bridge to Good Sam and must've been daydreaming. She waved apologies to the person in the car behind her and turned onto the bridge.

Maybe I'm too tired to work, she worried. But didn't really believe it—just a few years ago, she'd often worked double shifts without any problem at all. She turned the radio to a rock station and sang along during the rest of her trip.

The surface lots were full, so she had to park on the roof of the garage. The sun was still hot, and she was sweating by the time she got inside. She caught herself in a hallway mirror; not a beauty today—her hair was damp from swimming and sweat and her face wan. As she walked along the corridor to the PT office, she smacked her cheeks to put some color into them—and to get more alert.

"Ah, Judy," said Peggy. "Thanks so much for coming in. We were just too thin to make it today. I've got three patients with new legs that need walking and just didn't have the staff for it."

"Happy to come in. Are they all on ortho?"

"Yup. Here are the names. Just get their legs on, get them out of bed, and take them up and down the connecting corridor no more than three times. None have been up much yet, and I couldn't let them get behind."

Judy reviewed the list and picked up her things. "Oh, I know. Any trouble in the beginning, and some never learn to use the legs. Well, I'm off. See you Monday."

"Thanks again, Judy, you're a doll."

Judy went into the staff lounge to drop her purse in her locker, then headed for the orthopedic floor. She checked at the nurses' station to make sure all her patients were still healthy enough for walking, then settled down to work. Within an hour and a half, Judy walked with two of the patients and headed toward the room of Mrs. Mildred Elroy, who had lost her leg to advanced vascular disease. An enthusiastic smoker and drinker, Mrs. Elroy was sitting in her bed putting on makeup. She looked up and smiled as Judy came into the room.

"Hi, Mrs. Elroy, remember me? I'm Judy Haite, your physical therapist. Going to take you for a walk with your new leg."

"Hi, hon. You're the one with the funny story, of course I remember. Please call me Milly. I'm glad you're here—I was afraid I wouldn't get the practice today. I'm anxious to get out of here, and the doctor won't let me go to rehab until my stump can take the pressure."

Judy watched as Mrs. Elroy attached her leg, then helped her out of bed. She fitted a harness between them to secure the woman's safety as she walked. They made their way out of the room and headed down the main corridor.

"It doesn't hurt at all today." Mrs. Elroy smiled as she greeted a fellow amputee.

As they turned the corner, Mrs. Elroy's artificial leg slipped out from under her and ripped away from her stump. The sudden move caught Judy by surprise and instead of steadying the woman, she fell on top of her. Mrs. Elroy screamed in pain. Judy sat, stunned, unable to help.

Nurses ran to Mrs. Elroy. As they lifted her into a wheelchair, blood was seeping into the sock covering the stump. Mrs. Elroy was cradling her arm, rocking back and forth in the chair.

Judy started to cry. Then sob. She sat in the middle of the floor and couldn't do anything else. A nurse came up to see if she was injured, and Judy waved her away.

Finally she got up and started down to the PT office. Peggy wasn't there, so she got her purse, left the building, got out to her car, and sat.

She was still sitting in her car staring at nothing as the shift changed and employees came and went from the parking garage. About six thirty Peggy rapped on her window. Judy opened it, but said nothing.

"You're upset. Why don't you go home? Come in tomorrow late, and we'll talk. I don't know my schedule. I'll call in the morning and let you know when I'm free."

Judy nodded and put her window up. She couldn't let herself talk. She continued to sit until activity ceased in the garage. Then she backed her car and wended her way to the street level. She was able to give the attendant a smile as she left.

Judy didn't remember driving home. Sam was already there; she could see him digging in the backyard. She dragged herself out of the car and went inside.

After a shower she took a beer out on the patio and sat watching Sam planting lemon-yellow ground orchids. He was putting in what looked like a hundred plants under an oak in the corner of the yard. How had he remembered? They'd been at a tree event in Lake Worth a couple of months before, and she'd seen a couple of these orchids; she'd mentioned they'd be pretty if you had a whole sea of them. Lovely Sam.

Sam came in after hosing the dirt off his hands. "Hi, honey. Oh, hey, what's the matter?"

"Disaster at work. I let a nice old lady fall. Probably ruined her stump." Judy took a deep breath. "I've never had anything like that happen before. She put on her own leg, and I didn't check it. It just fell off when she walked. I feel horrible."

Sam came over and hugged Judy. She didn't expect him to say anything—he had learned that platitudes never helped her. "Why don't I mix us a proper drink?"

Judy sat waiting for Sam to come back. She had never felt this bad. She was proud of her profession and had excelled at every job she'd taken. Now she'd made a rookie mistake. She had to stop thinking. Nothing would help now.

Sam came back with margaritas and tortilla chips with hot cheese dip. They sat, drank, and nibbled. It grew dark. Sam got up, turned on the lights, and went inside. Later he came out with tomato bisque and grilled cheese sandwiches. He turned on the lights and the television. They sat, watched, and ate.

"Can I do anything to help?" asked Sam.

"Not really. It'll take time, I guess."

"Just let me know. I'm right here."

"Sorry to ruin your evening."

"That's okay. I just hate to see you like this." Sam reached over and squeezed Judy's shoulder.

They watched TV until ten. Then Sam went up to bed. Judy told him she'd be up soon, but knew she wouldn't. She went into the kitchen and poured a large margarita and went back on the patio and watched TV. All night she watched TV and tried not to think. And fought sleep.

About five she went upstairs and sneaked into bed. Sam was sleeping peacefully, a little grin on his face. Judy lay stiffly beside him and waited for the alarm. She feigned sleep, let him turn the alarm off, and then sat up and yawned. "Morning."

"Morning. Feeling better?"

"Some. Sleep helped." Judy got up and went down to make coffee. She brought it up, and Sam reached for it eagerly.

"I slept well, but I'm dopey as all get-out."

"Coffee is a great drug," Judy agreed. They turned on the TV and waited for the coffee to revive them. Then Sam got up, showered, dressed, and went downstairs.

Judy followed slowly in her bathrobe.

"Not going in to work?" Sam was fixing his cereal and juice. "Want some?"

"No thanks. I'm going in later. I'll eat after a swim, I think."

Judy swam, then sat outside by the pool reading. When she went in to get more coffee, Peggy called.

"Judy, this is Peggy. How are you this morning?"

"Better, I guess. Still stunned. I feel terrible about Mrs. Elroy."

"Can you be here at eleven thirty? Sorry it's so late, but I've got meetings all morning."

"I'll be there." Judy put the phone down. Was it her imagination, or was Peggy a little cool toward her? Probably she's just busy. Judy made a cup of coffee, took a couple biscotti, and went back outside. She read until ten and then went inside.

After a shower, Judy sat on the bed. Usually she worked Mondays from eight to one. So should she wear her uniform? If she met with Peggy at eleven thirty, her shift would be nearly over. Peggy must've called someone in to cover her shift. Judy could call Peggy back, but she'd probably be in a meeting.

Judy finally decided to wear her work shoes and carry her uniform. She could change if she had to work. That settled, Judy dressed in lightweight tan slacks and a crisp white shirt. She studied herself in the mirror and decided she looked pretty good. Her hair was lustrous, and her face was tanned, with a bit of red from this morning's sun. She waved at herself in the mirror and headed down to the car.

She reached the medical center at a quarter past eleven, so she went right to the staff lounge to store her uniform and bag. She'd pick up a pen and notebook and go straight to Peggy's office. The lounge was empty. She tried several times to open her locker, but it was stuck. This hadn't happened to her before, but others had had trouble with the old lockers. Judy shrugged and went to the PT office.

"Hi, Sally. I've got an eleven thirty with Peggy. Can I borrow a notebook and pen? Couldn't get my locker open."

The secretary looked up from typing. "Sure. Just take them out of the closet." Sally buzzed Peggy, then told Judy to go right in.

Expecting to see Peggy, Judy stopped in the doorway. Peggy was there, but so was Dr. Hughes, the chief of rehab medicine, and Jack Hewitt, one of the vice presidents.

"Come sit, Judy." Peggy motioned to a metal chair opposite the other three.

Judy sat and looked from one serious face to the other. For several seconds no one spoke. Then Dr. Hughes cleared his throat. "Judy. Mrs. Elroy is in surgery this morning. They have to amputate her knee and pin her shoulder. As you know, with an above-the-knee amputation and inability to use a walker, Mrs. Elroy's health is in peril. Would you please explain how in hell this all happened."

"Mrs. Elroy put her leg on, and she walked fine for about fifteen feet, but when we turned a corner, the leg shifted out from under her. I had the harness on, but the angle of her fall took me by surprise, and I lost my footing. Dr. Hughes, I'm devastated by the accident."

"Did you check the leg after she put it on?" the doctor continued.

"No. I forgot," Judy admitted. Oh, she wished she could lie, but Mrs. Elroy knew what happened, and Dr. Hughes probably did also.

"That was an unforgivable error. I can't imagine your doing it; you've always been so careful with the patients. Was anything wrong? Were you sick? You weren't drinking, were you?"

"Oh, no," Judy thought—I can't tell them about the nightmares or about…or about Joe. "I didn't sleep well the night before, but I felt I could work okay.

"Mrs. Haite, this is very serious," began Mr. Hewitt. "I'm quite sure the hospital will be sued for the mess you've made. The cost to provide free care to try to heal Mrs. Elroy will be astronomical. You made it all worse by running away, not caring for Mrs. Elroy, and not putting any note in the chart."

"If I can…" Judy started to speak, but Mr. Hewitt raised his hand to stop her.

"We've met this morning and decided we have no choice but to suspend you. It could very well be a permanent suspension. Here's a brochure detailing your rights to appeal our decision. We'll pay you for today and any other accrued salary; the check will be mailed. Your benefits will end at the end of next week. I advise you to contact an attorney—the family may sue you in addition to the medical center."

Judy sat stunned. She was being fired. Just like that. Should she get angry? Cry? She couldn't react at all. She was humiliated and just wanted to disappear.

Peggy said softly, "I've put a box of your belongings on the chair outside. I'm sorry, Judy, but we've had no choice."

Judy stared dumbly back at Peggy, stood, and left the room. She had to get out of there without being seen. But Sally was still at her post, and of course she had known everything. Sally looked up quickly at Judy, then down at her keyboard. Judy guessed no one wanted to see her either.

She picked up the box, set her face in neutral, and entered the corridor.

In a few minutes, Judy knew everyone in the hospital would know. She had to get out. Fired. Fired. She'd never been fired in her life. Or even gotten less than stellar reviews. She could never come back here. Could she still live so close? Maybe she and Sam could move back to Maine.

As she walked, she relived the day. Peggy was in meetings all morning all right, meetings about *her*. And she admired Dr. Hughes so much, and now he thought she was a nitwit. And Sally knew they were going to fire her when she came in. Only then she realized why her locker wouldn't work. "Oh, I'm so stupid," she moaned.

CHAPTER 16

Judy drove away from the hospital. When she came to the bridge to Palm Beach and home, she didn't turn left, but kept driving straight south along the Intracoastal Waterway. Her car automatically took her to Lake Worth, her home for ten years.

When she'd first moved to the area from Maine, her real estate agent had shown her several houses out west that she could afford. The houses were nice, but the land so flat, she didn't think she'd be able to find her way home at night. Or be able to distinguish her house from all the others once she'd found her street. The Realtor finally gave up and brought her to Lake Worth, "where all the other hippies live." Judy found a house near the Intracoastal in an older 1940s neighborhood. It was a mixed-income area with large two-story houses and little one-story ones. The architecture ran the gamut from New England colonial to Mediterranean. Some of her neighbors had actually been born in Lake Worth (most Floridians are not natives), and all in all it was a pretty friendly neighborhood. Judy felt lucky to have found it.

She drove down her old street. She'd been hoping Ginger, her best friend in the neighborhood, would be home, but there were no cars in the driveway. She sat for a few minutes. She was upset, but she was also hungry. She drove downtown, sat outside at a bistro, and ordered a simple lunch of pear and Stilton salad, bean soup, an éclair, and coffee. She ate slowly and tried to focus on what to do with the afternoon—not on what just happened at the hospital.

After eating she wandered through some antique stores, but couldn't even pretend to be interested. Finally she gave up and headed back to get her car. Just then her cell phone rang. She didn't recognize the number, but answered anyway.

"Hey, Judy. Where the hell are you?"

"Pardon?" Judy had no idea who was calling. A woman's voice.

"Judy. It's after three. You're supposed to pick me up!"

"I'm sorry. Who is this?"

"It's me, Terry."

"Terry? Where are you?"

"Where are *you*? You're supposed to pick me up at the airport."

"Sorry, Terry. We've got a bad connection. I'm on my way—got stuck in traffic. I'm about fifteen minutes from the airport. Where are you?"

"Delta."

"Be right there."

"Okey dokey. Bye."

"Bye." Oh, good grief. Judy had completely forgotten her friend Terry was coming for almost a month. Knowing Terry, she probably had forgotten to give Judy a date and time when she'd be here, but…This could be bad. Or not. Maybe having Terry around would take her mind off…off other things. Sam wouldn't be pleased; he was so happy to have just the two of them in the house again. But Terry could be fun, and she'd enjoy showing off Sam and their house.

Terry Biddle Lynch had been her best friend from her first job after college. They both worked at the hospital in Portland. Her nickname, Trouble, came both from her "TBL" initials and from her behavior. She'd park in a no-parking zone and be surprised her car was towed. She'd ignore plane schedules and be surprised to miss flights. Wheels fell off her cars. She ignored birth control and had a child. Once Judy was visiting and smelled smoke in the house; Terry said it was all in her head until flames erupted from the bathroom where Terry had left her hair dryer plugged in. Terry begged to come with Judy on trips to Europe, but Judy always found ways to discourage it. Terry finally got her cousin to go with her on a safari in Africa, and their plane was hijacked. Things were usually too exciting around Terry for Judy to take for long, but she was an old friend, and she hadn't seen her since she and Sam had been married.

Terry was out on the curb at Delta. Judy helped her with the luggage, and they hopped into the car and drove off.

"Well. Hello!"

"Hi, Terry. You look terrific." Terry still lived in Maine. She had short teased blond hair with dark roots. As always, fashionably dressed, she wore a short-sleeved beige linen suit with a low neckline, which she accented with lots of gold—earrings, bracelets, and ropes around her neck. Judy saw she still wore tons of makeup; she thought it made her look older and coarser—her skin underneath wasn't that bad. Oh, well, Judy never had learned makeup herself beyond lip gloss and sunscreen.

Terry ruffled her hair. "I can feel my hair go wild already. How do you stand this weather?"

"Got used to it. Sam taught me to avoid air-conditioning. It's the shock of going from one to the other that's bad. Usually I try to stay with whatever we have outside. Hey, what brings you down here? It sounded pretty hush-hush when you called."

"Consulting on a trial. Another of your county commissioners is being investigated by a grand jury." Terry was an attorney much in demand. Her expertise was in structuring (she called it wheedling) plea agreements. She would wear out prosecutors wanting to have highly publicized embarrassing trials of government officials and celebrities.

"When do you start working?"

"Tuesday. I think. I have to check in Monday to see how things stand. But at least I have the weekend off. Been out straight for months. How've you been?"

"Sam and I have had houseguests from hell—I'll catch you up later on that—and we're just getting back to normal after the hurricane and all. But we're fine."

"Just fine?" Terry raised her eyebrows.

"Oh, we're great. I'm just in a mood lately." Judy pretended she had to focus on driving, adding for effect, "Damn these drivers. Half can't see over the steering wheel, and the other half are psychotic!"

"I'm anxious to meet Sam. I really envy you. I keep catching men and throwing them back. Never found someone I've been comfortable with day to day. Know what I mean?"

"Oh, do I. Before Sam, usually someone would fall deeply 'in love' with me before I even knew he existed. We'd date for a year or so, then I'd feel smothered and break it off—usually not well either. Remember the time I hid under my desk when I'd told Anton it was over and he came to the office?"

They laughed and hashed over more old stories from back then for the rest of the trip home.

Once at the house, Judy got Terry settled in the guest room. They both swam for a bit, then lounged on the patio with martinis.

"This is the life!" Terry stretched out on the chaise. "What a beautiful room."

"I forgot you've never been here."

"Quite a change from Lake Worth."

"Quite. We love it here. Loved Lake Worth too, though."

※

Judy was in the kitchen getting dinner ready when Sam came home.

"Hi, hon."

"Hi. Day go okay?"

"Oh, yeah. Boy, I'm ready for a lazy weekend, though. We were busy all week."

"Had a surprise today. Terry's here. I forgot all about her visit, what with Joe and all."

"Oh, damn. Just what we need…"

"Shhh! She's right out on the patio."

"Oh, well. Any friend of yours…" Sam hugged Judy, then went upstairs to change.

They grilled scallops and had salad and asparagus for dinner. Sam brought out champagne he was saving. They had a lively meal, with Terry telling Sam all about Judy's days in Portland.

Judy sat and smiled, cringing from time to time from some of the anecdotes. She'd forgotten she'd ever been that young and stupid. Terry told of the time they'd rented a sailboat with their boyfriends. None of them knew how to sail. One of them *said* he knew, but could only sail with the wind. It happened the wind was offshore that day, so they headed straight into the Atlantic. A trip planned for a few hours turned into a night of terror before the Coast Guard finally rescued them. This was one of the first of the typical Terry disasters Judy had experienced.

Another time, again at the ocean, Terry convinced her that they should rent a motorboat for the day. They'd gone north up the coast and came back, weaving in and out among the islands. It was a calm day, and Judy had marveled at the clarity of the water. Afraid of heights, she was amazed to find her stomach lurch when she looked down through the water to the rocks below. They put in at a small island and sunbathed for several hours. On their way back to return the boat, they got hungry and tied up at a restaurant in Camden, right in the harbor. They'd lolled through lunch, then strolled through the town looking for earrings for Terry. It was several hours before they returned to the dock where they'd left the boat. In their absence the tide had gone out, and they found the boat hanging off the dock, with its contents floating far below and a large group of giggling locals waiting for them. Somehow adventures with Terry always involved cost and embarrassment for Judy.

The talk about boats was too much for Sam. "Hey, Terry. Would you sail around the world with me?"

"You serious?" Terry smiled and tilted her head.

"I just struck out with Judy. I want to retire and go island hopping. Even picked out a yacht—but Judy turned me down flat."

"It's probably my fault—we didn't have much luck with boats. But I've always wanted to do a long sail—with someone who knows what he's doing."

"So you'll do it with me?"

"I couldn't right away. And I couldn't go for more than six or eight months—my firm allows a sabbatical every five years to recharge. But, yeah, I'd definitely be interested in hearing more about this."

Judy watched them, fascinated. She couldn't tell if they were serious or just playing verbal badminton. But she was relieved Sam had taken to Terry. He sat and leaned toward her as she spoke, laughing and encouraging her to continue. As they chatted, Judy withdrew and relived the day. When they got upstairs, she'd have to tell Sam she was fired. He'd care only about her reaction—they didn't need the money, and he'd like having her available more often. She'd keep the discussion positive—pretend she was relieved to have more free time.

Judy's head snapped back. "Hey, guys—I'm going to have to go to up to bed; it's been a long day."

Terry and Sam wished her good night and went back to their conversation. They'd just discovered they knew several people in common.

Judy trudged upstairs. After a quick shower, she eased into bed. The sheets were crisp bright white cotton and felt good on her skin. She'd tell Sam about the job tomorrow. No rush. Oh, so tired.

Judy slept for just a few minutes, then jerked awake. Joe was there again. This time he was sitting up in bed smoking and wagging his finger at her. No sound.

What could she do? She had to sleep. She remembered when she had bad dreams in grade school, she'd been able to manipulate them or at least repeat the mantra "this is just a dream" while the bad dream was occurring. She'd have to relearn that trick. So she took a deep breath, closed her eyes, and went right back to sleep.

This time Joe was lying in bed, and she was trying to lift him into a more comfortable position. As she held him by his torso, his skin came off in her hands. He screamed in pain. Judy woke with a start.

Now her heart was racing. How could her brain do this to her? Pills. She needed sleeping pills. She got up and rummaged through the medicine cabinet. No sleeping pills, but she found a muscle relaxant she'd been prescribed for a wrenched back. The label said to take three tablets before bed. Judy remembered taking three the first time and being so zonked out that she slept in a chair—unable to get up and walk to the bedroom. So three should do it. She tossed the tablets into her mouth and gulped enough water to wash them down.

Back in bed she turned on the TV and tried to relax. She fell asleep in minutes.

She woke as Sam was shaking her. What was he doing that for?

"Judy. Wake up! You've been screaming bloody murder. Must be some nightmare." Sam smiled down at her.

"That's funny. I don't remember being in one. What time is it?"

"Eleven thirty."

So she'd had a half hour of sleep. Great. Now what? At least she didn't have to worry about being able to function at work anymore.

"Are you coming to bed?"

"Yup. You okay?"

"I guess so. Did I say anything?"

"No. Just screamed. Really loud."

"Sorry."

"Nothing to be sorry about. Are you okay? Really?" Sam sat on Judy's side of the bed and started to massage her neck. Judy knew he wanted sex, usually a nightly thing with them, but she just wasn't up to it. She feigned sleep until Sam gave up and went to bed.

When Sam began to snore, Judy went downstairs with her book. She read for a while, made coffee, and thought. She could get through the weekend without sleep. Then, when Sam and Terry were both working, she could take the muscle relaxant and sleep. She'd still have nightmares, but she wouldn't remember them. She might scream, so she'd sleep with doors and windows closed so no one would call the police for her. There, she had a plan. She could relax.

She was watching TV when Sam came down.

"Morning."

"Morning. Been up long?"

"No. I just came down a while ago." Judy got up and followed Sam into the kitchen. "Can I fix anything for breakfast?"

"I'll start with coffee. I can wait for food until Terry gets up."

They brought their coffees out to the patio.

"Aah. I love a day with nothing planned. Don't even have to wear a watch. I used to think battery-powered watches were the stupidest things ever invented for lazy Americans, until I got one and found how nice it was not to have to wear one every day." Sam grinned.

"Only problem is the day the battery dies. Always seems to happen when I really need to know the time. Amazing how many times I can look at a stopped watch and not realize it's not working.

"My mother says we look at clocks to see what time it isn't. Which reminds me…We have to make a trip to Maine soon."

"October would be nice—or is that too late?" Right now Judy couldn't imagine visiting Sam's mother, though she'd like to go to Maine. Sam's mother, Myra, had been controlling when he was a child and had only gotten worse. She treated them both as children needing minute-to-minute guidance…what to wear, what not to put ketchup on, what time they should go to bed. She drove Judy nuts. The last couple of years, Judy managed to finesse it by visiting her own folks most of the time Sam visited his mother. But this year her parents were in Florida. Oh, well, she'd figure out some escape later.

"My favorite month up there. I'll work out the dates and make arrangements."

"You give me the dates, and I can do the rest. I was fired yesterday—because of that accident—so I'll have more time."

"Was that fair to you? It was just an accident."

"I think they were freaked out about their liability. Oh, I should probably alert Mark White about this—they said I may be sued too." Judy felt lighter having this topic out of the way.

"You sure you're all right with this? Couldn't we sue the hospital for wrongful termination or something?"

"Technically they just suspended me, maybe to avoid a suit from me. But I'm pretty sure it's permanent. I'd rather just forget it."

Just then Terry came in, carrying her coffee. They chatted a while, then went in to cook breakfast together.

The weekend went smoothly. They took Terry around town, then out to Okeeheelee Park for a bike ride and picnic. They picked up some movies on the way back and spent the evening watching them and talking.

Judy pretended to sleep, then came downstairs and read or watched TV until morning. Sunday was more of the same: beach walk, restaurant lunch, swimming at home, light supper, and early to bed.

By Monday Judy was feeling pretty good. She wasn't sleepy, but did feel a bit lightheaded and was having strange shifts in her vision—like a film getting stuck in an old movie projector. Terry found she had to work on Monday, so Judy took the pills and barricaded herself in the bedroom as soon as Sam and Terry left the house. She put on the TV and stayed awake just until the first commercial break.

She woke up at three o'clock. Soaking wet and breathing hard, but no recollection of any nightmares. Five hours sleep. Great. This was going to work. She went down for a swim, made a peanut butter sandwich, dressed, and went out to shop for dinner.

CHAPTER 17

Later that night Judy felt really alive. When she and Sam got upstairs, they had some rollicking funny sex. Afterward they lay silent, both pleased with themselves.

"Wow. Maybe we should have *less* sex more often!" Sam leaned over and kissed Judy long and hard. "That was probably the best ever."

"At least in the top ten." Judy snuggled up next to Sam. The sleep she'd had that afternoon had revived her hopes. She could keep her secret from Sam and survive the nightmares. Piece of cake. Sam soon fell asleep, and she got up and went downstairs to spend the long night awake again.

The week went on, with Judy sleeping in the daytime and pretending everything was fine, but getting only two or three hours of sleep at night…and no more than an hour at a time. She experimented twice with drug-free sleep, but each time Joe came back with a vengeance. Judy was getting tired, so she started going upstairs early to rest, leaving Terry and Sam downstairs. Sam would come up, they'd have sex, he would sleep, and she'd go back downstairs to prowl through the night.

On Friday Judy began to feel sick. Dry scratchy throat, fever, and headache. She started making supper, but hadn't gotten far when Sam came home.

"What's up?" Sam came over to her as she leaned against the counter.

"Don't get close. Think I'm coming down with a cold or something. I feel rotten. I tried to get dinner, but I'm not getting very far." Judy felt her face. "Fever's getting worse. I've taken aspirin and even my magic NyQuil, but this thing keeps rolling in."

"Hey, sweetie, go to bed. I'll come up in a few minutes to get anything you need. I can finish getting supper later. What is it, anyway?"

"I've got a crab casserole in the fridge. Three fifty for thirty-five minutes should do it. Then just make a salad or something. The casserole is as far as I got." Judy washed her hands and headed toward the living room. "Oh, and Terry usually gets home around seven, so time supper for then, unless you're starved."

"Oh, I can wait. Get on now while you can still walk." Sam patted Judy on her shoulder.

"Sam, cut it out." She tried to go.

"What out?" Sam tipped his head to one side.

"You know my shoulder is my erogenous zone." She winked at Sam, then shuffled dizzily off.

Boy, she felt miserable. She got into bed, but couldn't get comfortable. Stupid cold.

In a few minutes, Sam came up with a hot toddy. "Here, this'll fix you up."

She sipped the hot whiskey drink. The steam cleared her nose. The liquid soothed her throat. "Better than drugs." She smiled at Sam, who was sitting on the bed by her knees.

"You get some sleep. I'll be up later to see what I can feed you." Sam squeezed her knees and left.

Judy finished the drink and scooted down in bed. She fell right asleep.

Joe was standing naked in his hospice room. The skin had fallen from his torso, showing crimson flesh underneath. He started to come toward her, but his foot fell off.

Judy jerked awake. Damn. She started to cry. Then stopped. I'm so pathetic…It's just a cold. I'll tough it out awake. So she sat up in bed and turned on the TV. She couldn't find anything to take her mind off herself, finally watching two hours of *Project Runway*. Then Sam came up with hot soup and toast.

"We didn't have chicken soup, but I know you like this." He laid a tray across Judy's lap. He'd made cream of tomato bisque. Had cut the crusts off the cinnamon toast. Not sure what she'd like to drink, he had tea, ginger ale, and V8.

"Yum. This looks good. Sam. And Sam, why don't you sleep in the TV room tonight? I'd hate for you to catch this too."

"Sure you wouldn't mind?"

"No. Really. Go."

"If you insist." Sam pinched Judy's cheek and went downstairs.

Judy leaned back in bed. Her fever was worse, so she took three aspirins before eating. This weekend was going to be a long one.

Twice she dozed, and twice Joe was there with his horrible tricks. At three in the morning, she took muscle relaxants and slept until six. She woke up crouched at the end of the bed. Must've been some nightmare. She wondered why she didn't remember it when she took the pills, but was grateful for them.

Sam poked his head in the door at seven. "How're you doing?"

"Better. I'll take NyQuil all day. It's just a cold."

"Want breakfast?"

"Tea and toast would be good."

Sam was back in minutes with a loaded tray. He'd made cinnamon toast and had even gone outside and picked a bouquet of herbs—rosemary, basil, and peppermint—and arranged it in a little ceramic pot. "I just looked at the calendar. We're supposed to begin cooking class today."

"What time?"

"Ten to four. Can you make it?"

"Sure. I'll be okay as long as you drive. What about Terry?" Right now going to the cooking school was the last thing she wanted to do. But it would keep her awake.

"I figure we can bring her. As long as we pay extra, I'm sure they'll find room."

"Sounds right. What are you doing until then?"

"I thought I'd clean downstairs. You never got around to your 'maid' day, and things are really scruffy. Are you staying in bed?"

"No. I'll get up. I think I'll go sit outside. I'm not feeling very ambitious." Damn, she thought. Always the cleaning. She felt like shit, looked like a hag, and all Sam could think of was sex and the damn housekeeping.

"We should leave at nine thirty."

"Oh. Okay."

Sam went downstairs. She heard the vacuum cleaner—that was a big reason she put off cleaning—if they'd only make a silent one. Maybe if Sam could outfit the house with a central system, she'd use it. Judy ate her toast and got ready for a shower, muttering. She'd meant to clean the house herself after everyone left, but the only thing she'd done so far was to take the bedding out of Eileen's room and put the sofa back together. She hadn't even emptied the wastebaskets yet.

❦

They didn't leave until ten to drive over to the cooking school in West Palm Beach—they'd forgotten to give Terry time to put on makeup. Sam and Judy wore jeans and old long-sleeved T-shirts. Terry wore skintight black pants, chain belt, nicely pressed white shirt, a fitted vest, and silver high-heeled shoes. In the car Judy felt trapped by Terry's perfume, but didn't say anything. She wished she'd mentioned it when Terry first came; it was too late now to do it politely. She wished she'd reach the age when she wouldn't have to worry about hurting someone's feelings. Just blurt out what bothered her. It probably wasn't going to happen for her.

The classroom was huge. They found six men and one woman scattered among the rows of stainless steel tables. Sam approached the chef, a tall, fat, red-faced man, who was sharpening his knives. "Good morning."

"Morning." The chef continued to work on his knives. Sam had his hand out to shake, but the chef ignored it or didn't see it.

"I'm Sam Haite. My wife and I signed up for the whole series. We have a houseguest this week, and I'm hoping she can join us. We'd pay for her class, of course."

"Just this one class or the whole course?" The chef finally looked up at Sam.

"Oh, just this one."

The chef smiled. "No problem. We've got plenty of product today. If it's just for today, we won't charge extra."

"Hey, thanks." Sam grinned and turned to find Terry and Judy at the front table. "Guys. It's okay for Terry to stay, but you two had better behave."

Terry laughed and adjusted her vest. "That's why we sat up front. If we were in the back row, we could get out of control."

Judy smiled and moved so Sam would be between her and Terry to get away from the perfume.

The chef passed out a booklet about fish and several recipes they were to prepare and gave them each an apron. A culinary student had prepped the ingredients for each recipe. Then he lugged in a grouper the size of a small child and plopped it on the chef's table. The chef used the giant fish to demonstrate how to properly clean and fillet any fish. Terry flirted with him, and he gave her the cheeks, the tastiest portion of all.

Next they were each given a perch to clean and fillet themselves. Judy managed to scale it without any trouble, but with the usual mess of flying scales. Terry yelped each time a scale landed on her or her clothes. She finally retired to the side of the room to pick the scales off her pant legs. Sam scaled and filleted his fish faster than the chef.

They had a break after this, and they went out to the courtyard. Judy was in a haze from the cold medicine and sat on a bench off to one side. The bench was shaded by an arbor and was next to a large herb garden. Butterflies and bees swarmed over flowering tarragon. Judy dozed.

She fell right into a dream. At first it was a rerun of the day she was fired. She came into Peggy's office. Dr. Hughes and Mr. Hewitt were there also, just as before. They looked silly: all three in black robes sitting behind Peggy's small metal desk. They weren't talking about Mrs. Elroy, though. No. Mr. Hewitt announced they were a tribunal investigating Joe's autopsy results.

Dr. Hughes began. "Did you see Joe the day he died?"

Judy had to say no.

Dr. Hughes tilted his head back; she could see his large hairy nostrils. "That's odd, Judy. The autopsy found your fingerprints on Joe's eyelids."

Judy was amazed. "I didn't know you could detect fingerprints on skin."

Dr. Hughes huffed. "Of course we can. The technology has been kept quiet, but is standard practice today."

Judy felt a trickle of sweat run between her shoulder blades. "Well, I visited Joe almost every day."

Dr. Hughes's head seemed to get bigger; his eyes bulged, and he waved a huge fat finger at her. "But he was given a bath not long before he died. The aide testified that she washed his face, including his eyelids, with soapy water. Your fingerprints were clear and had to have been made after that. How can you explain that?"

How could she? Where did they get her fingerprints in the first place? Should she ask? They had her. Would she go to prison? Oh, God. Doomed.

"Judy. Judy. Wake up!"

Judy woke up and looked around. Everyone was staring at her. "Wow. I was having a nightmare. It was so real, I was terrified."

Sam sat down next to her. "What about?"

"It was like a movie. I was accused of a crime, and the evidence was my fingerprints on the victim's skin. They can't do that, can they?"

"Hey, I don't know. They do on TV if someone grips really hard, but I don't know how real it is. Who'd you kill?"

"Oh, I don't know. It was just a confusing scene. Must be the antihistamines. Well, let's go back."

The rest of the class was a blur to Judy. She was anxious to be alone to research fingerprints. What if they *could* do it? Would they make everyone at the hospital be fingerprinted? Or worse, did police keep the prints they made of children in grade school? They'd come to her class once, and they'd all lined up and offered their tiny hands to the policeman, proud to be working with him.

On Sunday Sam went out golfing early. Terry nagged until Judy agreed to a picnic lunch on the beach. Judy busied about fixing lunch and then puttered around cleaning the kitchen. The house seemed nicely empty with just one guest. By eleven she was slowing down—too many days with too little sleep. And this day she'd be missing her drug-induced sleep again.

She wondered how long she could hold out. Curious, she went up to her study and googled *insomnia*. She didn't find anything linking fear of sleep and nightmares, except for references to horror movies and kinky sites.

The most frightening references included death by insomnia and didn't apply to her. There was a genetic disease, fatal family insomnia, in which a patient progresses into complete sleeplessness. It is untreatable and ultimately fatal in seven to eighteen months. The progression of the disease, however, hinted at what Judy had been experiencing—phobias, hallucinations, diminished mental acuity, and panic attacks. She found several references to laboratory animal research, shuddering while reading one in which puppies died after just five days of enforced insomnia. In experiments of sleeplessness in humans, the longest trial lasted eleven days with no serious side effects. In studies of the general population, increased death rates are found among those with four or fewer hours of sleep and eight or more hours. Six to seven hours of sleep was associated with the lowest death rate. Additional Web sites linked insomnia with serious mental disease. Insomniacs were found to be unable to assess risk. Unable to appreciate their own weaknesses, they possessed an exaggerated self-confidence. Judy felt wiggy, but not crazy. And her self-confidence was rolling on the floor. So the quick survey made Judy feel a little better: she wasn't going to die from this.

One reference, however, confirmed one of her fears: a 1930 American Bar Association report on "tormentum insomnia" stated that forced insomnia had been the most effective torture since the 1500s and certain to produce any confession desired. So she was at risk of blabbing to Sam.

As she jumped from word to word, Judy found links between "insomnia", "guilt", and "confession". Apparently confession can dissolve the pain of guilt, but it has to be a good confession, an admission of wrong without any excuse: I did it. It was wrong, I'm sorry. Could it be that simple? She wasn't close enough to the ministers at the Palm Beach church to confess to one of them—and it wasn't like in the Catholic Church with the confessional boxes and a regular setup for confessing. Plus, in the movies at least, the church official often leaked details of crimes to the police. She'd already dismissed Sam as confessor. Who else? Terry was attorney, and that would complicate her life. Margarida? Poor Margarida would be horrified. Eileen was a logical choice, but Judy couldn't see it bringing either of them any comfort. Her parents? No. Her brother Frank? Of anyone he might understand, but he really cared for her, and she didn't want to jeopardize that.

Just then Jack jumped up and sat on the keyboard. He was covered with sticky seeds from one of the bushes next door. She started picking them off—but he thought she was playing, rolled over onto his back, and grabbed her hand with his front claws. He gave her some soft rabbit kicks with his hind legs.

"Hey. Hey. Simmer down, Jacko." Jack relaxed and stretched out, letting her rub his belly.

"Jack. I've done a very bad thing. I killed Joe. I lay on top of that poor old man and squeezed the life out of him. I should not have done it. I may tell myself that I did it out of pity, but I'm afraid I did it mostly to get all of those people out of our house."

Jack was sound asleep. Judy sat back in her chair, still patting him. "I murdered Joe, and I'm sorry. I murdered Joe, and I'm so very, very sorry."

She took a deep breath. Somehow confessing to a cat didn't feel quite right. She *was* sorry, but she still didn't want to get caught. She quickly googled fingerprinting on a victim's skin and was relieved to find that, while possible to do, it was tricky to perform and seemed to be relegated to investigation of crime scenes, not general hospital autopsies.

It was strange. Her mind was both foggy and alert. Allaying one fear it quickly uncovered another. What if she was suspected in Joe's death? On TV they always took the suspect's computer away. Now hers showed a specific interest in fingerprints on a dead body. And what about Sam? They used the same computer. Real smart, Judy!

She exited the computer in a hurry when Terry yelled up that she was ready to go.

☙

They drove south along the coast. Judy hadn't been watching much local news, so when they passed the area where a condo had toppled into the ocean, she pulled over to look. In her mind she'd pictured the scene of a building that had fallen on its side more or less intact. In reality the pile of rubble was barely recognizable as from a building at all. There were bits of colored fabric, but most of the ruin looked like a natural seaside jetty—rough stones tumbled into the water, with waves splashing onto it.

"Wow." Terry craned to look.

"Wow is right. Horrible. I wonder if any bodies are still in there. I understand now why there weren't any survivors." They sat for a few minutes, then drove on. Not talking.

Judy took Terry to the Boynton Beach inlet, one of her favorite beaches. The sun was hot, but a brisk breeze off the ocean kept them cool as they walked along the water's edge. The noise of the surf made conversation unnecessary.

They walked about half an hour north to a dune in front of a little lemon-yellow beach house. In all the years Judy had come here, it had always been deserted—both the beach house and its parent house across the road. When Judy first lived in Lake Worth, she used to half-pretend to live here. The little house was in a pine grove. It always seemed just painted, with shining clean windows and inviting white wooden lounge chairs on the porch. Judy had never walked into the woods to the little house, only dreaming of owning it and spending rainy afternoons curled up inside with a good book and a cup of tea. And the servants to bring them.

When they reached the dune, they unpacked blankets and sat back in the sun.

"So. How's work going?" Judy adjusted her hat so she could watch the little sanderlings at the water's edge.

"Inch by inch. These things can't be rushed. Are you on vacation?"

"No. I'm retired now."

"I thought you were still working part time at Good Sam."

"Not anymore."

"How come?"

"Fired. Sort of."

"You? No. What happened?"

"Dropped a patient. I made a stupid mistake and didn't check to see that her leg was on properly."

"You can't get fired for one mistake. Can you?"

"Officially I'm suspended. But they want me gone."

"Need any legal help?"

"I might get sued. We've got a good attorney." Judy sat up and began unpacking the food, wishing for a change in subject.

"Are you planning to work somewhere else? I can't imagine you not working."

"I guess I'm in shock right now. We'll be going up to Maine in October. I won't really think about work until we get back."

Judy poured them bloody Marys and plunked large celery stalks in each. "Well. Cheers."

"Cheers."

The sanderlings continued scurrying back and forth at the ocean's edge.

"Those birds are always so busy," Judy mused. "I can't imagine how they get enough to eat to keep up that running." Boy, that was a weak attempt at changing the subject. This was the first time she'd spent any length of time alone with Terry since she picked her up at the airport. Taking a deep breath and a long swallow of her drink, she sat back against the dune. Relax. The beach was therapeutic.

"So what have you been up to?" Judy crunched into the celery.

"Work mostly. I'm the only single person and still the only woman at the firm. Half are sure that I'm gay, and the other half hit on me whenever they can. So I try to stay out of the office—and out of town—whenever I can."

"Any pets?"

"God, no. No plants either. I live in a glass and steel building down by the wharf. Never there. Don't know a soul in the building except for the manager."

"Do you still sail?"

That got a belly laugh from Terry. She sounded like her old self. "Oh, no. That was the one and only time for me. I don't get outdoors often. Just being here is heaven. I should do better, but I'm in a rut, I guess. I'm thinking maybe I should take Sam up on his plan."

"I'd be scared to death to go with him. Read much?" Judy the inquisitor. But she couldn't help it—Terry seemed disinterested in Judy's life.

"Haven't picked up a non-law book or magazine since college. I do grab a DVD every once in a while, so I've seen the Oscar winners at least. I never watch TV. I get up early, work, maybe go to a bar, get home late, sleep. Day after day."

"How are your folks? Do they still have that cabin in Castine?"

"They let that go. They're all well. They live about thirty miles from me, but I don't even get home for Christmas every year. The minute I'm home, my mother starts being a *mother*—drives me nuts." Terry sighed and stared out at the ocean.

"Remember the time we grossed out those guys in Castine?" asked Judy, changing the subject to cheer Terry up.

"I almost grossed myself out." Terry laughed.

They'd been at a meeting of the hospital association. One night they ended up at a bar/restaurant built out over the ocean. Several drunk obnoxious administrators joined them at the large table. The men went for conventional fare: fried clams and French fries. Judy and Terry started with raw oysters and were surprised that several of the men reacted as if they were scarfing down earthworms. Always willing to push the limits, Terry ordered sea urchins for the two of them. One of the men ran to the edge of the dock and threw up. The rest quieted considerably. While Terry was reading the menu (aloud of course) to decide on their third course, the men beat a hasty retreat.

"What a great way to clear a room. Have you ever met any of those guys again?" Judy asked.

"Oh, sure. And they haven't forgotten."

They sat in silence. A long silence. Judy could think of nothing else to say. She and Terry had been out of touch too long. They hadn't spent time together for years, and though they'd been in the same house now for over a week, Judy felt she didn't know her any better. Terry had become totally immersed in her work, which Judy didn't share. She'd tried to talk about music, books, theater, food... but none were things they had *ever* shared. She now recognized that Terry was simply an old friend from work. They no longer shared that work or their colleagues and had nothing else in common but their past. And it wasn't enough for a long visit.

CHAPTER 18

Monday morning. Judy was making breakfast when Sam came down. She had made waffles, his favorite, topped with strawberries, blueberries, and whipped cream. And Maine maple syrup—Sam had a friend who shipped it to them by the half gallon. Judy just had coffee.

Sam eyed his plate and looked at Judy. "I'd rather have sex, but this is nice."

"Sam, c'mon. We've had sex every day except during the hurricane. Maybe once when I had the cold."

"Yeah, but it doesn't seem like it. Something's wrong. I can feel it—you haven't been…Oh, I really don't know how to describe it… You're just not there. Are you that upset at being fired?"

"I really don't know. I thought I was dealing with it, but I have been out of sorts. And I'm not sleeping very well."

"Maybe you should see a doctor."

"I think time's the doctor. I'm sure I'll be myself soon."

"You'd better," Sam growled.

Sam was so seldom in a bad mood that Judy was concerned. She'd been spoiled by his generous cheerfulness lately. Should she tell him about Joe? No. That's the insomnia speaking. Just hold on, she told herself. He'd been like that several times before: Sam wanted his sex when he wanted it—with no excuses from her. Once she'd strained her back at work, and Sam was a bear for weeks. But he always came back to his sweet self.

Sam ate quickly and left for work. Judy waited for Terry to leave so she could sleep, but Terry worked out of the house all day.

Judy frittered away the time with grocery shopping and a long walk. She made a vegetarian lasagna for dinner. Sam loved it, and she wanted to do something for him. And tonight, when they had sex, she'd make sure she was enthusiastic—or fake it.

Sam was still grumpy and distant when he got home. He ate with her and Terry but left soon after to play tennis. By the time he got home, she and Terry had had too many margaritas. They were sitting on the patio drinking and giggling like schoolgirls.

"Hey, Sam," Terry yelled when they heard him come into the kitchen. "Come out and join us."

He came in and looked at them. "You guys are too far ahead of me. I'm going up to work on the books." Sam smiled coldly and went back inside.

"Uh, oh. Trouble in paradise," giggled Terry.

Judy thought she'd better stay downstairs for a couple of hours before facing Sam. His mood had sobered her faster than coffee. Terry went up to bed around eleven. Judy tidied up and followed her. She expected to see Sam in his office, but the lights there were out. Going into the bedroom, she found him fully clothed, stretched out in the middle of the bed, sound asleep.

Afraid to wake him, Judy went downstairs and spent the night watching TV and playing solitaire on her laptop. The night went by slowly. Around two a heavy thunderstorm began, bringing a steady hard rain. Jack howled outside, then came in and she toweled him off. They sat side by side and watched movies until dawn.

It was still raining when Judy crept upstairs and through the bedroom to take a shower. She thought she'd get cleaned up and then invite Sam for sex. The hot water eased her fatigue. She shampooed her hair twice and then added conditioner. Then she stood under the rushing water for several minutes as the hot water massaged her tight neck. She towel-dried her hair instead of using the hair dryer to avoid waking Sam. Sitting on the edge of the tub, she went through three towels before her hair was dry. She stopped; her arms were beginning to tire. She was really getting out of shape—if she wasn't going to do therapy work, she'd have to go to the gym.

She put on the light cotton robe hanging behind the door and walked over to the sink to brush her teeth. Looking at the mirror as she brushed, she really didn't look at herself at first. Then she realized she'd changed. Her face had lines—on her forehead, her eyelids, and from her nose to her chin. Plus, there were bags under her eyes and gray splotches on her cheeks. God, she looked terrible! And… Grabbing her hair, she examined it closely. Gray hairs. Hundreds of them.

She looked in the mirror again. The gray didn't show, but it made her hair look dull, and strands were flying all about. She looked old, a hag. Then her optimism peeked through: maybe it's just from stress and it would change back. Or even better, maybe this was her punishment for Joe. That would be fair. After all, she'd cost him maybe a day or two of life.

When she took off her robe to get dressed, she discovered the back was all bloody. Damn. Her period was early again and heavy, as it had been lately. Menopause was marching through. She'd heard some women practically crack up at the mere idea of "the change"—

but for her, menstruation was a constant reminder of her inability to conceive. It would be a relief when all of that was over.

Cheered up a little, she threw on a sundress and went into the bedroom. Sam was stirring, so she took a deep breath and smiled. "Hey, honey. Want coffee? Breakfast?"

Sam took his face out of the pillow and squinted at her. "Yes to coffee. Can wait for breakfast." He smiled. "You better today?"

"Yup. Full of moxie. Geez, I really don't like that stuff, though."

"What?"

"Moxie."

"C'mon. It's our state drink."

"Florida?"

"No. Maine. We live here, but our state is Maine."

"You really feel like that?"

"Ayah. I love it here, but I dream sometimes of going back. The only really bad part is the winter is too long—but money helps that a lot."

"Full time?"

"Maybe. But just spending more time up there would be nice."

"We could be snowbirds."

"Or the opposite. Come down here in summer and go north in winter. I really like Palm Beach best when it's empty."

"Really?"

"Maybe. What about that coffee?"

Judy went down and returned in a few minutes with coffee. They sat back in bed to drink it.

"Any plans today?" Judy asked.

"Taking the day off. Tennis in about an hour. Then I'm free. Want to go out for lunch?"

"Sure. Should I meet you? Where and when?" Judy was relieved. When she came out of the bedroom, she'd almost proposed sex despite her period. Now she hadn't the energy—she'd used it up trying to be cheerful. If Sam and Terry both went out, maybe she could get some sleep.

"Let's go retro. Benny's at three." Benny's on the Beach was part of the Lake Worth fishing pier. The pier had been under construction for several years to repair damage from the last bad hurricane and had just reopened.

"Good idea. Three then. But first let's have some lovin'—I missed you last night." Sam made a goofy smile, wiggled his ears, and reached for her. He threw Judy on the bed and started to pull her dress up.

"No go—just started my period." Judy wriggled free and scrambled across the bed to stand on the floor.

"Oh, c'mon. That's no problem."

"Sam. I've got cramps. I'm bleeding heavily, and I hate it when you make me do it then. It's messy and for me, not sexy at all."

"Dammit, Judy. Don't be such a prude!" Sam stood up red-faced.

Judy walked to the door. "Maybe I can't help it, Sam." And she left, going quickly downstairs.

Sam put his cup down and went in to shower. In a few minutes, he dressed and followed Judy downstairs. He walked through the kitchen and without a word, left the house—slamming the outside door as he left.

Terry was fixing herself toast as Judy refilled her coffee cup. "What was that all about?" She scrutinized Judy's face for clues.

Judy waited until she was sure Sam was out of earshot. "Terry, it's just that Sam's so hungry for sex. He's always pestering. And often he seems so impersonal about it. Like anyone would do."

"How often do you two do it?"

"Almost every day. I just started my period today and turned him down. So now he's sulking."

"Every day? Wow, that's well above the national average—but I wouldn't mind." Terry smiled. "But you were always a prude about messes and smells."

"It doesn't bother you?"

"Depends on the guy. And sometimes whose laundry I'm messing up. The other day I went home with one of the attorneys at work and we had a gay old time. His sheets, mattress, and blankets were a mess, though. It was funny; afterward he turned into a fussy old maid about it. His Hudson Bay blanket…his silk sheets…lordie!"

"How well did you know him?" Judy was curious. Sam was the only man she'd had sex with without knowing him for months.

"Just met him that day. Judy—you just take all that sex stuff too seriously. Jesus, look at the kids today."

"I am what I am. It's just too personal with me. Maybe I started too late—I knew too much—first I was scared of pregnancy, then herpes, then AIDS. Kids now are like little animals. Sometimes I envy them, but…Oh, well." Judy smiled and plopped down on the couch. "What's up for today?"

"Going in to work this morning; no idea how long. Don't make any plans that include me. I'm bushed. When I get back, I think I'll do the "sit outside and nap" bit. Maybe I'll go into town later and find some action."

Judy poached an egg, made toast, and brought her breakfast out to the patio to eat. She'd read the paper and then go up and sleep until two. Then she'd be in good shape to lunch with Sam—if that was still on.

After Terry left, Judy took three muscle relaxants and watched the *Today Show* until she dropped off.

Joe was in bed with her. His flesh was still raw, with beads of blood glistening in a faint light. He leaned toward her; reaching out his scrawny arms, he drew her to him. His face was too close to hers when his tongue licked into her mouth. She couldn't wake up. Joe rolled on top of her and started to lick her neck. He got on his knees and…

Judy woke up in mid—scream. Sweating, she looked around the peaceful bedroom. The TV was still chirping away. Oh, God. The pills hadn't worked. She'd only been asleep for twenty minutes. Now what?

She got up, threw on shorts and camisole, slid into leather scuffs, and went downstairs. Grabbing a backpack, she loaded it with a beach towel, a thermos of ice and vodka, two cans of spicy V8, some crackers, and a package of sliced Swiss cheese. She grabbed her keys and hurried out to her car.

She drove to the beach at the Boynton Inlet. She was dismayed to see the parking lot packed with cars. Oh, well. She snatched her backpack, crossed A1A, walked over the canal, and headed up the beach to her dune and the little yellow beach house. Good to see that people were lazy everywhere—just a few had straggled beyond the beach area directly across from the parking lot. By the time she got to the dune, the beach was deserted. She spread out her towel and lay down.

It was hot and not enough breeze came off the ocean to cool her. She lay sweating, trying to calm herself for half an hour before she gave up and went into the ocean. The water was nicely cool with slow swells. She lay on her back resting her head on her arms folded behind her neck. Bobbing up and down in the water lulled her as she drifted slowly out into the ocean. Every once in a while, she opened her eyes to see where she was. It was so peaceful—maybe it would be best if she just floated off to nowhere. After an hour she could still see the beach house, but it was tiny. She shut her eyes and drifted further. Suddenly Joe was back on top of her. He was saying something, but she couldn't make it out—he had no teeth at all, and his tongue just fluttered his lips. His breath smelled like rotten meat.

    She woke up sputtering under water. Thrashing about, she surfaced and tried to calm herself. She found the direction of the shore, but didn't see any detail. She was a long way out, but was able to fall into an easy breaststroke and make for land. It seemed forever before she could see the beach house. She changed direction to head for it and finally made it to the beach. No one was around—the lifeguarded beach was a mile away. She sat in the shallow water to catch her breath, then scrambled to her dune. She mixed a drink and sat eating crackers and cheese. She finished everything, and more than a little drunk, sat and watched the birds. She wasn't thinking. She couldn't think.

    She didn't sleep, but she wasn't awake either. She leaned against a dune and watched the sea and sky change from blue to gray. Suddenly she realized it was getting dark. By then she was dry, so she picked up her things and headed back to the car. Driving home, she wondered if the beach had done her any good. She did find out she didn't want to die right away. But she hadn't used her brain to figure out how to get sleep without nightmares. She'd have to go back online to see if there were any herbs or drugs that had a side effect of reducing REM sleep and dreams. Then figure out how to get the chemical. Feeling that she again had a plan, Judy reached Sunshine Street and home.

Both Sam and Terry's cars were there, but no lights were on in the house. Maybe they had both gone out. Once inside, she turned on the lights in the kitchen. Usually Sam left a note on the counter if he was out, but no note. She emptied her backpack and took care of the trash.

Turning on lights as she walked to the stairs and up to the bedroom, Judy's mind was calm, planning what to fix for dinner before she started researching the drugs.

The bedroom was as she left it. She took off her clothes and put on a robe. Heading back downstairs, she hesitated, then opened the door to Terry's room—maybe there would be a clue where the two had gone.

Her brain was slow to interpret the image. Why was Sam doing Pilates on Terry's bed? Then reality hit. Terry and Sam were having languorous sex. They looked as if they'd been at it for some time, as Sam seemed content and waiting for Terry to climax.

Stunned, Judy closed the door quietly and went back to their bedroom. Shattered, she wanted to make a scene. To scream, cry, throw things. But she was deadened. She sat on the bed for a while then got up, dressed, and went downstairs, turning the lights off as she left.

Outside, she got in her car and drove off. She drove across the bridge to West Palm, down the Intracoastal to Lake Worth, across the bridge, and then back north to Sunshine Street. She parked a few houses down and watched as the lights came on in her house. She waited half an hour more, then called Terry's cell.

"Biddle."

"This is Judy. Don't say a word until I'm through. Tell Sam you have to help a client in Orlando or Tallahassee or something. It's an emergency, and you'll have to leave tonight. Pack your bags and leave. I never want to see you again. Oh…and don't let Sam know I know what you just did. If you do, I will kill you. And that's a promise."

"Oh." Then the phone went dead.

Judy sat in her car and waited. Almost an hour later, she saw Terry and Sam come outside. Sam helped Terry load her bags. He walked back to the house, stood, and waved as Terry backed out of the driveway. He then turned and went inside.

Judy waited ten minutes before driving into the yard.

Sam was pouring himself a whiskey in the kitchen. "There you are."

"Here I am."

"Where were you?"

"Beach."

"I mean, at lunch."

"Ohh! How could I forget! Sam, I'm sorry. I took a snack to the beach and fell asleep. Forgot all about lunch. I just woke up."

"No harm. We can go tomorrow instead. Want a drink?"

"I guess not. Oh, maybe a little Irish Mist."

Sam poured her drink, and they went out on the patio. The ceiling and walls were open. Sam made a little fire, and they sat watching it.

Sam was the first to go up to bed. Neither of them had mentioned Terry. Judy sat watching the fire for another hour, thinking. What to do?

So angry, still shaking. At first she wanted to go upstairs and wallop Sam with his golf club. But a little island in her brain wondered, was this her fault? A combination of Joe's death, her refusal to join him in an adventure, and her so-called friend Terry. But in the end, she decided it was more Sam's fault than hers. She had every right to be angry.

But now what? Kick Sam out? Run away herself? Stay and fight? Stay and pout? Too many thoughts swirled through her head. She finally decided that all those days without sleep made it impossible for her to make a good decision—if there *was* one. Maybe she should just go away for a bit and cool down.

Tomorrow she'd pack her car, take Jack, and drive up to Maine. No explanation for Sam. Beyond that she had no plan.

The fire died down, and Judy finally slept.

CHAPTER 19

A light breeze brushed her face. Birds twittered far off. Judy slowly opened her eyes and looked around. She was on the patio. It was hot, and her clothes were soaked in sweat. But she felt… peaceful. Glancing at her watch—nine thirty—she sat up and blinked several times to clear her eyes. Then raised the back of the chaise to the sitting position and thought.

She'd slept the whole night through, the first time since Joe's nightly mischief had begun. Slowly she remembered yesterday… She was going to pack the car, take Jack, and escape to Maine. First she needed coffee. Standing, she yawned and stretched. Somehow everything looked brighter than she remembered. And more in focus.

She found a note in the kitchen from Sam. Tennis, back at noon. Well…coffee. She heated water and ground the beans. While the coffee seeped through the filter, she opened the fridge and several cabinets trying to find something that called out to her. Ah! A hunk of Brie. She spread the cheese on two slices of mountain bread and popped them into the toaster oven. When the cheese was bubbling and beginning to brown, she took the toast out and spread super-sour orange marmalade on top. Coffee and Brie toast, breakfast of… Well, a great breakfast for anyone.

The paper must be upstairs, so she went back to the patio and turned on the TV and watched the *Today Show*—most of it promissory notes of what they were going to show later that morning or some other day. Irritated, she snapped the TV off and sat in silence. The coffee was good, and she drained the cup. The cheese toast looked and smelled wonderful, but she found she wasn't hungry and just had a few tiny bites, then gave up on it.

Maybe running away wasn't so smart. She had been white with anger last night, but now she was already mourning her life with Sam…How could he have done this to her? To them? Just because she wouldn't have sex one morning, he did this? Her friend Terry was a terrible flirt, but Judy had never thought Sam could be tempted. And so quickly. Or had he done this before? And what about diseases…Until now she'd always felt so safe with Sam. She was a firm believer in the germ theory of disease—it made her shudder just to see someone on TV open a refrigerator and drink directly from a milk carton. An STD would be both dangerous and embarrassing—she just couldn't risk it. What to do?

Grrr! Judy hated confrontation. Maybe the years of living alone made it even more difficult for her to speak openly—which was a definite disadvantage in an argument. And she tended to focus on what the other person wanted rather than what she wanted. Often she didn't even know *what* she wanted. Plus arguing with Sam, and many men, put her at a vocal disadvantage: she had a soft voice that, when she got angry or needed to be forceful, betrayed her by getting high and squeaky. While Sam had a deep voice that, in an argument, got deeper and had a physical quality—the few times he'd boomed at her, she'd fled in surrender.

But she'd have to talk to him, not just run away.

That decided, Judy went up, showered, and changed into a wispy cotton sundress. A washed-out coral, the dress was one of her favorites—it was light and cool, but the fabric was dense enough that she didn't have to wear underwear. Natives had taught her to ditch the under layer of clothing during the hot summer months. At first the prude Mainer inside her rejected the idea, but over time she slipped into the habit almost year-round.

She came down the stairs barefoot and sat in the kitchen booth to decide what to cook for lunch. She'd pick something she liked more than Sam did. Maybe that would give her some kind of psychic upper hand. Shrimp? That was his least favorite seafood. She'd marinate it in Chinese sweet chili sauce; he preferred teriyaki. Brown rice; he liked white. Cauliflower; he hated it, especially cooked—she'd puree it. And stir-fry veggies with lots of onions; he like the veggies, but would pick out the onions. Oh, this was so silly, but she needed to get back at him somehow, and this was all she could think of.

Sam came in at noon, hungry. He arched his brows when he saw the meal, but picked out the onions and wolfed it down, finally speaking. "As soon as I'm finished, I've got to hit the yard. I've let it get away from me."

"How was tennis?"

"Okay. Hot." He cleaned his plate, threw back the wine, and headed outside.

Judy picked at the food; something was missing. She finally gave up and took a book to the patio. She read while glancing up from time to time at Sam puttering about the yard. He didn't seem to have much to do...He'd trim a few inches from a bush, grab at a weed, and then stand and search for some other imperfection. He was nervous. Judy enjoyed this, and her courage grew.

About four a thunderstorm forced Sam to give up and come inside. Judy had the ceiling and walls up and was nursing a gin and tonic. Sam got a drink and joined her. Neither spoke for a good five minutes.

"Well," Judy started.

Sam glanced up at her from his examination of the beads of sweat on his glass, but said nothing.

"Let's talk about the elephant," Judy began, her throat tightening.

"What?" Sam flushed.

"I know about you and Terry." Judy got braver.

"Oh." Sam sat back and grimaced. He ran his hand through his hair and took a big gulp of his drink.

"I had planned to take Jack and drive up to Maine this morning while you were out, but I thought we should talk first."

"Oh."

Judy had never seen Sam so lifeless. "I'm just going to blurt it out, Sam. Have you ever done this before? Can I trust you not to do it again? Do you have any idea what this does to me? To us?"

"Judy, I'm sorry. No. This is the first time I've had sex with anyone else since the day we first met. I've never even been tempted. But you were so weird this summer…and Terry…"

"So it's my fault?"

"Well. No. But…"

"But what? I'll tell you one thing, Sam. I will not have sex with you again until I have letters from your and Terry's doctors with proof that you are disease-free."

"Don't you think that's a little excessive?" Sam sneered.

"You don't know where Terry's been. She is such bad luck. Oh, God." Judy hugged herself and tried not to cry.

Right now Sam was not her handsome husband: his face was rigid, his lips thin, pale, and set in a straight line—even his eyes seemed smaller. He took nervous sips of his drink and shifted in his chair. He stayed silent for several minutes, looking at Judy.

"What do you want?" he finally asked, standing up and going to look out at the storm.

"I don't know. I need to get away from the house. I've loved it so, but right now it's not the haven for me it's always been."

"Do you want me to come too?"

"No."

"Where will you go?"

"Up to my parents' cabin, I guess. I'll call later and make sure no one else is using it. Then I'll pack and maybe start up early tomorrow."

"Well, if you have to, go. But can't you just stay here? I can move to another bedroom."

"I'll sleep out here tonight. Then I'll go."

"I still don't get it, but okay. You go up there now, and I'll be up in a few days."

"Call before you come. I may not be ready. And remember—not until you test negative."

"Oh, okay." Sam rapped his knuckles on a table and left the room.

They stayed apart the rest of the day—each fixing supper for one: Sam a can of baked beans, Judy a tuna sandwich she nibbled at, then shared with Jack. While Judy packed her car, Sam left for a few hours. Judy was bunked down on the patio when he returned. She pretended to be asleep when she heard him come out. He rattled around talking to Jack and moving furniture, trying to wake her. He finally gave up, and she heard him go through the house and up the stairs.

The next morning Sam woke Judy with a breakfast tray and coffee for himself. He sat quietly while she pushed the food around the plate.

"I wish you'd change your mind."

"I know you do, but…"

"Do you want a divorce?"

"For God's sake, Sam, *I* don't know! I'm upset. I don't know how long I'll be upset. Maybe I'll get over this; maybe I won't. I just want to get away!" Judy slapped her hand on the table.

"All right. All right. Whatever you want. Are you still taking Jack?"

"Yes. I'm going to be alone at camp; he'll be good company."

"I guess that's it."

"I'm going to take a shower, then I'll be off."

"Do you need anything?"

"Just don't let Jack out."

Judy left her dishes on the patio and went upstairs. She felt free—and so healthy—two whole nights of sleep! She took a cool shower and shut Sam out of her mind. Didn't wash her hair—no time. Toweling off quickly, she dressed in her best long-distance driving clothes: white jeans (Banana Republic—soft cotton, roomy), un-ironed long-sleeved blue cotton shirt, and the leather sneakers she'd found in Italy years before. No socks, no bra. She looked around the room to see if she'd forgotten anything, grabbed a few towels for camp, and hurried downstairs.

She stopped in the kitchen to take some Mountain Dew and carrots out of the fridge and went outside. As she was storing the last of her gear, Sam came out with Jack in his carrier.

"Thanks, Sam."

"You're welcome. Drive safely."

"Will do. Bye."

"Bye."

Judy backed out of the yard. Sam stood watching. Sad. She felt homesick already for Sunshine Street. It reminded her of when she'd finished college and drove off to Portland one day, car packed, to look for a job. Was this going to be the end of Sunshine Street for her, or just a vacation?

CHAPTER 20

Her sadness followed her out to the turnpike, but when she got onto the highway and up to speed—radio blaring and Jack yowling—she felt better. On the road again. It had been years since she had taken a long road trip by herself. It was when she first came down to Florida—it took three days. Never interested in geography, she'd no idea Florida was so far away from Maine. Judy started with country and western; it kept her moving, but almost hurt her head, so in about an hour she switched to a public radio station. Jack gave up his protest and settled down to sleep. Her phone rang. Sam. She didn't answer it. She didn't want to talk to him. Actually, she couldn't think of anyone she *did* want to talk to, so turned the phone off. She wasn't much of a phone talker in the best of times—probably inherited from her father, who every time it rang announced, "There's that damn contraption again." If the call was for her, he'd add the command "and keep it short, dammit." Judy still seldom initiated a call, instead wrote letters, notes, or e-mail to deal with the world.

She had no destination in mind for the first day, maybe Georgia—she liked the red clay. She hoped her car could make the trip; usually before going more than a hundred miles from home, Sam would take it in for a tune-up. Sam. How could she be so mad at him when his sin was so much less than hers? Or was it? Murder versus adultery. What a pair they were. Only she knew about both their sins; Sam only knew about one. Her obvious path was to forgive Sam, the lesser sinner. But his had more directly hurt her. Her killing Joe hadn't affected Sam at all—except for the way she acted, which, if she had to be honest with herself, had probably helped Sam slide into adultery. And Terry. She had welcomed her, had even been relieved that she and Sam hit it off. And she knew Terry, knew how much trouble she was. Was everything her fault then?

Judy shook her head and put her mind back on driving. Early afternoon she got off the turnpike around Buford and followed 1A up the coast. After lunching on carrots and soda, she was hungry and tired. She finally found a small motel that looked reputable. She pulled in, got a room key, then drove on to find a restaurant. Settling for Chinese, she got takeout and headed back to the motel. She unpacked Jack's stuff and some of hers, then settled on the bed with food and TV. The food was surprisingly good—Szechwan chicken and pan-fried noodles, extra crispy—spicy but not aggressively so. She missed the Suffering Bastard she and Sam usually ordered when they ate Chinese. Warm Mountain Dew didn't add anything to the meal. She enjoyed the first few mouthfuls, but then stopped, appetite gone. She bundled up the trash and took it outside, then opened a can of food for Jack, took a quick shower, and got into bed. Jack made a lot of noise scattering litter around the room—he was a true outdoor cat and hated litter boxes. But then he settled down next to her, and they both fell asleep.

The next thing she knew, it was five o'clock and she was wide-awake. This sleeping all night was such a treat. She dressed in the same clothes of the day before, scooped her stuff out to the car, got Jack, and took off to find a place for breakfast.

Meandering up 1A she found a small diner with an almost-full parking lot. She smiled at the wonderful coffee and bacon smells that hit her when she opened the door. She picked a stool at the counter between two skinny people and ordered bacon, eggs, English muffin, tomato juice, and coffee. The coffee was as good as it smelled—strong and not bitter. Most of the customers seemed to know the waitress and one another—there was cheerful kidding riding on top of the country and western music coming from an old jukebox in one corner. Her food came quickly. The bacon was thick with just the right combination of chewy and crispy. She nibbled at a slice of bacon, ignored the rest, had three cups of coffee, and ordered a large cup to go.

After a quick trip to the bathroom, Judy got back into the car. She gave Jack a piece of bacon and sat back while he ate it.

Is this all she needed? A cat, good bacon, coffee, and cheerful strangers? It was so peaceful. When Jack finished his bacon, he stood, stretched, turned around three times, and curled up to sleep. Judy started the car and headed north. She stayed on 1A for an hour, then drove over to I-95 for a day's mind-numbing drive, spiced occasionally by idiots racing past in the breakdown lane. Stiff and tired, at six o'clock she headed back to 1A, found a restaurant, and had a little soup. Resting in her car, she fell asleep. She woke at dawn and got back on the highway. Never looking at a map or really knowing where she was, she continued north, driving seriously fast.

A late breakfast at a truck stop: crowded, dirty, screaming kids, weak coffee, overcooked eggs, and a doughnut. She only sipped the coffee; the eggs and doughnut were bathed in fat. Then back on the road. Early evening she pulled off the road somewhere in New York and found a two-story log motel that looked like a ski lodge. The sign out front advertised twenty-four-hour room service. Judy pulled her car up to her room and unloaded Jack, his stuff, and a suitcase. Time for a rest and change of clothes. First, though, she put a harness on Jack and carried him to a field at the back of the motel. Jack was on a long spring-loaded leash so he could explore freely while she sat against a tree and smacked at mosquitoes. She'd forgotten about these—in Palm Beach spraying, careful yard care, and the ocean breezes kept the pesky insect population to a minimum. She'd have to remember to add DEET to her shopping list for camp. At least it was summer, so the black flies would be gone—they could drive a sane man mad. It was cold out—maybe sixty-five or seventy. Used to a constant ninety to ninety-four degrees in the summer, Judy shivered as a heavy dew started to fall at dusk. The mosquitoes finally won, and Judy got up and returned to her room.

She fed Jack, read the room service menu, and ordered a small steak, mashed potatoes, baby beet greens, mixed salad, chocolate cake, martini, Heinekens, and coffee. It sounded like too much food as she ordered, and when it came, she nursed the alcohol but barely touched the food. Eating had become too much work. She'd fill her fork with something she truly loved, but as it reached her lips, she just couldn't put it in her mouth. She didn't understand. She loved to eat, but just couldn't. Well, maybe sitting and driving wasn't enough exercise to require food. She sighed and licked a bit of frosting off the cake. She turned on her phone—there were several messages since she'd left Palm Beach. Someone from the hospital, Sam, and Eileen. She didn't plan to return any of the calls, but as she sipped the last of her coffee, the phone rang. Sam. She answered this time.

"Hello."

"Hello. You okay?"

"Sort of."

"Where are you?"

"Motel somewhere in Pennsylvania or New York, I'm not sure. It's green and hilly. And lots of mosquitoes."

"Any more thoughts about us?"

"I've been trying not to think. Maybe I've simmered down a bit."

"Can I come up now?"

"No. And have you been tested yet? And Terry?"

"I've made an appointment, and I called Terry…"

"Good. That's really good. When's your appointment?"

"Couple of days. Results take a while, though. Why don't I come up there after they take the blood?"

"No, Sam."

Sam was silent for about thirty seconds. "Well, good-bye then."

"Bye." She hung up.

⁂

Judy slept until ten the next morning. She took Jack out on a leash, then came back and ordered coffee to go—no sense in wasting anymore money on food. She had the car packed by noon and went back on I-95. She probably could make it to camp in a day if she pushed it. But she'd need time to shop before she went out there, so decided to take it easy and spend two more days driving.

New Hampshire felt almost like home: drivers became sane, almost polite as the traffic lessened. She put Bach's *B Minor Mass* in the CD player. Civilization. She smiled—almost home. As soon as she crossed into Maine, she got on 1A and looked for a place to stop.

About an hour later, she found an inn standing on a hill all by itself right on the ocean. The inn also rented little cabins, and Judy took one of those—afraid they wouldn't let Jack into the main building. She unpacked, then went outside and sat in a very uncomfortable Adirondack chair to watch the sea. Oh, for a glass of champagne! Or beer. She should've stopped to buy something. She put Jack in the cabin and went over to the inn.

The inn looked much like the house in *Psycho*—except it was in good shape, painted a bright white and surrounded by towering pine trees. Several late-model cars were in the gravel parking lot off to one side. Just inside the door was the cubicle where she'd registered. She walked down a short corridor through gleaming old oak double doors into the lobby. From the Victorian exterior she'd expected fussy old furniture, antique rugs, and lots of velvet. Instead the interior had plain wooden floors, simple graceful wooden furniture, and no rugs at all. Later she learned the furniture was made at a local shop and was for sale at the inn.

A woman at a small desk looked up as Judy came in. She was dressed in jeans and a plaid short-sleeved shirt. Young, no makeup, short blonde hair.

"Hi. I'm over in one of the cabins. I'm wondering about food—and is there a bar? I don't see any signs."

"There's a bar right behind me…on the other side of the wall. And the dining room is down there at the end of the corridor. Both are open until eleven thirty. You can eat at the bar if you'd like. Or we even offer takeout so you can eat down at the shore."

"Wow. Sounds good. Thanks."

"Enjoy your stay."

"It's beautiful here."

'We enjoy it. This used to be my grandmother's house. My husband and I took years to fix it up. We just opened this year."

"I wish you good fortune." Geez. This child is the owner. Judy walked around to the bar, a small room with a tiny bar, no stools, and six tiny tables. Sliding glass doors led to additional tables on a deck overlooking a field of wildflowers. Several people were at tables talking quietly. She could hear wind chimes from the deck, but there was no TV or music playing.

Judy ordered a gin and tonic and stood at the bar sipping it. The young bartender was probably the owner too.

"Is it possible to bring a beer or something back to the cabin? I forgot to buy anything on the road."

"Sure. Just stop by on your way out, and I'll fix you up. Or do you want it now? If you'd like wine, Josie, our cook, has a nice selection of half bottles."

"Champagne?"

"Sure. If that's what you want."

"Okay. Sounds good."

About a half hour later, Judy was sitting on the deck, and Josie, a little gnome of a woman, came out with a narrow wicker basket with checkered tablecloth tucked around a half-bottle of Cliquot.

"There are glasses in your cabin. Enjoy." And Josie skittered back into the building.

Judy thanked the bartender and went back to her cabin. With Jack on his leash, a blanket and the basket, she inched her way down the steep path to the shore. No beach, all rocks and seaweed. Low tide, salt smell, heaven. She found a grassy area that was almost level, anchored Jack's leash, spread out the blanket and tablecloth, and sat down. The sun was low but still warm. She opened the champagne, filled a glass, and leaned against a rock. The champagne was just right, not sweet or sour, fruity. Jack came over and sniffed her glass.

"Shoo!"

Her phone rang. Sam again. Judy didn't answer—just sat back sipping the last of the champagne, with Jack purring by her side.

"Jack, if I could purr, I would. It's so peaceful here." She picked up the basket, stood, and stretched. The sun was getting low in the sky. "Let's walk."

Walking north along the shore, she scattered crabs foraging among the rocks. When they came to a gray sandy clam flat, Jack chased from clam squirt to clam squirt much as children play in the street fountain in West Palm. Seaweed wrapped around her ankles, tripping her up and soaking her jeans. The sun got lower, and she was chilled, so she picked up Jack and headed back.

Once in the cabin, more surprises. No TV. No radio. No clock. She hadn't noticed the little stove before. The glass-fronted stove had wood laid for a fire. Going into the bathroom, she had expected either a plastic bathroom-in-a-box or a standard toilet and metal shower. Instead the bathroom was outfitted with an old claw foot tub that was long, skinny, and high. She'd never seen one like it. The bathroom walls and floor were tiled in rose, and the ceiling had a hand-painted mural of angels and cherubs playing with all kinds of fanciful sea creatures.

When Judy got into the tub, she found that she could float—she lay on her back and cruised back and forth, pushing off with her toes and fingers. She stayed until her fingers pruned. Fully relaxed, she dressed in a T-shirt, robe, and slippers. She took the pillows and blankets off the bed and went outside. Padding the chair with the pillows and wrapped in the blankets, she watched the light fade. The phone rang from inside, and she let it. It got dark, really dark. The inn had dimmed its lights, and no others were visible. Stars emerged, hanging down from the sky. Jack jumped onto her lap, so she knew she was anchored for a while; she hated to disturb him. So she dozed. No dreams. Cozy.

She woke up when Jack jumped down to chase something in the grass. Back inside she lit the fire, remade the bed, and sat reading. Jack dozed in front of the fire.

The telephone rang again. Damn! Sam again. She let it ring.

Peace disturbed. She didn't want to think about Sam, so she turned off the light and curled up on her side. Jack knew his place and hopped onto the bed and let her hug him as she drifted off to sleep.

―――◈―――

The sun woke her up, hitting her square in the face. Just seven. Glad she didn't oversleep, Judy got up, sponged off, dressed, and gathered her stuff together. She left Jack in the cabin and walked over to the inn. The dew on the long grass drenched her slacks. The air was cold and clear. Just a few white clouds flitted across the pale blue sky. No one was in the lobby, so she went through to the dining room. Much like the bar, the dining room had sliding glass doors on two sides that led to an open porch with several tables. Inside there were nine large round tables, four occupied. This time the view was of the ocean and the outer islands. A lobster boat was pulling traps right in front of the inn.

Judy started when the young bartender asked where she'd like to sit.

"Can I sit outside?"

"Sure." He led her to a table, took her coffee order, and went inside. He was back quickly with coffee, a menu, and a place setting. "It's weird, but no one's ever had breakfast out here before."

"It's so nice out—I hated to come inside."

"I know the feeling. I grew up lobstering. At first, working inside here—especially with the views—drove me crazy. But I'm getting used to it. And proud of what we've done."

"So you're the owner?"

"Yes. Me and Sally, my wife. I'm Dick, by the way. The cook, Josie, is Sally's aunt. People from town help out, but we're the main staff. I'll give you a few minutes to read the menu."

She laughed out loud when she opened the menu. It was one of those large, padded things, but inside was a note stating to order whatever you felt like eating. The rest of the space was filled with photographs of the area and suggestions for sightseeing.

Dick came back. "Do you know what you want?"

"I liked the menu. I think something light. So…Maybe an onion bagel, toasted with butter and cream cheese, smoked salmon, orange juice, and more coffee. That should do it. Oh…and I'd like to settle the bill now too. I want to get going fairly quickly."

"Right you are." Dick went off.

Judy sat daydreaming of spending a few months here. What a lucky stop. When the food came, she forced herself to eat a bit of it. Why should eating be such a chore? She laughed at herself. Was there such a thing as dietary schizophrenia? She still thought of food, enjoyed ordering it, admired it—but eating it had become so hard.

Back at the cabin, Jack was happy to see her. She tethered him outside while she picked up and loaded the car. They were back on the road by nine.

She was going to her parent's cabin at Mud Pond in Washington County—the most eastern of the coastal Maine counties. In the fine tradition of Maine, Mud Pond was a pristine, spring-fed lake named to discourage people from discovering it. Home to handsome loons, one could find trout, salmon, and white perch if you knew where and how to find them. Judy's father always prattled on about which lure to use for which fish—and all the lures had names. Judy had her own method: big ugly lures for big ugly fish like bass, and small pretty jewel-like red, silver, and gold lures for pretty fish like trout and salmon. Her family only caught fish they planned to eat right away—and they frowned on "catch and release"—could never understand why you'd torture fish for sport.

She was hungry for the Maine of her childhood and drove slowly through the towns scattered along 1A. Some towns looked prosperous, mostly tourist towns. The land was reclaiming some of the others, buildings leaning as if wishing only to rest on the ground. She drove into Camden about three. The main street was jammed with tourists, but the park at the edge of the harbor was deserted. The harbor itself was clogged with sailboats, kayaks, and a few working boats. Settled against a tree Judy nursed a bottle of water. Then she lay on the blanket with Jack and dozed. She woke up groggy. A few teenagers were playing Frisbee with their dog. More boats were coming in, then leaving the harbor. A cool breeze was coming off the water.

"C'mon, Jack. Gotta go. First, though, I've got to walk out the kinks in my back." She left Jack in the car with the windows cracked and walked up to a used bookstore in the center of town. Just as she came through the door, her telephone rang. Eileen. Stepping outside, she answered.

"Hello."

"Judy. Is that you?"

"Yup."

"Oh, good. Sam and I have been trying to reach you."

"My cell's been out of whack," Judy lied easily. "I haven't had much luck calling out either."

"Well, I'm glad I got through. Not glad, really. I have bad news."

"Are you okay? Sam?"

"Yes, yes, yes. But Margarida died. I don't know when exactly, but Sam found her body yesterday. He hadn't seen her for a couple of days, and she didn't answer the phone, so he went over. I guess he has a key. He said she was in her bed with a beautiful smile on her face."

"Oh, how sad. How very sad. I know she was old, but I thought she'd go on forever—she had so much energy. And never complained about anything. I don't even recall her ever mentioning going to a doctor."

"We're all broken up about it."

"When's the funeral?" Judy hated funerals and was frantically trying to think of an acceptable reason for not going back. Usually the person who died was the one she'd like to see, not everyone else.

"Strangest thing. She didn't want one. Connor was buried in upstate New York somewhere, and she wanted to be buried with him as quickly as possible. She'd told Sam about this years ago, so he knew what to do. There will be a little ceremony up there, but there's no one she knew still living in the little town. But it's all in her will; she just didn't care for any ceremony. And no memorial service either. She just wanted to float up to heaven."

"Good old Margarida." Judy smiled, but her voiced cracked. "You were kind to call. Everything else okay?"

"Getting used to the condo. Miss the old neighborhood, though."

"When's your house going to be ready?"

"Maybe never. They keep finding things that aren't up to code or some such thing, so I'm thinking seriously of buying this condo.

We're down by the beach and closer to the stores, so we're enjoying it. Or I am. I don't know if Marilyn ever enjoys anything."

"So she's still there?"

"Oh, yes. But I think she'll be off in a week or so. There's a big meeting at her work, and she needs to 'whip her staff into shape'—so she says. Well, I'll let you go. Where are you, anyway? Sam was sort of vague about it."

"Maine. I've been on the road, going up east to my parents' cabin."

"Oh, that's nice. Weather good?"

"Beautiful."

"Lucky you. Well. Sorry about the news."

"Thanks again for calling. Bye."

"Bye."

She sat stunned on the steps of the bookstore, then realizing she was in the way, got up and walked back to the car. She started the car and began to drive…and cry. Then bawl. She had to pull over as she was ambushed by wracking sobs.

CHAPTER 21

Judy sat at the side of the road thinking about Margarida. This was the saddest she'd ever felt about a person's death. Maybe because somehow Margarida was so innocent. She'd thought the best of everyone. Her language was squeaky-clean (she called her breasts "fronts"). She believed in governments, the Olympics, churches, Boy Scouts, TV advertising. It was like the death of a family dog—pure grief.

Judy called Sam.

"Hello."

"Sam, it's me. Eileen just told me about Margarida."

"I tried to call you. I wasn't surprised—she'd been having heart trouble…but it's certainly sad. She was such a sweet lady."

"And Eileen said no funeral or anything?"

"That's right. She was so eager to see Connor, she didn't want to waste time with funerals. She did specify a few prayers to be read as they buried her, but that's all. She was a little worried that she'd be so much older than Connor when she got to heaven, but figured God had some way to fix that. She was hoping they'd both be young."

"Well, I just wanted to touch base. Right now I'm at the side of the road crying."

"I've been doing a lot of that too. You okay?"

"I will be. Well, I'm going to go. Take care."

"Um…Bye, I guess."

"Bye." She hung up.

Downhearted, she got back on the road and drove straight up 95 to the supermarket in Brewer, the city across the Penobscot River from Bangor. Appetite completely gone now, she quickly loaded up a cart with camp basics and cat food. An hour east of Brewer on Route 9, she stopped at the little store on the hill, her favorite worm store. She found the Styrofoam containers of earthworms stacked next to the beer. She bought a couple and topped off her tank. A little later she stopped at a farm stand and got some early corn, green beans, tomatoes, and spinach—her eyes wanted them, and she hoped they'd spark her appetite.

She had trouble finding the turnoff to the lake. Route 9 had been improved in the years since she'd been out here, and her landmarks were gone. She drove well past the lake, then turned back and found it. She had to slow to a crawl to navigate the poorly maintained dirt road. Boulders jutted up right next to holes filled with muddy water that could be anywhere from an inch to two feet deep. The hump in the center of the road was a foot or two high, so she had to keep switching from side to side of the road to avoid wrecking the car. She finally skittered down the last steep hill and landed on the road rimming the north side of the lake. This road was in somewhat better shape, padded with years of pine needles and leaves. Now she could see the lake, dark blue like the sky. She opened her windows and smelled the cool air…pine, wood smoke, and berries. After half a mile, she turned into the faint driveway of the family cabin, got out of the car, and walked down to the lake. Quiet.

The cabin was on a hill, a single-story log structure her father had built years before. The logs had darkened with age, so the cabin now blended into the surrounding pine woods. Wild rosebushes covered the hill sloping to a narrow strip of sand. In the lake, rocks the size of cars leaned against the beach. Small pine and spruce trees grew between the rocks at the lake's edge. A small dock and float were anchored to a flat rock at the edge of the property.

Judy walked out on the dock. While it was peak vacation season, no one seemed to be in at any of the camps at that end of the lake. Retired employees of a local paper company owned most of the camps; the company went bankrupt and stopped their pensions years ago. Most of the men had to go back to work and found employment out of state—they held onto their camps, but seldom used them.

When Judy was growing up, it was common in Maine for families to have a camp somewhere for summer family fun and winter hunting and fishing. It was not a sign of wealth—most were simple structures, often with only one or two rooms—and land had been cheap to buy or rent from the paper companies. With 3,000 lakes and ponds, 32,000 miles of rivers and streams, and 3,500 miles of ocean frontage, there was ample space for them throughout the state. It was not until Judy was an adult that she discovered that not everyone in the country had a seasonal home.

Judy loved the lake. The family's cabin was in a cove toward the east end. The lake was three miles long and no more than a half mile wide…not large enough to satisfy thrill-seeking speed boaters, so craft usually seen were quiet ones—sailboats, rowboats, and kayaks. This day no boats were out, but two loons were in the cove fishing.

Judy took some deep breaths, then climbed up to the car and started unloading. The key was in a can under the steps. She unlocked the door and stepped inside. The logs smelled so good. The cabin had one large room with a high peaked ceiling and windows along the lake and east sides. The west side had built-in sofas with three sleeping cubicles above them. Each cubicle had a single mattress, storage shelves, a light, and a window. Her father had taken the idea from photos of old Scandinavian houses. Toward the rear of the camp, with a lower flat ceiling, a large kitchen opened to the front room. At the very back were the bathroom and her parents' bedroom.

A red Swedish wood stove stood against the east wall of the main room. Antique skis, snowshoes, and fishing gear hung on the walls. A large round pine table with stubby legs was in the center of the room. Redwood armchairs, sold as outdoor furniture, with bright red canvas cushions were scattered about the room. There was no TV, but a large, ancient, shortwave radio stood atop a bookcase that contained mostly nature books and a row of bound leather volumes of the camp's logbooks—camp rule dictated that each visit to the lake was recorded in some detail.

This was home—she'd been coming to this cabin since she was eight or nine. Her parents now lived in a condo, having sold the home she grew up in ten years before.

In less than half an hour, Judy unpacked the car and put stuff away. She tethered Jack outside—afraid if she let him roam free, he might try to take on a bear or wildcat.

She took a chaise from the shed next to the cabin and brought it and a beer to the beach to watch the sun go down. The breeze fell, and the lake became glass. The loons began their schizophrenic cries—mournful croons and lunatic laughing. Jack came down and sat on her lap, cowed by the new sounds and smells.

Sun down and moon up, Judy stood and stretched. "Well, Jack, how about supper?"

The radio brought in an NPR special on rock and roll. Cheered, Judy sang along as she fed Jack and started her supper—one ear of corn, a hot dog, and a cucumber. She ate just part of the hot dog—it tasted of odd chemicals. The corn turned out to be one of those so-called "sweet" hybrids, and she dropped the ear after one bite. Finally she gave up and opened another beer.

The windows were all wide open. She turned the radio off so she could listen to the silence. Jack found a cushion and fell asleep. She settled in a chair and read for two hours or so. It wasn't quite cool enough for a fire. Tomorrow she'd build one outside to cook on. Maybe go fishing.

The following day Jack woke her up at dawn. It was chilly in the camp, so after she tied him outside, she lit a small fire. She had coffee, managed to eat half a plain doughnut, and promised herself to take a vitamin pill later. Then she locked the camp, put a short leash on Jack, and went for a walk along the camp road. The lake was just a few miles from the ocean, so a heavy fog was still touching the treetops.

For a cat, Jack was pretty good on a leash—he'd stop and scratch from time to time, but didn't have to smell every tree and bush as a dog would. She saw only small game—rabbit, squirrel, and hedgehog. She heard partridge gurgling in the bushes but didn't see any.

Twice they walked down to the lake's edge for Jack to drink—he growled as the waves lapped his nose.

Judy strolled back toward the cabin feeling serene—a feeling that changed to vigilance when she saw a vehicle parked next to hers that she didn't recognize. She hoped it wasn't one of the other campers looking for company. As she got closer, she could see Sam's back as he peered into the cabin. Damn. She hated surprises. She and Sam had an agreement that he wouldn't come yet. She wasn't ready to forgive him. And he wouldn't have any testing results yet—so why did he come?

She was standing next to her own car, and without thinking, got into it and backed out onto the road. She knew the area and Sam didn't, so she headed west along the lake, away from the main road leading back to Route 9. A rough logging road further west would link her to Route 9 if she wanted, but a half mile from her cabin, she drove into the yard of Romeo Gagne's camp. She hid the car by driving around to the front of the building. She knew no one would be at the camp, as Romeo had moved to France years before. Soon she heard another vehicle drive slowly by. She assumed it was Sam. Then quiet. Jack sat in the passenger seat and gazed at the lake. She didn't dare turn on the radio. There was nothing to read in the car. She had an almost-full tank of gas, but no money, no wallet, no phone, and no food.

This was so stupid! It reminded her of the time she and her older brother had locked their parents out of the house for a joke. But her parents got so angry, they didn't dare let them in. She was trying to avoid a confrontation with Sam, but instead was probably escalating the situation. Maybe he had just come up to Maine to commiserate about Margarida's death. He must've seen her drive away. Now he'd be boiling mad, so she'd better avoid him for a few hours at least. In about half an hour, she heard a vehicle coming back toward the camp, driving even slower than before. That must be Sam. After he was well past, she took Jack out of the car to explore Romeo's camp. A small rowboat was under the main building, complete with oars and oarlocks. She dragged the boat to the lake and set off toward the west end. Her plan was to row around the long end of the lake, poke down the inlet, and maybe just drift for a while. If she got really hungry, there were always berries.

A few people were out fishing. Jack sat up on the little bow seat sniffing the air. The sun rose higher and burned off the fog. A family of ducks tempted Jack, but he stayed in the boat making throat trills. She had rowed past Emile LaGasse's place before she noticed him out there waving. She turned the boat around and landed on his beach.

Emile was sitting out on his porch smoking a pipe. When Judy was a child, he had a little shack here. Over the years he had constructed a two-story year-round house and became the lake's first permanent resident. The joke on the lake was that no one had ever seen him working on it—he was always outside sitting and smoking.

"Mornin', darlin'." Emile stood and came down to the boat.

"Morning, Emile."

"Who've you got here?"

"This is Jack."

"Sam just stopped by lookin' for you—he said he was your husband."

"I'm not surprised."

"Well, c'mon, sit a spell." Emile smiled and beckoned Judy to follow him up to the porch.

Emile was maybe eighty—eighty-five. Short, five-six tops, skinny, bowlegged, and stooped. He still had a thick head of black hair and his teeth, though yellow, were his own. He had on his summer uniform: red plaid flannel shirt, khaki cotton pants, red suspenders, and a wool red plaid cap. His winter uniform swapped the cotton pants for heavy green wool and added a red plaid wool jacket and leather mittens, and he turned down the earflaps on his cap. His high, laced, leather boots served him year round.

They sat. Emile smoked. Jack pulled at his leash—he wanted to explore.

"Why don't we put Jack inside so he can stretch his legs?" Emile got up and opened the door.

"Okay."

"And how about coffee? I just made molasses cookies."

"Sounds great."

They filed into the house. Emile's house would have been right at home on Sunshine Street. A gray, graceful New England-style home with white trim, white porches, flower boxes dripping with nasturtiums. Flowerbeds filled with zinnias and lilies bordered the house; in place of lawn, Emile trimmed blueberry bushes back to a foot high. They walked into a kitchen that had a bank of glass-fronted refrigerators and freezers, a triple-wide cooktop—the kind with no visible burners and several ovens tucked in among furniture-grade cabinets. China cabinets displayed crystal, Chinese pottery, and bone china. Bowls of fruit and flowers adorned the slate countertops. A large wire rack of sugar-topped cookies cooled next to the largest espresso machine Judy had ever seen in a person's home.

"When did you get that?"

"Restaurant in Machias went out of business last fall. Got it for a song." He chuckled. "Makes a good cup too. What's your pleasure?"

"Plain double espresso."

"You're no fun. I do good things with chocolate."

"Plain espresso, please. And I just had a huge breakfast—maybe I could take a cookie home." The cookies looked and smelled delicious, but Judy was afraid of hurting Emile's feelings if she wasn't able to eat one.

"Okeydoke." Emile took beans out of the refrigerator and tossed some into a compartment of the machine, pressed a few buttons, then turned to pick out cups. They heard Jack running up the stairs."

"He's not shy, is he? Hope he didn't hear a rat up there."

"Rat?"

"All kinds of critters try to get in, and some succeed. I should get a cat myself to take care of them. I have one of those traps that don't hurt 'em, but it usually takes a while to catch them—they're so damn clever—take the food and run. Anyway…Here we go…" Emile took his cup, grabbed a cookie, and they headed back outside.

"So, how was winter?" Judy sipped the coffee and stared out at the lake.

"More snow than usual. I got stuck in here for three months—nothing could get through. The town tried to get its plow down here, but it didn't get one hundred feet from Route Nine. And power was out most of the time. Good thing I laid in lots of food. It was peaceful, I'll say that. Since no one could get in, I didn't have to listen to those damn snowmobiles. Had to shoot a couple deer—they were starving to death anyway. Put up the steaks and made mincemeat."

"No one was in all that time?"

"The warden flew over twice just to make sure I was alive."

"How's everything else out here?"

"Folks still jarring over the road—no one wants to give money, and it really needs fixing up, or we'll have to go back to using horses."

"Who's collecting?"

"Me."

"Did my father give you anything?"

Emile chuckled. "Ansel? Goodness no. He's never even paid the Association dues. I stopped mailing him bills years ago. It's voluntary, you know. And ole Ansel will never volunteer to part with his money."

Judy smiled. Emile knew her father for sure. "I don't have my wallet with me, but I'll drop something by before I go. What's a good amount?"

"Happy to have anything. Fifty would be nice."

"Okay."

They chatted on about individuals at the lake: who died, had babies, moved in, or bought a new boat. Neither mentioned Sam again. Finally Judy got up to leave.

"Hold on a minute." Emile went back into the house and came back with a bag of cookies and a little basket filled with eggs. "Hens been laying real good. I don't need the basket back. I make them just to pass the time at night. Oh, wait another minute."

This time he came back with a quart canning jar and two small glasses. "Here, try a sip of this. I've been working on my recipe. This is blueberry brandy with a hint of raspberry."

His hands shook as he poured. "Damn little glasses."

Judy sipped. "Wow. Hundred times better than the stuff we get at the store."

Emile stood proudly. "I thought so too. Here, take the rest."

Judy thanked him, they went in to get Jack, and then she got back in the boat. She kept going west; it wasn't time to try going back yet. At the end of the lake, she rowed up the inlet and pulled in at a grassy area.

"Might as well take a nap." She had a few sips of the brandy. Jack came over and sat next to her, and they both fell asleep. When she woke, a monarch butterfly was flitting over her face. Shooing it away, she sat and looked around. Jack was still asleep. Only eleven o'clock. If she rowed the long way round the lake, she'd get to her cabin after one. If Sam's car was gone, she'd bring back Romeo's boat and get her car. And if Sam was still there? She supposed she'd have to land at the dock and deal with him.

As they rowed, a light breeze came up. Jack was back in the bow playing figurehead. At the end of the lake, a cluster of ten or eleven tiny camps had wide beaches, and several children were out playing. When she started down the south side of the lake, there were just a few deserted camps, then none at all. This was where the road ended at the foot of a steep hill. From this point to the other end of the lake, there was old forest, no beaches and no camps. The lake was shallow on this side and thick with lilies and sharp grasses. The forest looked like something you'd expect in a swamp in the Deep South…trees leaning against one another, vines dragging them to earth. She jumped when a great blue heron took flight…This prehistoric-looking bird was the largest at the lake. She stopped rowing and drifted to watch the bird skim the trees and disappear.

When she was opposite her cabin, she couldn't see from that distance whether Sam was there or not. At least no one was out on the beach.

She reached the east end of the lake and lay back in the boat and let it drift back toward the cove. Jack came down from his perch and lay beside her, purring. She was in no hurry.

CHAPTER 22

Judy didn't get back to the cabin until two-thirty. Sam was gone, so she rowed over to Romeo's, put the boat away, and brought her car back. In the cabin she stored Emile's gifts and got a beer. Back on the beach, she tried to relax. What would she do if—or when—Sam came back? She had to stay firm on the medical issue. She'd have to keep the cabin door locked all the time—whether or not she was inside. Inside, if Sam got angry or even worse, physically threatening, he'd have the advantage, so she'd only meet with him outside, preferably away from the cabin. At night she'd barricade the door so he couldn't push it in.

She still didn't know how she felt about forgiving him for his tryst with Terry. She'd have to make her ambivalence clear to Sam—even if he did get medical clearance, she may not want him back—at least not right away.

It helped to have a plan, even one so flimsy. She went in and changed into a bathing suit. She was shocked by the cold water and came out before the water even reached her knees. (When she had first moved to Florida, she'd only swim in the winter; the water—ocean or pool—was as warm as spit the rest of the year.) But after several attempts, she finally got all the way in and swam out to the middle of the cove. The rest of the afternoon she swam, read, and gloried in the humidity-free air. About five she changed into shorts and a T-shirt and went into the woods to gather fallen wood for a quick fire. She got a hot fire going in the stone fireplace on the beach and grilled a hot dog. The hot dog was lunch and dinner. After she had a few bites, she threw the rest into the fire, went up to the cabin, and poured a small glass of brandy. She promised herself that tomorrow would be different—she'd start making real meals and make sure to catch some fish.

As she was getting ready to return to the beach, her phone rang. Probably Sam. But it wasn't.

"Hello."

"Mrs. Haite?"

"Who's calling, please?"

"This is Sandra Bragg, Mr. Hull's secretary." This Sandra had a snooty voice.

"Oh. Yes, this is Judy Haite."

"I'm calling to let you know you're scheduled to give a deposition in the Elroy case. You're to appear at the office of Hull and Dunning on Datura Street at one p.m. Tuesday."

"No."

"No?"

"I'm out in the Maine woods. It's impossible for me to be there."

"I'm afraid you must be there."

"Sorry, but I can't be."

"Mr. Hull said you had to be there."

"I can't be—so figure something else out."

"But, but…"

"Good-bye." Judy hung up.

About ten minutes later, the phone rang again. Must be that Sandra again.

"Hello."

"Why'd you leave like that?"

It was Sam. She'd have to get better at checking caller ID, but the numbers were so small…

"You were supposed to call to see if I wanted you up here. I don't like surprises."

"You're being impossible. I managed to get my blood drawn early and then flew up to see you, and you just take off."

"Sam. I'm being me. And you're being you. You don't have your results yet. I've always worked in hospitals, and I don't plan to get sick or die from an STD. You were unfaithful. You have to prove to me that you and Terry are free from any venereal disease before I'll talk to you about the future. Chasing me up to Maine doesn't help at all. Taking me seriously will."

"You're being ridiculous!" Sam yelled this time.

"So you keep informing me."

Sam hung up. Her beautiful, sweet Sam. God, what a mess.

The phone rang again. This time she checked—it was that Sandra woman.

"Hello."

"Hello, Mrs. Haite. This is Robert Hull. Sandra told me you were being difficult."

"Not difficult. Just unable to leave the Maine woods at this moment to make an appointment I knew nothing about."

"Maine woods?"

"I'm at a cabin near Canada. I won't even have a car for a week or two. And I don't know when I'll be able to drive." Spinning lies.

"Well." Silence. "Well, we'll have to arrange something else then. We'll be in touch." He hung up.

Judy had forgotten about the accident after the…after the Joe thing. She hoped Mrs. Elroy had recovered okay. Tomorrow she'd have to call Mark White to see what to do.

Well, until then there was nothing she could do about any of this. She rummaged through the bookcase and found her father's tiny volume of poems by Du Fu, a Chinese poet from the 700's. Her father used to read the simple poems to them at night after they were up in their cubicles—beautiful poems of nature and the poet's struggle to survive in an area of shifting politics and conflict. Snuggled in her cubicle, Judy had felt so safe comparing her family's life to Du Fu's.

Judy hugged the battered book. Such good memories. Judy's father had read to her and her brothers every night before bed. This tradition ended at home when they were older, but whenever they went tenting or were at the lake, someone, usually her father or brother Frank, would read the others to sleep. The reader would stop from time to time to make sure someone was still awake. Judy smiled, remembering the struggle to keep the reader going.

She took the book and her glass of brandy and went back down to the beach. She read until it got too dark, then sat and watched the sun go down. She let Jack go loose, and he settled onto her lap and started purring.

Jack was the first cat she'd had since she was a kid. Back then all of their cats had eventually died from distemper. She thought back to the day she and her brother were kneeling against the back of the sofa watching the rain. His cat had been missing for days. Suddenly Spot came through the flowerbed to the window and fell over dead. She remembered only that fragment—not whether they went outside to check on the cat. Or how they reacted. Only the drenched cat reaching the window, putting up a paw, and keeling over.

Jack stopped purring and looked up at Judy. "Good boy." She scratched his chin, and he resumed purring. Is this all she really needed—a cat? She'd read a story once in which a man never dated a woman who had a cat. Not that he didn't like cats himself, but because a woman who had a cat wouldn't need him.

❧

The next morning Judy had a tiny bowl of Cheerios and coffee. Feeling virtuous, she left Jack in the cabin and took a brisk walk to the east end of the lake and onto the barrens. Blueberry growers burned the fields every year to keep growth of other vegetation down. There were a few white birch trees among the boulders; otherwise it was all blueberry bushes covering the rocky, hilly terrain. In its way it was beautiful—being able to see so far after being closed in by the surrounding forest. When they were kids, she and her brothers pretended they were on the moon when they played on the barrens. She'd remembered to put a plastic bag in her pocket and stopped near the end of the barrens to pick blueberries. They were falling off the bushes, and she had the bag filled in minutes.

Judy walked around a looping logging road back toward the cabin, breathing deeply first, clearing her mind. Then made plans for the day: one, call Mark White about the deposition; two, go fishing; three…no three.

White wasn't in his office, so Judy left a message. Then she took worms, rod, and a small box of lures out to the beach. She uncovered her mother's rowboat (her father had a larger boat with outboard motor) and got oars, oarlocks, net and life preserver out of the shed. She went back in the cabin for a water bottle and an apple. Jack seemed happy sitting on the windowsill, so she scratched his chin and left him there. She also left the phone behind—she wanted to fish, just fish.

She threw a line out as soon as she got to deep water and started to troll, going east, where her luck would be best for catching white perch. The other end of the lake was where she was more apt to catch salmon or trout. But she was hungry for white perch. Wild white perch from cold-water lakes is a sweet fish, Judy's favorite of all fishes. The little ones were irritatingly bony, but even those give some tasty morsels. After an hour of no luck, she ran into a school of perch—threw back the first few undersized ones, then caught two fat fish about ten inches long. While large enough to fillet, Judy planned to pan fry them whole—the crispy skin was the second-best part of the fish.

Having caught enough for lunch, Judy rowed back to the cabin. She cleaned the fish on the dock, then went inside to soak them in milk. Later she'd toss them in corn meal, then pan fry in an iron skillet on the beach. Spinach salad would complete the meal. Happy about lunch, she stored the fishing gear, got a beer, and went out on the beach with Jack.

Just as she got settled, the phone rang. She made it back to the cabin in time to pick up the call.

It was Mark White.

"Hello."

"Hello, Judy. I got your message. I haven't called Hull yet. Did he tell you anything about what was going on?"

"No. Just that it was a deposition for a suit in Mrs. Elroy's case."

"Is she suing just the hospital or are you included?"

"Don't know."

I have my notes from when you called right after the incident. But tell me again what happened."

"Mrs. Elroy put her artificial leg on herself. I forgot to double-check it before she got up to walk. She did okay until she turned a corner. The leg slipped off, and she wrecked her stump."

"Do you have any reason why you forgot to check it?"

"I hadn't had much sleep the night before. I was called in to ambulate a few patients. But I've worked with a lot less sleep before with no problem, so that's no excuse. Maybe it was that Mrs. Elroy seemed so competent. But I can't think of why I forgot to check. I made a mistake."

"I appreciate your candor, Judy. Now, what exactly did the hospital do to you? Were you really fired? I can't tell from my notes."

"They told me I was suspended, but didn't give any mention of how I could get un-suspended. At the time I felt I was fired. My salary stopped, and so did my benefits. They haven't even paid me for my accrued vacation time."

"What do you want to happen?"

"Mostly I just hope Mrs. Elroy has recovered. I made a mistake, but people make mistakes all the time at the hospital. Mistakes that kill people. I've never heard of any other employee treated like I was. I should be covered by the hospital's insurance. If employees weren't covered, they wouldn't work in hospitals. If I'm not covered, the hospital should've informed me when I was hired."

"When you were suspended, did you sign anything? Or did they give you anything in writing?"

"No. Nothing to sign. They did give me a pamphlet about my rights."

"Do you want to go back to work there?"

"God, no. But I want the option to work somewhere else or do private work. A suit against me would be a problem. You know how people are."

"Well. I guess I'm up to speed. I want to check some case law, then call them. I'll keep you posted."

"Thanks. And don't forget, I'm out here at the family cabin in Maine, and I'm not going back to Florida for some time."

"I got that part of your message this morning. Anything else?"

"No. Thanks."

"No problem. Take care. Bye."

"Bye."

Judy went back to the beach. At two she had lunch. The fish was perfect, what she'd dreamed about for months. But once again, while her mouth and eyes eagerly anticipated the food, somewhere or something in her chest prevented her from managing more than a few tiny bites. What was happening? She knew anatomy—there was no physical reason she could think of that prevented her from eating. She could still drink—coffee and liquor posed no problem—so no anorexia. And nothing hurt, like an ulcer. Maybe it was some weird infection—of her inner ear or something.

CHAPTER 23

Judy drove down into Millbridge the next day. She had a couple of paperback books and went into the library to swap them. She continued south to the ocean, then drove east toward Machias, stopping from time to time at antique stores and yard sales. She didn't see anything she wanted. She stopped at Tunk Stream to watch huge salmon swimming upstream—too big for her. Later she stopped at a small liquor store to pick up a few things. She wasn't back at the cabin until after three. She'd left her phone at the cabin; White, Hull's office, and Sam had all called.

She called Mark White first.

"Well, I talked to Hull several times today. You are included in the suit, along with the hospital. But there may be a way we can get you out of it. You won't like it, but…Are you sure you don't want to come back down here and work on this?"

"I'm sure. What's your idea?"

"As I talked with Hull, I got the distinct impression they were primarily interested in the hospital's deep pockets, not yours. By the way, they don't seem to know how wealthy you guys are. Anyway, it turns out that Mrs. Elroy feels sorry for you. She liked you."

"How is she?"

"I wouldn't get an honest answer out of them at this point, but she did have another surgical procedure, and she is using an artificial limb."

"That's a relief!"

"Anyway, Mrs. Elroy thinks your knuckles should be rapped, but isn't so interested in a financial settlement. If you would go along with a side agreement to forfeit your PT license in Florida and take a refresher course in patient safety/accident prevention, you could reapply for your Florida license or get one from any other state. You needn't give a reason to the Florida licensing board for forfeiture—just say you're moving, retiring, or some such. And they'd keep the agreement secret, out of the press."

"Do you really think that this would work? I mean, is this a real proposal or just something you guys threw around?"

"Oh, no, it's a real deal. We can draft something today, have you review it, and get it finalized in a week. Then you're off the hook."

Judy didn't hesitate. She hadn't planned on going back to work soon anyway. "Great, let's do it. E-mail me the stuff. I don't have the Internet out here, but I can find a connection somewhere."

"I'm glad you agree. Otherwise a suit can drag on forever. You could be back in business before the suit even makes it to court."

"Thanks, Mark."

"You're welcome. Glad to help. Bye."

"Bye."

Whew! That's over. Judy didn't know how weighed down she'd been by the accident and looming lawsuit. And what a relief none of this would become public. She'd been humiliated enough in that meeting at the hospital and could only imagine what a public trial would bring, especially down there—the newspapers were meticulous in reporting details of medical mishaps.

She didn't know why Hull called—but she felt she could forgo returning that call. Was she ready to speak to Sam? No. Maybe later, at night.

Judy smiled. She picked up Jack and twirled around the cabin. There was light at the end of the tunnel. She'd survived Joe. She'd escaped a lawsuit. Maybe she could come to an agreement with Sam to put their life back on Sunshine Street.

Perhaps, unknown to her, the worry of the lawsuit was preventing her from eating. Now happy and feeling hungry, Judy decided to try her favorite camping meal. She cut a potato in small tidy cubes and fried them carefully in butter and olive oil. When the potatoes were golden and crispy, she seasoned them with salt, pepper, and a dash of cayenne and divided them in half. She dropped an egg on half of the potatoes and cooked them until the eggs were scrambled but still slightly wet. In a side pan, she fried a slice of Spam. She added sliced tomatoes to the plate and sat at the table ready to celebrate. It smelled so good, but she couldn't even lift the fork. She almost cried before dumping the plate of food into the garbage.

Frustrated, Judy took a beer and went to the beach and swam until a thunderstorm came up at dusk that forced her back inside. She paced around the cabin at loose ends—one big problem with being at camp alone was there weren't any card games. Her family loved to play whist, thinking bridge a bit stodgy, and would stop and play at a drop of the hat—one only had to make eye contact and nod at a deck of cards to pull everyone into a game. Finally she pulled out a jigsaw puzzle, mixed a gin and tonic, and spread out the pieces.

Jack jumped onto the table to help. After two hours Judy hadn't even found all the straight-edge pieces, so she scrambled what she'd done and put everything back in the box. She wanted to do something but didn't know what. Good news did that to her. If times were tough, she'd focus, buckle down. Good news gave her energy but nothing to do with it.

The weather cleared after dark, so she finally decided upon a walk. Maybe stop by and chat with Emile, if she got that far. The rain brought new smells to the woods, maybe just a hint of rotten wood and mushrooms. She walked about a mile in the pitch black—it was still cloudy, so there was no moon. Clipping happily along, she heard a deep huffing sound. A bear? Moose? Something large. She stopped, turned, and walked as quickly as she dared back to the cabin. She wasn't afraid of these animals if she could see them, but at night they were scary. Once in the cabin she laughed at herself—it was probably just a bullfrog. Oh, well.

Riding her cheerfulness she dialed Sam's number.

"Hello."

"Hi, Sam. It's me, Judy."

"Hi."

"You called."

"Right. Look. I'm here at my mother's and will going back to Palm Beach in a couple of days. Before I leave, I really would like to spend some good time with you. Maybe go fishing or something. We don't even have to talk about it."

"It?"

"My Terry mess."

"Gee, I don't know, Sam."

"I promise I'll behave. I just want a pleasant day with you. Plus, I should have my results by then."

"Well…maybe. Not tomorrow. But all right, day after tomorrow. Not here. I'll meet you at Beddington Stream and Route Nine. We can go after some brook trout. I'll bring the gear and lunch. How's that?"

"Great. Thanks. What time?"

"Meet you there at ten?"

"Okay."

"Night, Sam."

"Night, Judy."

&

The next morning Judy got up before six, had coffee, pumpernickel toast, and a glass of V8. She tidied up the kitchen, swept the floors, and took Jack for a walk. Back at the cabin, she apologized to Jack, shut him in, and left for Bangor.

Bad timing—traffic was heavy on Route 9. Usually she drove at noon or five o'clock, traditional mealtimes kept by most of the drivers out here. She had to pay attention on the hilly road, but still had moments of pure pleasure when the forest hugging the road opened to views of a tiny settlement hugging a valley or a stream snaking through swamps and hills. Some of the thrills of driving Route 9 were gone, with the improvements made to widen the road and flatten the hills and curves. In the old days Judy used to pull off the road from time to time to let a car get in front of her to act as a shield against vehicles driving toward her in the wrong lane. People would pass anywhere after enduring miles and miles of following logging trucks grinding up the hills, barely avoiding going backwards on the steep ones. Now there were passing lanes every few miles.

In Bangor she parked in front of the library, an imposing marble edifice that made books somehow more precious. Going up the stairs brought back fond memories of her childhood. She and her friends used to walk downtown almost every week in the summer to get books. And to be shushed by the librarian. In high school she'd been tossed out several times for talking too loud. Later, as an adult, she'd gone into the library to see if they had a copy of Matilda, Who Told Lies and Was Burned to Death. She thought she'd get it for one of her nieces. The librarian scoffed at her, looking at Judy as if she were a pervert. However, a younger librarian chuckled and produced the book with a flourish. She often wondered if the book remained on the shelf after she left.

Inside, the building was busier and noisier than Judy had ever remembered. She found a computer station, retrieved the draft settlement from White, and printed it out. She sat in the main reading room and read the document twice. It looked okay to her; it left to her the choice of the safety course and its length. She signed it and put a nickel in the machine for a copy.

Next she walked the few blocks to the post office and mailed the signed agreement express mail. Business done, she stood outside the post office for a while, watching people come and go. Strange, whenever she came home she rarely met anyone she knew. She didn't know many people in Palm Beach either, but there she didn't expect to.

Her parents were in Florida looking after Aunt Helen—so no duty calls. No other relatives lived in the area. Judy sat for a while in the car deciding what to bring for the fishing lunch with Sam. She finally opted to try crab, so drove out Route 1 to the fish market. She got a container of nice pink leg meat. She also picked up white bread and a few other things on the way back.

She got to camp in time to swim for quite a while before dark. After the first few days at camp, she was sure no one was in the cove, so she swam naked. It felt better, plus she didn't have to deal with wet swimsuits all day. Jack was happy to be back outside. She let him loose, and he chased after chipmunks and chickadees before settling in the shade by the water.

When it was dark, she went in swimming again, then still feeling ambitious, went in and baked some blueberry muffins with heavily sugared tops. She nibbled at a muffin top and drank two beers.

Still craving activity, she took the rowboat out for a spin around the lake. Emile was out on his porch, so she stopped in to chat for a few minutes. They swapped fishing stories, and she gave him the check for the road.

She resumed rowing around the edge of the lake. She was the only person on the water, though she could hear loons around her and some coyotes yipping at the south shore. When she got back to camp, she was finally tired enough to sit and read. About midnight she took a small glass of brandy up to her bed and was asleep in minutes.

Jack woke her up batting her eyelids. She tried to interest him in sleeping longer but looked down into the kitchen and saw his bowl was empty. Once she'd fed him, she was wide awake. She made coffee and took it and a muffin back to bed. It was strange not having a newspaper. And at camp she rarely even heard news on the radio. Was it necessary to spend that time every day trying to keep up? When she left camp, she'd have to experiment with staying out of touch. She could use the time to read more serious books on politics and history.

Jack would be cooped up in the cabin while she went fishing, so she clipped on his leash, and they went for a long walk. It was a perfect day—cool, clear blue sky, light breeze. For a while she stopped and watched a raven's nest. There were two huge adults and two chicks that were almost as big as their parents. The chicks were out of the nest and moving clumsily in the pine tree's branches. Judy hoped she'd be able to see them try to fly.

When she got back to the cabin, Judy busied about packing a lunch in a cooler and putting together fishing gear for her and Sam. She brought spinning and fly rods, lures, flies, worms, creel, and a net.

She was ready way before time to go, so she went down to the beach to swim. She was finally used to the cold water; her only deference to it was to flop on her back to enter the water—fewer nerves to react to the cold.

Using a crude Australian crawl, she swam to the center of the cove, then traced the west shore back to camp.

She put on long pants, long-sleeved shirt, red bandanna soaked in bug repellant, and hiking boots. She scrounged in the coat closet and found an old Red Sox cap to complete the outfit—the cap would keep the brush out of her eyes.

She loaded the car and headed for the stream—five miles out the dirt road and ten miles east on Route 9. Traffic was light in this direction, and she reached the stream fifteen minutes before ten. Sam was already there, sitting on the hood of his vehicle watching traffic. She pulled in next to him. He came over to her car and leaned into the passenger-side window.

"Morning, honey."

"Hi, Sam."

"Hey, have you lost weight?"

"I don't think so." She had, but didn't want to talk about it.

"I don't have any gear."

"I told you I'd bring stuff for both of us. Do you want flies or worms?"

"Better start with worms. My fly-fishing technique is rusty as hell."

"Well, let's unload and get going."

Judy gave Sam fishing gear and took hers. "I put lunch in a backpack cooler. We can leave it here or lug it in. What do you think?"

Sam hefted the backpack. "Doesn't feel too heavy, I'll carry it."

"Okay." Judy checked to make sure they had everything. "Well, let's go. The other side of the stream has the best path. We have to cross the bridge—watch out for traffic, the shoulder is really narrow." Judy felt so awkward. Silence between her and Sam was usually comfortable; now she was babbling nonsense—as if Sam couldn't cross the road by himself.

They crossed the bridge and headed south upstream. For a short while, the going was easy—a well-worn dirt path through shoulder-high grasses. The stream widened here, and the water was shallow. Not a good place to stop and fish. Soon they entered the dark forest. The trees grew right to the stream's edge on both sides, shading it. The path rose steadily until the bank was ten feet or so higher than the stream bed. The fir trees grew too close together to cast from the bank. To fish they either had to drop a line to a pool directly below, or scramble down to a boulder to cast out into the stream.

Occasionally they'd see a trout jump for a fly or swim up small rapids. Judy and Sam separated and concentrated on fishing. Sam caught a few trout too small to keep. Then Judy landed a twelve-inch beauty.

"Rats."

"Why rats?"

"I was enjoying fishing, but this is all I need to eat."

"You can help me catch mine. I seem to be attracting just the babies. Plus, I could eat more than one."

"You sure?"

"Yeah. Plus, my mother loves trout. Go ahead. We'll stop when we have three or four big ones."

They continued walking upstream. Twice they had to go inland to get around areas flooded by beaver dams. On the second detour, they climbed a small hill. Judy shuddered.

Sam saw her. "What's wrong?"

"This is bear country. Look at the trees."

The bark from all the trees was stripped from knee high to well over Sam's head. And unlike the dense forest they'd been pushing through, the brush was cleared from the entire hill.

"Is this dangerous?" Sam looked ready to run.

"Just keep your eyes open, city boy. Around here the only black bear attack I remember was against a man baiting traps with peanut butter. Since then I've always made sure not to pack it for snacks and not to have PB breath when I go into the woods."

"What do I do if I meet one?"

"I forget all the rules. If you see babies, be sure not to get between them and their mother. And give them the right of way. I've come nose to nose with only one. I was wearing a baseball cap, and I'd been looking down at the path instead of ahead and felt this strange quiet. I looked up, and I was just a few feet from a big one. He looked at me as if I were the dumbest thing on earth."

"What'd you do?"

"Took a quick right off the path. It was dense brush like we've been pushing through, but I sliced through it like a hot knife on butter. I didn't run, but I walked really fast. Never saw the bear again."

"Were you scared?"

"Oh, yes. He was *so* big. But they're vegetarians—I think. I've picked blackberries with bears before—but in big patches, they weren't really close. And they were so intense; they're really cute when they're busy at something."

"Really cute. You're crazy."

They went through the bear area and continued fishing. Sam kept catching little ones and tossing them back, despite changing lures. He even tried fly fishing at one spot. By two o'clock Sam was tired, sweaty, and frustrated.

"Let's eat."

"Oh. Okay. There's a clearing just up ahead from an old beaver flood."

They found the grassy spot in ten minutes. The field was teeming with Indian paintbrush and daisies. And bees. They settled under a large pine tree. Judy took out a large sheet and unpacked the food.

She mixed crab, mayo, and some diced celery and made them sandwiches. Sam opened the beer while Judy put out chips, bread and butter pickles, asparagus spears marinated in dill and lemon vinaigrette, muffins, and coffee.

Sam ate hungrily, and conversation was limited to his grunts and "Please pass the…" He didn't seem to notice that Judy mostly drank her lunch while pushing food around her plate.

"Nap time." Sam stretched out and closed his eyes. Judy sat finishing her coffee. This day had gone better than she expected. Sam hadn't mentioned the "Terry thing" once. While Sam slept, she bagged the garbage, then cleaned the trout and put it on ice. She let Sam sleep until four thirty, then shook him awake.

"Rise and shine."

"Ugh. I could've slept here all night. It smells so good." Sam shook and rubbed his face, now puffy from sleep. "Is there more coffee?"

She poured him a cup and put everything else back in the pack. "We'd better start fishing our way back. The bugs will get bad when the breeze dies." Judy sprayed herself with another coat of repellant and handed the can to Sam. He sprayed his hands and swiped his neck and face.

"I'm already itching like crazy."

"I should've brought the Dawn."

"Hunh?"

"Read it in a column somewhere. Liquid detergent is the best thing for itches. Really. Course, you end up with little blue blotches all over you."

"I'll take your word for it." Sam dumped the rest of his coffee and stood. "Well, guess I'm ready."

They headed back, fishing just the deeper pools. Just before they came out to the end of the forest, Judy hooked another big trout. She stopped to clean it and put it on ice.

"Two—zip." Sam took the worm off his hook and shrugged his shoulders.

"I've always been lucky."

"I don't get it, though. We had the same lures, same worms, same stream."

"Luck, pure luck."

"Well, at least let me help you eat 'em."

Damn. Judy had agreed to the fishing expedition. Now he'd want to come back to the camp. She should've released her fish.

"Why don't you take both fish to your mother's—they're big enough for the three of you."

"C'mon, Judy. I'll come back with you. Go swimming. Sit on the beach. When we get hungry, we'll cook the fish, eat. Then I'll head out. Promise."

"Keep it light?"

"Scout's honor."

Sam looked so handsome, she could roll in the grass with him right now. Maybe he was right, and she was being an old prude. Maybe that was one source of her anger—old—she was so different from teenagers and younger adults who thought nothing of hooking up or whatever they called it. She'd missed Sam. Being honest with herself, camp was lonely—even with Jack. "Oh, all right."

CHAPTER 24

Back at camp Sam stripped and dove into the lake. Judy went up to the cabin, got Jack and tied him outside, and brought a towel down to the beach for Sam. She went back to the cabin, locked the door behind her, put the fish away, and stored the gear. She changed to a T-shirt and shorts and, barefoot, took a book down to the beach. On the way she unlocked the shed and pulled out another chaise. She placed the chair four feet from hers and settled down to read. She looked up from time to time to watch as Sam swam across the lake and back.

Sam came dripping back to the beach. "God, that water's cold."

"I know. It's taken me a while to get used to it. We've lost our subcutaneous fat living in the tropics. Plus the lake is cold anyway—even for the natives."

Sam dried off and lay back in the chaise, eyes closed.

Judy watched him. The sun accentuated the gold in his hair, eyelashes, and emerging beard. He looked like a Norse adventurer resting after a conquest.

After an hour Sam stirred and raised the back of his chair to sit up. "I'm hungry again. Oh, and I forgot to bring something to read."

"It's a little early for supper. I'll get snacks, and I picked up some new magazines in Machias. Want a drink?"

"Sure. Can I help?"

"No. Stay there. I'll be right back."

Judy went up to the cabin and filled a basket with small bags of chips and the magazines. Feeling lazy, she made two large gin and tonics. On the way out, she locked the door and pocketed the key. While she was thawing toward Sam, she wasn't sure she wanted him to stay the night. She edged down to the beach with the basket over her arm, balancing a tray of drinks.

"Aah. That was quick." Sam reached for a drink and took the magazines and a bag of chips.

"I would've made a lousy waitress. I almost lost the drinks coming down the hill."

"I'm always amazed in a restaurant when some little woman carries one of those huge round trays loaded with food through a door too narrow for it… You know, they have to tip the tray to get through."

"Me too." She couldn't think of anything to talk about except Terry.

Judy tried to read. She was feeling so awkward with Sam—before you knew it, she'd be babbling on about the weather. They sat and read for an hour or so, then Judy decided an early supper would be best. Then Sam would leave while it was still light out, and there wouldn't be an issue about keeping him outside. She got up and gathered their glasses to go up to the cabin.

"I thought we'd cook out here. I'll bring the food out, and you can gather the wood and build the fire. Use the fallen stuff, not the logs by the camp. They're for winter."

"Oh, okay."

She went up and filled a basket with food and put it, a folding table, dishes, and wine out on the steps. Sam came up and helped her carry everything down to the beach.

"I'm surprised your father hasn't put in some kind of dumbwaiter to get stuff to the beach," Sam kidded.

"He wanted to, but Mum wouldn't let him. He's always antsy to improve the camp…except for refusing to install a telephone. She's the old explorer—fought getting electricity. But she approved the gas toilet. When we were first here, we tented and had a chemical toilet. Dumping that into the barrels in the ground was a real treat."

"I bet."

Sam had a huge pile of wood and a good fire going. Judy put the foil-wrapped potatoes at the back of the grill in a rustic oven. "We'll give these some time, then I'll add the corn."

Sam opened the wine, and they sat watching the lake. After a while Judy got up and put the corn on the grill and then walked out on the dock. She didn't hear Sam come down behind her. She jumped when he spoke.

"It's so peaceful here."

"Yes. I love it. On the Fourth of July, sometimes people are down here, and it's noisy. Or seems noisy by comparison. But usually it's deserted."

"Aren't you ever worried being by yourself?"

"I've camped out here all my life. There's never been any trouble. I do worry when my folks are down here—it's so far from medical help."

"Can I stay the night?"

"No, Sam. We agreed."

"I don't want to drink and drive."

"So don't drink."

"You're a hard woman."

"Sam. We agreed to keep it light. If you're really worried about driving, you can sleep in your car or out here on the beach."

"Okay, okay." Rebuffed, Sam went back to the beach.

She followed and checked the potatoes. "These are getting there. I think I can cook the fish now." She put a large iron fry pan on the grill. The fish had been sitting in milk, and she picked them up to shake off the excess. She had a plate of cornmeal and was ready to coat the fish when Sam came over to supervise.

"Why don't we fillet the fish? They're big enough."

"The skin's too good to throw away. Plus, it wastes too much of the meat that way."

"If you say so." He came up behind her and put his arms around her. Part of Judy wanted to melt, but she elbowed him in the side.

"Watch it, Sam. Cut it out! Let me go!"

"No." He twisted her body so he faced him, squeezing her into his chest.

"Dammit Sam!" His arms were so strong she couldn't move. She tried to bring her arms up to push against him but she was pinned. Frantic, she stomped on his foot with her heel.

"Ow!" Surprised he let her go. "I'm not going to hurt you. Geez, Judy, you're being hysterical. Don't you miss me? Don't you miss sex? It's been ages."

"Of course I miss you. And sex. But I've told you time and time again my conditions to even think about getting back together. You keep acting as if you've done nothing, and I'm the one doing something wrong. Plus, I really didn't want to talk about this today."

"Oh, damn. I need to go to the bathroom." Sam started up the path.

"Go outside."

"Can't. Got to poop."

"Go outside anyway."

"There's no TP."

"Use leaves."

"Hey! There's a bathroom up here. Dammit…" Sam pulled at the doorknob and then rattled the door, trying to open it. Damn thing's stuck."

"It's locked, Sam."

"Whaaa?" Sam turned around. "Jesus, Judy. What's going on?"

"Just go in the woods, Sam."

Sam glared, but urgency won out, and he crashed into the woods. A few minutes later, he came down to the lake and rinsed his hands.

"I'm not some kind of monster, Judy."

"No. But you're a large, sexy, stubborn man. You've been violent before. And what about your gorilla act just now?"

"Jesus. You think I'll rape you in there?"

"You've come close before."

"If I were going to rape you, I wouldn't have to do it in the cabin, you know."

"Sam. Cut it out. The fish is almost done. Let's eat."

"I still can't believe you locked the damn door. Do you have a gun too?"

"Of course not. Well…They keep a shotgun down here somewhere, but I hadn't planned to use it." Judy arranged the food on the table.

Sam finished almost the whole bottle of wine by himself before he began to eat. He cleared his throat and glared at Judy. "I'm going to stay the night. Inside. And as your husband. And I'm not getting any damn test!"

"I thought you'd already been tested—that's what you said on the phone." Judy was dumbfounded.

"I just told you that. And I never called Terry either." Sam grinned and looked proud of himself.

She looked at Sam. No longer handsome, his eyes were glazed and his orbits, instead of being oval, looked round. His cheeks were red, his skin shiny with sweat. His hands clenched his fork and glass.

He added, "You frigid bitch."

At that moment her love for Sam died. Just as suddenly, whatever had caused her loss of appetite evaporated. Not knowing what to do or say, she began to eat. The corn was a delicious sugar and gold, slightly underdeveloped. The potatoes were fluffy and dripping with butter and sour cream. The trout, though not quite as tasty as the white perch, was perfectly cooked. She thought desperately how to get out of this situation. The boat would take her too long to pull out and launch. If she tried to get to the cabin, he'd follow. Even if she made it and locked the door, he'd probably smash a window and get in. He could swim better than she could. Maybe just run into the woods and hide until he came to his senses. She knew the woods and he didn't. Otherwise she knew she'd either have to agree to have sex tonight or be raped. She never should have let him come back here. She took another ear of corn.

Just then Jack came onto the beach, begging for food. Judy picked out some pieces of fish, checked for bones, then put a small plate for him down onto the sand. Suddenly Sam began coughing. Violently. He stood, waving his arms, and came toward her, splattering Judy in the face with bits of fish from his mouth. She ignored him and went to the lake to rinse off.

He was still coughing and retching when she came back. His face was beet red. He gulped some wine, but coughed it right back out. Judy saw that he could breathe okay, so she wasn't that worried. But Sam was getting frantic. He flailed his arms, tried sticking his fingers in his throat. He looked at Judy, pleading with his eyes for help.

Maybe he had a fish bone stuck in his throat. One way to dislodge it is to eat bread soaked in oil. She had bread and olive oil in the cabin, but didn't move to go get it. Or she could try to sweep his throat with her finger. But she made no move to help.

Jack finished his fish and went onto a rock to preen.

Sam hacked and hacked. Suddenly bright red foam started to bubble from his mouth. Sam wiped his face with his hand and stared at his red fingers.

"Sam, I don't know what to do. There's probably no local 911 out here. Maybe we should drive out for help." Judy poked at her fish carcass for more meat.

Sam coughed even more violently, his whole body rising with each explosion. The red foam changed to frank blood pulsing from his mouth. He was losing a lot of blood, but Judy knew that he wasn't anywhere near bleeding to death.

Suddenly Sam fell to the ground. Judy bent over him to assess the situation. He now was trying to breath, but couldn't. Perhaps she could do a tracheotomy. She had a sharp knife in the cabin and lots of tubing in the shed. She hesitated, kneeling beside Sam with a hand on his chest. Was she waiting for St. Blaise to rescue Sam? Judy continued to watch Sam as if they were simply on TV. It just didn't seem real. The blood was too red. It had all happened too quickly, and her brain was stuck in quicksand. Finally she stood and sprinted up to the cabin.

She grabbed her phone and paused. She didn't know the ranger's number; he was the closest source of help in the area, ten miles or so east on Route 9. She wished there were a landline; the operator might be able to help. Her cell's 911 linked her to a voice who didn't understand where she was or what she needed. Her call was finally transferred to the Maine State Police. It still took forever to describe where she was and how dire the emergency. She was sweating when the call was over. The sudden silence was proof that she'd been yelling at the phone all this time. What else could she do? She went up to her car, started the engine, and turned on her high beams. Then she ran back to the cabin and got a knife. She stopped at the shed and picked up a short length of copper tubing her father used to install the gaslights.

Returning to the beach, finally ready to try to save Sam, Judy found a corpse. While she was away, Sam had bled even more and now lay flaccid, pale, and covered with partially coagulated blood. Jack was sitting at his head, sniffing. She felt Sam's neck. No pulse. She thought that maybe if she cleared all the blood away from his mouth, she could try CPR. She peeled his shirt back to his armpits to get rid of the blood and tried several percussions. More blood, now almost black, oozed from his mouth and nose, but his heart didn't react. Sam was dead.

Judy sat in the sand next to him, stunned. Why hadn't she tried to help him earlier? Had she wanted him to die? She really didn't know. Her whole day had been dictated by fear. Fear of confrontation. Fear of Sam's size and anger.

It took an hour for the state police to arrive. Judy heard the siren approaching the lake. She heard the car head the wrong way on the camp road. She heard it stop, turn around, and come her way. Then it sped past the cabin and didn't return for almost ten minutes. A deputy finally appeared on the path above the beach. He was a giant in form-fitting pale blue. He started to speak, then saw Sam and strode over to the body. Hand on carotid artery, he boomed, "I'm afraid he's dead, ma'am."

"I know."

"What happened?"

"He choked on something. Couldn't stop. We were eating fish; it might have been a bone. He choked and choked, then blood just gushed out, and he couldn't breathe. I couldn't think of anything to do to help him."

"Sorry, ma'am. This has happened before out here. Even in town it would be hard to save someone in that kind of trouble."

They were silent for a few minutes. The deputy didn't seem to know what to do next. He finally called to have the body removed. "We'll take him to the hospital morgue in Machias. They'll let you know when you can have the body—probably take a few days. Will you still be out here?"

"I don't know. But I can be reached on my cell. My wallet's in the cabin—I'll give you my card."

They walked up to the cabin. Judy found her card and gave it to him.

"I'll stay here until they come. Can I get you anything?" The deputy looked helplessly around the cabin.

"Thanks. I think I'll make coffee—my brain is numb. Can I get you a cup?"

"Sure, if it's not too much trouble."

Judy made the coffee and brought it to the table with a couple of muffins. They sat drinking. The deputy ate two muffins. Each time their eyes met, he jerked his away. The deputy looked about fifteen years old to Judy. His face was covered in peach fuzz with bright red cheeks, blond hair, blue eyes. He looked like he should be drinking milk, not coffee.

Close to midnight the ambulance pulled into the driveway. The path was too narrow and rough for the gurney, so the driver and the deputy carried a stretcher to the beach. Judy stood outside the cabin watching as they carried Sam's body up the embankment and out to the ambulance. The driver backed the ambulance carefully out the driveway and slowly drove away.

The deputy walked over to Judy. "Is there anyone we should notify?"

"His mother. She lives in Shellport. I don't have the number in my cell, but she'd be in the book: Myra Robbins. His father died in the Korean War, and she remarried."

"We'll call her tonight. Here's the number at the coroner's office. When you've made arrangements, just have the funeral home call them."

"Oh. All right. Thank you."

"Night, ma'am. Sure you want to stay out here tonight?"

"I'll be all right. I've really nowhere else to go."

Judy walked the deputy out to his car. Then she turned off the motor of her car and went down to the beach to retrieve Jack.

She stood holding Jack and looking out at the lake. The full moon was perfectly mirrored in the middle of the lake. The night was magical. Off to the south a band of northern lights danced in the sky. She stood watching them flare—reds, blues, and purples—while patting Jack with an empty mind.

Jack squirmed to be let go, so she carried him up to the cabin. She'd pick up the mess on the beach the next day. She turned on the radio and rinsed the coffee cups. She'd had only part of a glass of wine at dinner, so she poured out a few ounces of brandy and sat at the table.

She should've gotten Sam's mother's phone number and called herself rather than having the police do it. But she hadn't established any relationship with the woman in her years married to Sam. Sam said she'd been happy when he got divorced and didn't want him to remarry. They saw her rarely. The first two years they were married, they came to Maine every August. When they were at his mother's place, she put them in a room with two narrow single beds. There was another room with a full-size bed, but she always managed to have a sewing project scattered on top, which for some reason couldn't be moved. Myra never spoke directly to Judy. If Judy came down in the morning before Sam, Myra would look up from the newspaper and point with her chin toward the coffee. That was the extent of her hospitality.

If Judy cooked herself something for breakfast or took a snack from the cupboard, Myra would watch, then complain later to Sam that now she couldn't bake as there weren't enough eggs. Or she'd planned to have chips with tonight's hamburgers, but now there weren't enough. The last four years they both came up to Maine, but Judy let Sam go to his mother's alone while she stayed in Bangor with her parents.

Judy felt as if she should do something, but it was after one and everything could wait for morning. She had a little more brandy, kept the radio on, and went up to bed. She hadn't expected to fall asleep, but did so in just a few minutes.

Judy didn't wake up until after eight thirty the next morning. Jack was on the windowsill watching something outside.

CHAPTER 25

Curious, Judy walked over to the window to see what Jack was looking at. The sky was overcast, and it was trying to rain, spitting just a bit. At first when she looked out, she didn't know what she was seeing. The beach below was covered with black birds—ravens, crows, grackles—fighting over the leftover food and the blood on the beach. She'd never seen so many birds at once. A blanket of writhing birds. It reminded her of the metal garbage cans in summer when she was a kid—maggots squirming on the bottom, several inches deep.

Well, it seemed she wouldn't have much to clean up later. She decided not to disturb the birds and went into the kitchen to fix coffee. Coffee, muffin, and juice would be breakfast. She ate sitting at the table. Then she had a second cup of coffee. She felt far away, not tied to this place or this time. She knew she had things to do—she just didn't know what yet. Arrangements, the deputy said.

She sat. Time passed. A heavy rain started. She loved the sound on the roof. Arrangements. Funeral stuff. And then what?

Another cup of coffee. Should she call Myra? Or Mark? Anyone else? Calling Mark would be the easiest thing to do. She checked her watch, eleven thirty, and dialed. The secretary put her through.

"Hey, Judy. I got your agreement and took it over to Hull and swapped it for their agreement not to go public. It's all sewed up!"

"That's nice, Mark. But not why I called. Sam died last night."

White didn't answer right away. "Good gracious, Judy. I'm stunned. What happened?"

"He choked on a fish bone. It was awful. The bone must've pierced an artery—there was so much blood. It was so sudden. It was…" She couldn't think of anything else to say.

"Judy, how terrible. Where's the body?"

"The Machias hospital morgue."

"Have you thought about the funeral?"

"Mark, I can't think at all. I've been sitting here for hours just watching it rain. I know I should do things, but…"

"Well, take a deep breath. Where do you want the funeral?"

"I don't care. I really don't. I hate funerals."

"Does he have family up there? Doesn't his mother live in Maine?"

"Yes. His mother. But she doesn't live in a town Sam had ever lived in. He didn't know anyone else there. And he didn't have brothers or sisters. The only relative he ever talked about was his mother. And her husband."

"So, do you want the funeral back down here?"

"Not really. I don't think I could go back to the house with Sam gone."

"You have to do something, Judy."

"I suppose I could make Myra happy and let her plan the funeral. She will be devastated by this. Maybe that's best."

"You'll call her?"

"I guess I have to."

"Judy, have her charge everything to our firm. We'll take care of it."

"Oh. Okay."

"What about newspaper notices?"

"Myra can do that too."

"Well, that's a start. Now I'll get the death certificate and work on settling up the estate. It should be pretty simple. He left everything to you and his charities; you already co-owned most of the assets, so taxes will be minimal. But we'll have to go over all that at some point."

"All right. Oh, Mark, I really don't want to go back there. Ever. Can you have someone close the house and put everything in storage?"

"I'll have them clean the fridge and make sure the grounds are tended. But why don't you wait a while before deciding anything that extreme? And don't you have a cat in the house?"

"I really don't want to go back there. And Jack's up here with me."

"Wait a while, you'll change your mind."

"Oh, all right. Is there anything else I should do today?"

"Just call Sam's mother. Then just take care of yourself. Look, I'll call every day to check on you. And I'm so sorry, Judy. It's hard to believe."

"Thanks, Mark. Bye."

"Bye. Take care."

Just call Myra. An upset Myra. Well, better do it now, or she'd lose her nerve. She called for the number, then dialed. The phone rang six, seven, eight times.

"Hello." The voice was hesitant. Judy couldn't tell if it was a man or a woman.

"Myra?"

"No. This is Henry." Henry was Myra's husband. They'd married in the 1960s. He must be well in his nineties by now.

"Henry, this is Judy."

Silence on the other end.

"Sam's wife."

"Oh. Sam's wife, Judy."

"Yes. That's right. Is Myra there?"

"Well…"

She waited; he said nothing more.

"Henry. I'd like to talk to Myra about what she'd like for the funeral."

"Oh, yes, I suppose."

"Henry. Is Myra there? I really need to talk to her."

"Well…"

Was Henry senile? Sam had never said anything.

"Henry, talk to me."

"Well…Myra's not doin' too good. It might be best if she calls you later."

"All right. But make sure she does call me. It's important." She waited for Henry to pull together paper and something to write with, then gave him her cell number.

"Bye, Henry. And be sure she calls."

"Bye." He hung up.

Judy doubted Myra would ever call. Henry might not even relay the message. Damn. This was even harder than she feared. If Myra didn't call today, would she have to drive down there to talk to her?

She made a decision. It was unlikely that she could get Myra to handle the funeral. She got the number for a florist in Shellport, who gave her the name of the business that did most of the funerals in town. She called and made arrangements for them to pick up Sam's body when it was released. They would call her with the date of the funeral. The details could be decided later.

They would also arrange for a death notice in the Maine and Palm Beach papers. Judy took down an outline for an obituary and would call back when she had the information. That could be a problem. Judy didn't have any of their papers at camp and wasn't sure of proper names and dates. She'd have to call Pocket Pets—they'd probably have his resume. Plus, she needed to tell them anyway about Sam's death.

Judy called Pocket Pets and told Dave what had happened. He promised to e-mail Sam's resume and anything else he could find about Sam's life right away. She wished she and Sam had a better Internet service; all they had was dial-up at home, and her cell phone was a no-frills model. At some point she'd need to get to a connected computer to get the stuff from Dave. Maybe Emile would know of someone at the lake with a connection. She'd walk down there when the rain let up.

She waited until four, but the heavy rain persisted. She finally dug her father's yellow slicker out of the closet—it skimmed the floor when she walked. She added a baseball cap and boots to complete the outfit and headed out to the road. The rain was blowing directly into her face, taking her breath away. She finally had to turn sideways and push against the wind. Her head was soaked in minutes, and the water ran down her neck, sopping into her T-shirt.

Emile came to the door as soon as she knocked, herded her inside, and tossed her raincoat and cap to the floor.

"Here, darlin', sit by the fire." He scurried away and returned with a large towel. "I've got plenty of shirts, want to change out of that?"

"I'll be okay, Emile. I'll get just as wet going back."

"Why didn't you drive?"

Judy snorted. "Too stupid, I guess. Didn't even think of it. I never drive when I'm out here."

"Hang on a sec." He left and came back with a white T-shirt and one of his red plaid flannel shirts. "Go on and change into these. Oh, don't bother moving. I'll go in and get something to warm your cockles."

Judy stripped off her shirt and changed into warm clothes—they must've just come out of the dryer. She was sitting comfortably in an old leather chair when he returned.

"Hot lemonade. My mother used it to cure all ills." He handed her a steaming cup of colorless liquid with a strip of lemon peel floating on top.

Judy took a big sip and clutched her chest, gasping. "Jesus! Lemonade and what else?"

"Mostly rum. Cures anything and prevents everything."

"Except drunkenness. I do feel better." Judy curled up in the chair holding the hot cup in both hands, inhaling the fumes.

"Child. I heard what happened last night on the scanner. I'm real sorry. I didn't know Sam, but…"

"Thanks. I think I'm still in shock. I came down here hoping you'd know someone with an Internet connection out here."

"You came to the right place, sweetheart. I've got the whole shebang out back in the office."

"I had no idea. I need to get to my e-mail. I'm trying to write Sam's obituary, but I'm stymied when it comes to some details. We had so many lives before we met."

"Well, sit here and warm up. I'll turn the beast on and get a connection for you." Emile scurried to the back of the house.

Judy sat sipping the warming drink, watching the fire. The heavy rain continued outside, but she could barely hear it in Emile's solid house. The timing of the rain was good, she reflected, as the beach would be washed clean by morning. She shivered, remembering Sam's body, the blood, and this morning's black birds.

Emile came back. "It's ready to go. I turned on the printer too."

"Oh, thanks. I'll go back there now—it shouldn't take me long."

"Can I feed you?"

"Oh, no. I'm not hungry. But I'm warm and a little bit boozy, thanks to you."

Dave had sent Sam's resume plus copies of a few newspaper articles about Sam he found in the office. Judy googled Sam's name, but nothing new came up. She printed out what she had and returned to the living room.

"Thank you so much, Emile. I think I have enough info, even if Sam's mother never calls."

"Come back anytime. Oh, wait a minute. Here you go—if I'm not home, use this key. Come anytime. Instruction for booting up the machine and passwords are taped to the hard drive."

"I don't know how to thank you."

"Just let me help you, it makes me happy."

Emile gave her a large plastic bag for the papers. She started to put on her raincoat, but he stopped her.

"Hey, this thing is sopping wet on the inside. Take one of mine."

Judy liked being taken care of. "Thanks."

"Plus, I'm running you home. Don't want all that rum to go to waste." Emile took an old black slicker off the coat hook and helped Judy into it. "Let's go, little lady."

CHAPTER 26

Back at the cabin Judy sat at the table and drafted the obituary. It sounded okay to her, but she'd wait until morning before calling it in—maybe Myra would call before then. She used the traditional format for men: education, business, and organizations first, then family. Women's obits tended to begin with family, even for successful businesswomen.

It continued to rain and got dark early. Judy made a roaring fire in the stove and pulled a chair in front of it. The rum wore off, and she got hungry. It was after ten; Myra hadn't called. She was hungry but not hungry for anything particular. It would've been the perfect time for a frozen meal if she had one. She opened the cupboards, but nothing called out to her until she found a small can of stewed tomatoes. Pirate eggs. She'd make pirate eggs.

Pirate eggs was named by her mother to sell a meal to her kids they'd otherwise not touch. It was a staple toward the end of a week when food had run low. Judy poached three eggs in the tomatoes and served them on buttered toast. She'd learned to love the contrast of the acidic tomatoes with the bland egg and toast.

She sat at the table and hungrily ate the eggs. There was one muffin left, and she ate that. Still hungry, she popped corn and doused it with melted butter and Parmesan cheese. Then, wanting something more, she had a beer.

After midnight. Judy sat by the fire, sometimes thinking of all that had happened, sometimes thinking of all she had to do the next few days, and sometimes not thinking of anything at all. She kept poking her conscience at her delay in trying to help Sam. She finally gave up. She loved him; she feared him. And fear trumped love in the end. Plus…"frigid bitch"…*that* was mean.

She was afraid to go to bed. She'd slept well the night before, but the Joe nightmares hadn't started right away. Would Sam begin to torment her tonight?

Jack had been sleeping on another chair. He got up and batted his head against her legs. She picked him up, scratching his chin, and walked over to the window. All she could see was the deepest, purest black. She shivered, hugging Jack, who was squirming to get free.

"What'll we do, Jack? Think we should get a kitten?"

She turned on the radio—loud—took a large brandy and climbed into bed. She flipped through some magazines and finally lay down to sleep with all the lights on.

Sam was on the beach smiling, his arms stretched out to pull her to him. They were on a large beach towel—the size of a queen-sized sheet—decorated with fresh water fishes. She couldn't identify the beach. The sand was pure white and powdery, like flour. She laid her head against his chest. She smelled salt and Sam.

She woke smiling and stretched lazily. Jack jumped up on the bed, and she scratched his chin. After a while he sprawled onto his back and slept. There was still some brandy in her glass, and she sipped it while watching the night disappear. At dawn a breeze came up, and she could hear waves breaking onto the shore and the rowboat banging against the dock.

She was still in bed late that morning when the phone rang. She didn't move to answer it. The phone rang several more times throughout the day. Once she got out of bed to feed Jack and go to the bathroom, but she refilled her brandy glass and climbed right back into bed.

She didn't read. The radio was still on, but she was no longer aware of it. The day was a bright gray one—the sun almost but not quite out. The loons crooned from time to time. And she heard a motorboat on the far side of the lake.

It got dark. She climbed down for more brandy and refilled Jack's dish. She let him out and waited an hour for him to come back. Then she went back to bed.

That night she slept, but had no dreams. Again she left the radio and lights on. Jack seemed to sense something was strange and slept with her all night.

The next morning early, the phone rang several times. Around noon someone knocked on the door. She didn't answer. An hour later the knocking came back. Later still she sat up in her bed as the glass in the door smashed and Emile entered the camp.

"Hey, darlin', you're not answering your phone. I was worried."

"Don't worry, Emile. I'm fine."

"Why don't you come down here for a minute?" Emile craned his neck to talk to her. "I brought some fish chowder I just made. And biscuits. From scratch."

"I think I'll stay up here."

"Will you eat?"

"Not right now."

"If not now, when, sweetheart?"

"Later." Judy smiled and leaned back against her pillows.

※

Emile finally gave up, put his chowder into the refrigerator, then stood for several minutes, watching as Judy fell asleep. Finally he shook his head and opened the door. "I'll fix the glass tomorrow," he said softly to no one and left.

※

It was getting dark when Jack jumped up onto Judy's belly and woke her with a start. It took a few seconds for her to figure out where she was—then it all closed in on her again. Joe. Then Sam. Had she really let Sam die? Maybe it was arrogance to think she could've performed life-saving surgery in the scant time she had. Maybe she was letting Joe-guilt fog her mind. Maybe not.

Just then the phone rang. It wouldn't stop, so she climbed down from her bed and answered it.

"It's me. Mark. I've been calling all day. Were you out? How are you?"

"I just got back. Sorry, I forgot to take my phone." Lying was so easy. "What's up?"

"The funeral home just called me. They're in a panic. They're still waiting for the material for the papers—they can place the obituary tomorrow if we give it to them in the next hour or so. Here's their number…"

Judy interrupted, "Mark, I couldn't call. I don't know why. I'll have to spell out all the names and…"

"Why don't you just read it to me? I can record it and feed it through the computer—then I just have to proof it. Our transcription system's pretty good."

Judy sat at the table and read what she'd written. When she finished, she realized she didn't know where or when the funeral would be and had to ask.

"Day after tomorrow. Ten a.m. at the funeral home. It's right on Main Street…just after the state liquor store. You can't miss it—take a right off Route 193 on Route 1, and it'll be on your right. Oh, and Sam wanted his ashes scattered into the sea. They'll give you the urn after the service. I wish I could be there for you, Judy, but I'm swamped down here with a court case."

"Oh, Mark. That's all right. I wouldn't expect you to come all this way."

"Well, I'd better get cracking, or we'll miss the presses. I'll call tomorrow."

"Good night. Thanks for everything."

"No problem. Bye. Chin up."

"Bye."

The camp was suddenly quiet and cold. Judy started the fire up again and sat by it drinking brandy. She felt hollow but not hungry. Although Emile *did* make a good chowder—he always added crabmeat to the lake fish. Maybe she'd have it for breakfast. Another funeral. Not today. The day after.

She let Jack out and climbed the ladder back into her bunk.

❦

She was awake but still in bed when Emile came by to fix the window he'd broken in the door.

"Mornin', darlin'. Okay if I fix the window now? Hope I didn't wake you."

"Morning, Emile. No. I was just lying here thinking. Sure, go ahead. Sorry I haven't any coffee to offer."

"Oh, I'm full up with coffee."

"Brandy then?"

"Wouldn't say no. Would you like a drop to get you started?'

"Sure. Just a drop, though. The jar should be on the counter. The glasses are in the cabinet right above it."

Emile scurried about filling two tiny gold-rimmed glasses with brandy. When he handed a glass to Judy, he tilted his head. "Could I get you something to eat?"

"No, thanks. I'll get up after I've had this." Judy sat up in her bunk leaning against the wood plank side and watched as Emile deftly replaced the glass in the window. "This is like having a box at the opera."

Emile straightened up. "Darlin', I've been thinking...How's about my driving you tomorrow?"

Judy noticed his kindness in avoiding the word *funeral*. "Thanks, Emile. But I think I'll drive alone. Sam wanted his ashes scattered into the ocean, so I thought I'd go east along 1A and find the place we used to bring steamed lobsters on a picnic."

"Well, you be sure to call if you change your mind. I figure I'll leave about nine, nine fifteen."

"I will. Thanks, Emile."

Emile gathered his tools and left, nodding to her, lifting his chin in the way of the old-timers.

Judy sat and thought about the funeral. She'd have to go through her clothes for something somewhere near appropriate. She had a black blazer with her. Maybe with black jeans and her new black T-shirt, she could get by. They might not be proper attire, but she wasn't about to drive anywhere and go clothes shopping today.

She had better get them out now and make sure they were clean, though.

Suddenly she sat up. Jack. She'd let him out the night before and then gone to bed. Now wide—awake, she climbed down, slipped into jeans and sneakers, and opened the door. She expected to see Jack on the steps, but he wasn't there. She whistled. She called. She clapped her hands. Jack was good about responding to her, but this time no Jack. Images of Jack and a bear, a fox, a raccoon whirled through her head. No sounds of Jack coming. It was still and crisp outside. She went back and grabbed a jacket, then walked down to the lake, along the beach, and then up to the road yelling for Jack. She searched the woods and the road for any signs of him—dreading any bloody evidence of her faithful pet.

After an hour, she gave up and turned back to camp. Jack must be dead. He always came when she called. Crying, she was reaching grief she had not felt when Sam died. Why hadn't she stayed up to let Jack in? She knew the dangers in the woods. And poor Jack. Despite his boldness he was, after all, a pampered city cat.

The only noise was the crunch of Judy's feet in the gravel scattered over the ruts in the dirt road. When she turned into the driveway, down to the camp, the noise disappeared as she padded onto layers of pine needles. Her head hung low she watched her feet.

She almost stepped on Jack when she climbed the camp stairs. He sat there, proud as punch, cleaning a bloody paw. At his feet were the hind legs of a baby rabbit.

Judy dropped onto the steps and wept. Relief. Joy. She scratched Jack on the head, walked around his proffered gift and went inside, smiling at herself. A cat! She was such a silly cow.

Maine was having one of its cold summers. A lot of rain balanced by those cool crisp no-humidity days Judy dreamed of during Palm Beach Augusts. This day was one of the good ones. The air still, the vivid blue sky cloudless. Judy set up a chaise on the end of the beach furthest from Sam's accident and gloried in the sun's warmth. From time to time, she went up to the cabin for food or beer, but spent the rest of the day reading on the beach. She'd found an old P.D. James's Inspector Dagleish and a Highsmith's Ripley. The murders in the books didn't bother her at all. The familiar characters and familiar structure of the books were soothing.

She napped late in the afternoon and woke up with the sun almost down. She went up to the camp and checked out her clothes for the funeral: black stretch velvety jeans, her new black T-shirt, and the L.L.Bean black woolen blazer. She examined them for spots, then draped them over a chair back. She had no jewelry or handbag at camp, so she'd have to distribute a credit card, cash, and keys among the pockets.

She didn't think about the funeral itself until she was in bed later, with Jack "heat seeking," stretched out alongside of her. Would they expect her to speak? Would the service be long? Would the minister know anything about Sam? Right in the middle of a thought, she fell asleep. A deep dreamless sleep.

CHAPTER 27

Jack was busy bathing himself on the windowsill when she awoke. Seven thirty. It was chilly, but she decided there wasn't enough time to bother with a fire. She let Jack out, made tea and toast, and brought it back up to the warm bed. She forgot to turn on the radio, so she sat eating while looking out the window toward the back of the cabin. All pine trees. A big blue jay hung onto a swaying branch just a foot or so away from the glass, looking back at her.

It was after eight when she roused herself and climbed down from the bed. She ran a tub of hot water and sat in it until she was limp. Her hair was still wet when she dressed and got Jack back inside. She'd plan to leave at nine, but the cabin was chilly, so she decided to leave early—maybe stop along the way for coffee and doughnut. She made sure Jack had plenty of food and treats, locked up the cabin, and left.

The sun was bright as she drove to the main road, then headed west to Route 193, a north/south road to the coast. Miles of blueberry barrens were interspersed with homes, a few newish ones with manicured lawns, but most shacks no bigger than the rusted bodies of trucks and tractors hovered around them. She passed through dark woods crowding the road, over pretty little brooks, and through a few settlements—groups of houses but no stores or businesses.

Before she reached the turnoff to Shellport, she reached the road to Tin Mountain and without thinking turned onto the dirt road and drove five miles to the mountain's base. Tin Mountain was a low but steep rocky hill that she had climbed several times with her brothers. Her father, Ansel, would drop them off at the main road at dawn and pick them up at dusk. They'd spend the day exploring the mountain, foraging for berries, and sometimes fishing along the brook at the base of the mountain. If they caught anything, they'd cook it over a twig fire built on a rock ledge.

Judy left the car and followed the trail to the mountain's top, a sloping granite ledge with blueberry bushes growing between the cracks. She sat and leaned against a rock and watched the land below. Scrub brush grew in the swampy area, with a small pond in the distance. There was a slight breeze…She smelled raspberries. She closed her eyes and faced the sun. Not sleeping, but not awake, she breathed the sweet air.

***

Suddenly she jerked upright and looked at her watch—ten thirty. She'd missed the funeral! At first she was relieved, happy even—snow day at school, the rare calling in sick at work when she was fine, calling off a date she'd begun to dread. Who would care? Sam was dead. His mother hated her. Emile would be disappointed, but he would understand. Wouldn't he? And Mark White would probably find out. But he was really hired help when it came right down to it.

She stood up and walked in the direction of the raspberry smell and found some heavily laden bushes not far down the side of the mountain. She ate hungrily, staining her hands and shirt.

She went back to her "chair" at the top of the mountain. The rest of the day, she debated with herself. She ripped herself to shreds, and no one took the other side of the debate. She'd thought she was a loving wife, a smart, sane dedicated health worker, an even-tempered, law-abiding sane person—but she wasn't. Who was she? A murderer? She'd killed Joe and maybe Sam—plus, she'd aimed her car with evil intent at Hewitt. How could she work in hospitals after this? She had no friends, Terry and Sam being her last. She seemed to care more for a silly cat than her husband. Could she love? She might be a good sister, but her brothers required little from her, they had their own lives. A good daughter? Whenever she was near her parents, she thought only of escape.

Then she stood up and paced across the granite slab to organize her defense:

- Joe. She'd killed Joe so the family could have a funeral and her friend Eileen could begin to pick up the pieces of her tattered life. He was just 'rotting away in hospice anyway.
- Mr. Hewitt. Hewitt didn't count—she'd braked in plenty of time. She was just venting.
- And Sam. That was all his fault. He hadn't gotten tested. He hadn't even contacted Terry. He came up to Maine when she specifically told him not to. And then he drank all that wine, *plus* the beer. No wonder he choked. He probably put a big gob of fish in his mouth and swallowed it whole. And he would've raped her. She was sure of it.

She walked to the edge of the cliff, stretched out her arms, and screamed, "It's not my fault!" Once. Twice. Then many, many times she screamed—encouraged by the faint supporting echo from the valley. Finally, a little dizzy and feeling foolish, she went back to the rock and slid down against it. Well, that's not entirely wrong—it's not *all* my fault. She sat, grasping her knees, and rested her head on her arms. And drifted off to sleep.

When she woke, it was getting dark. And chilly. She climbed slowly down the mountain to her car and drove back toward camp.

It was pitch dark as she maneuvered down the camp road, but when she reached the cabin, lights were on. Had she left them on? Then she saw an unfamiliar car parked at the edge of the driveway. She parked her car and got out.

When she entered the cabin, her parents were sitting at the table littered with empty dishes. They must've been there quite a while.

"Where have you been?" Her father stood, hands on hips.

"Mum, Dad. What are you doing here?" Judy was confused…This was a living nightmare.

"What you should have been doing—attending your husband's funeral." Ansel punctuated each word with his whole stiff body. "Where were you?"

"I didn't make it." Judy's voice was soft, meek.

"Well. That was obvious. What were you thinking?"

"A lot, actually. I was thinking all day long."

"Don't get fresh with me, young lady."

Judy was fascinated. Her father's usually red face was now close to purple. Or fuchsia? She looked around for Jack. "Where's Jack?"

"Who's this Jack? Are you living out here with someone?" Greta looked at Judy while she spoke, but turned her attention back to her tea and doughnut when she finished.

"Jack's my cat, Mother." Damn. Why are these people here? As she thought that, she realized that it was perfectly normal for them to be at the funeral, staying at their own cabin and wondering where she'd been. "Where's my cat? Did he get out when you came in?"

Ansel picked up his pipe and sucked noisily on it. "We took that animal to Mr. LaGasse when we came. You know your mother's allergies—you shouldn't have had it in the cabin. The animal will be fine down there."

Judy slid from widow, grown woman, petulant teenager, to upset six-year-old. "I need Jack with me. If he can't be here, I'll go stay with Emile."

"I don't like this at all. I think you should stay here with us tonight, and we'll all go home tomorrow." Her father stood straight, commanding the troops.

"Why? I'm fine here. I'll be fine at Emile's."

"Oh, no, you aren't. You missed your husband's funeral, for God's sake! We held it off for two hours, but the minister finally had to go ahead. And that woman, that Myra—and her lunatic husband. They pissed and moaned the whole time during the delay. And they live just down the road. They didn't want to wait even five minutes."

"And look how you're dressed. And you have lipstick all over your face." Greta stood in support of Ansel.

Judy looked in the mirror next to the door. "It's raspberries."

Ansel came over and grasped her arm. "Judith. Be reasonable. We have Sam's urn in the car. We'll take you home. Later, when you're ready, we'll take you wherever you want to scatter the ashes... maybe have a little ceremony. We've talked to Mr. LaGasse. He'll have your car brought back to Bangor next week and clean up the camp."

"Dad, Mum. I've got to go get Jack. It's been a long, hard day for all of us. Are you staying down here tonight?"

Ansel looked up. "We have to. I've had a beer and a half, so can't drive—especially out here."

"Okay then. I'll just stay down at Emile's tonight. I'm sorry I put you through this." She didn't stop to gather anything to take with her and didn't listen to their complaints as she fled the cabin.

Outside it was quiet, dark, cool. She took a deep breath and headed for her car.

❦

Lights were shining from all the first floor windows of Emile's house when she drove up and parked in the gravel next to his pickup. The light from the house onto the white sand at the lakefront would make a perfect Christmas card scene. She saw Emile peer out of the kitchen window to see who was coming. When she got to the door, he had it open. He'd swapped his red plaid shirt for a red plaid flannel robe, but still wore pants and boots. Behind him the house glowed from the fireplace and numerous lamps—all shaded in a Chinese red.

"Darlin'. Come for Jack?"

"You and Jack, Emile. My parents are staying at the cabin tonight."

"Come in. Come in. Go sit by the fire—Jack's already in there." He swept his arm back dramatically to draw her inside.

As Judy sat down in the big wide leather chair, both she and the chair let out sighs. Jack snapped awake and came over to be scratched. Peace.

"Here you go, darlin'." Emile handed her a glass of brandy. "Have you had supper yet?"

"No." Supper? She hadn't had lunch either.

"Now don't go telling me you're not hungry. You've had a long day, I expect." Emile squeezed her shoulder and headed back to the kitchen.

She relaxed. Jack jumped up beside her and fell asleep with his head in her lap. The kitchen noises were soothing.

Emile returned carrying a tray table he planted in front of her. "My lobster stew. Just made it today. You should like it—Jack did."

"Thank you, Emile. It looks lovely." And it did. The red bowl of stew was on a white plate edged with a row of small toast rounds topped with olive oil and Parmesan cheese.

"Now, darlin', eat. Don't talk." Emile shooed Jack from her chair and turned on the radio low, jazz. He sat in the leather chair next to hers and turned his attention to filling his pipe.

Judy took a deep breath, sat up, and began to eat. And ate without stopping. She cleaned the bowl and ate all the toast. The brandy was gone too. Just as she finished, Emile magically replaced the bowl with a deep dish of fresh raspberries and a warm white sauce.

"Mmmm. What's in the sauce, Emile?"

"My cheating custard. Just heated up a little vanilla ice cream. Has to be a good brand to work."

"Nice."

Just as she finished the berries, a cup of espresso appeared on the tray.

Before he sat back down, Emile moved her tray table to one side and slipped an old worn leather ottoman under her legs. Judy slouched back in the chair sipping coffee, while she and Emile watched the fire.

Emile finally cleared his throat. Judy looked over at him. She wanted to talk. She wanted to tell him everything.

"Emile. I've been so bad."

Emile held up his hand to silence her. "Judy, darlin'. You can't be bad. You're just having a run of awful luck, that's all. I worried when you weren't at the funeral, but I know you had to be wherever you were."

"I turned off at Tin Mountain. Just sat there all day."

"Probably as close to God as that ceremony. You just weren't ready to be with folks yet. I can understand that."

"But I was bad before that. Really bad. I…"

"Lord, child. None of us is good all the time."

"But I've done awful things."

"Do you feel bad about them?"

"Oh, yes. Yes."

"Can you undo any of them?"

"No."

"Then what's done's done, child. Nothing you can do but live with it and try to do better. We only get this one life, and it's pretty sweet despite the trouble. Take some time out here at the lake. Stay here if you want. Get closer to the ground and that cat of yours. You'll be all right. The place'll fix you up in time.

"But I've…"

"Hush, child. Confess only to God, not man." He grinned at her and stood up. "This old man needs sleep. Why don't you stay right here tonight? You can sleep on the sofa. I'll build the fire up and get you some blankets."

When Emile came back with pillows and blankets, Judy moved to the couch and let him tuck her in. She stared at the fire for a while, then closed her eyes. Tomorrow she'd ask Emile for help. He didn't seem to want to know any details, but maybe he'd be able to help her dig out of this dark hole she'd made. And tomorrow she'd have to get Sam's ashes from her parents…and…She was sound asleep long before Emile finished cleaning up in the kitchen.

CHAPTER 28

Jack was sleeping with his head in her lap as she stirred. She could hear Emile in the kitchen, and bold smells of coffee and bacon filled the room. She ruffled Jack's head, and he jumped down as they both stretched. She turned to get comfortable on the sofa and looked out at the calm lake. She was amazed at how peaceful and what—happy?—she felt after the emotions of the day before. She didn't have any of that rumpled, slept-in-my-clothes feeling either. She miraculously had the desire to live outside of herself, get out of the mess that had followed her for weeks now. Taking stock, she realized that even if she *had* committed a crime, she'd never be accused of one. So she'd go on. Be a widow. Be a millionaire—maybe do some good with all that money. (And she had no idea how much she'd have—Sam always just said "millions".) And definitely stay away from Palm Beach. Forever.

Emile came in bearing a loaded tray. "Mornin', darlin'." He pulled a table over next to her and set the tray down carefully on it. Coffee, scrambled eggs, bacon, orange and grapefruit sections. "Do you need cream, sugar, ketchup, anything?"

"Oh, Emile. This is perfect. Nope, don't need a thing."

Emile sat in his leather chair next to her.

"Aren't you having anything?"

"Darlin', I've been up for hours. Just heard you stirring, so thought it would be safe to cook your breakfast."

"Lake looks calm."

"Oh, it is. Supposed to be a fine day…not too hot, no thunderstorms. Pretty near perfect, if they're right. Of course, I've often thought those weather people are linked to the tourism folks—if there's bad news, don't tell it. But my bones say it'll be nice. By the way, you look pretty chipper."

"I feel totally different from yesterday. I've been sitting here just marveling at it."

"So, what's on your agenda?"

"Well, I suppose I should go down and apologize to my parents for yesterday and get Sam's ashes from them. Then, I don't know. If they leave the cabin, maybe I'll stay there for a few days and start working on what to do next. Maybe I'll move up to Maine. Maybe build for myself out here."

"Don't move too fast, girl. You already have a place out here. And winters are tough if you're planning to stay year-round."

"Yeah. You're right. I'm just giddy that I feel so good this morning."

Judy ate hungrily, drank three cups of coffee, then sat back. "Well, Emile, I'm ready for the day. Thank you so much for everything. I don't know what I would've done last night without you."

"Come back any time, darlin'."

"I'll hold you to that. Plus, I'll be back soon for Jack."

Judy stood and hugged Emile, and he followed her to the car and waved her off the property.

Judy drove slowly, giving her parents as much time as possible to leave for Bangor, but when she got to the cabin, their car was still there. When she got inside, though, they were in the last stages of packing. Her mother was washing up some dishes, and her father was putting their luggage closer to the door. A copper vase was in the middle of the table—she assumed it to be filled with Sam's ashes.

Her father looked up. "So you came back. We wondered where you'd gone."

"Dad, I told you I was going over to Emile's to be with Jack. He fed me and I fell asleep. And Dad, before you go wild, I want to apologize to you and Mother about yesterday. I was more upset than I knew how to deal with, I guess."

Her mother came into the main room wiping her hands on a dishtowel. "You apology is accepted, Judy. But your behavior was atrocious. You should be acting like an adult by now."

"Well, we're off. The ashes are on the table. Stop by on your way back to Florida if you get a chance." With that, Ansel shouldered the bags and left.

"Bye, Dad, Mum."

"Good-bye, Judy. Behave yourself out here. Don't forget to put the key back under the stairs when you leave. Don't worry about our coming back out here anytime soon. We hardly ever do these days. Ansel likes to stay home and watch TV." Greta gave a grimace-like smile and followed Ansel to the car.

Judy went out and stood on the steps and watched their car back out, then head for the main road. Silence. Back inside she smelled her mother's perfume and opened all the windows. It was early, nine thirty. She sat at the table and picked up the urn.

Funny custom, but Sam wanted his ashes spread in the cove, so she decided she might as well do it now. First, though, a bath and change of clothes.

⁂

The drive to the coast took less than forty minutes. At first she was afraid she wouldn't find the right cove, but her body knew just where to go. There were no houses along this section of Route 1A; the road was too close to the sea on one side, and a large bog was on the other. At a tiny gravel turnoff, she parked, took the urn, and scrambled over the rocks to the water's edge. It was high tide, and a light breeze was swirling in many directions. When she took the lid off the urn and tried to scatter the ashes over the water, most blew back onto her. Well, that didn't work. So she knelt down and held the urn just above the icy water and poured the ashes in one big blob into a protected space between two large rocks. The ashes formed an island for a few minutes, then got wet and sank. She looked at the urn, shrugged, and threw it as far out into the ocean as she could. On the way back to the car, she brushed the ashes off her clothes.

That's that, she said to herself. Then she started to think she should've said a prayer or invited Sam's mother or…She shook her head, took a deep breath, and got in the car.

It was early, but she was hungry again. She figured she'd go back west toward Bar Harbor and get some takeout. Fried clams or something. She drove until she came to the turnoff for Mount Desert, the island that included Bar Harbor and Acadia National Park. She drove over the winding roads, not getting lost only because she had no destination in mind. As she came along one cove, she saw a sign for an open house. Something to do before she ate. She drove down the elegant drive and came to a large two-story stone house with a large veranda and several outbuildings—all in stone with green trim. When she got close to the house, she could see it was perched on a small hill that sloped to a tidy bay. Several cars were parked outside.

She met the real estate man on the porch. "What a charming house." She smiled at him. He stood to greet her. He was shorter than Judy, pale, maybe sixty or so. Dressed in a tweed jacket that looked too hot, yellowing white shirt with a shiny maroon polyester tie, rumpled gray corduroy trousers, and nice-looking leather oxfords, unshined.

"Hello. I'm Tim McKay. The house used to be the rectory for the Episcopal church. Built in 1915. Sold about ten years ago, and Earl Sockings had it updated—put in all new appliances, redid the wiring, even put in solar panels on the south side. But pretty much left the interior intact."

"Where's the church?"

"Oh, burned years ago. There was a big forest fire. Stopped just at the ridge up there."

"Okay to look inside?"

"Sure. Want company or not?"

"Not right now."

"Sure enough. I'll probably be right out here if you have any questions."

Judy went inside. It was as if she were entering a house she knew from another life—or maybe from a book she'd read. The house had a whiff of a men's club and was warm, welcoming. The walls were mostly mahogany wainscoting with some walls painted a dull cherry red, others a light new-leaf green. Fireplaces, wood stoves, and gas logs were scattered throughout. The kitchen was large, sunny, and had a huge pantry and a big Viking stove. The pantry smelled like her grandmother's sugar cookies. She went out the back door by the kitchen and found the veranda surrounded the house. On the south side, part of it was glassed in for a green house. At the north another section was screened in for a sleeping porch. The house was furnished with plain wood furniture, much of it Craftsman style, with newer leather sofas and chairs everywhere, most brown but some red. There was a library with real, much-read books, a fairly new sound system, and a huge television. As she wandered through the house and out into vegetable and flower gardens and out to the dock, the number of people milling about increased by the minute.

Judy was totally enchanted with the house. She walked around to the front veranda and found Tim McKay where she'd left him. "Nice." She smiled.

"It's one of the best on the island. I wish I could afford it."

"How much?"

"Depends on what you want. There's a boat, and the property includes the whole cove I could sell separately, lots of garden tractor-type things in the shed, the furniture, probably some valuable books, all the kitchen and dining room things, linens…I have a full list back at the shop."

"How much for all of it?"

"Two point five mil. It's a bargain. Really. Sockings died, and his family is scattered and just wants to get rid of it."

"Okay. Get all of these people to leave, and I'll buy it."

"You serious?"

"Oh, yes. I'm serious."

She had McKay call her bank. Satisfied she could close the deal with a personal check, McKay walked to the end of the drive and took down the "For Sale" sign. It took him another half hour to clear the house and ground of all the people.

"None of them was serious. See the same ones every time a nice house goes up for sale. Bunch of Nosy Parkers is all."

He and Judy sat on the veranda at a table and took care of business. In less than an hour, the house was hers. Then McKay handed over the keys and told Judy to contact him at her convenience so he could go over the property with her and also give her names of the best service and fix-it people in the area. Then they shook hands and he left.

Judy walked through the house again. Relieved, she loved it even more than during her first tour. No buyer's remorse. Then she locked up the house and went back to her car. She was hungry.

⚜

Less than a mile past the house, she came to a small clam shack and bought a takeout order of fried clams, coleslaw, and fries. At the market next door, she picked up a six-pack of beer. Sam Adams, Boston lager. She was back at the house in minutes. She didn't bother to unlock the house; she just walked to the back and settled into a chaise on the veranda. The food was a little limp from the container, but delicious. She ate it all and settled back with a second beer.

The sun was getting lower, but still had heat. A small inboard craft, red and white, rocked at the dock. It must be hers. She felt like a lottery winner. Those first few days when you could buy or do anything you chose. It was a good feeling.

ACKNOWLEDGEMENTS

Special thanks to Julie Gilbert and The Writers' Academy at the Kravis Center in West Palm Beach for the opportunity to play with words!

9/12

14147630R00177

DISCARD

Made in the USA
Charleston, SC
23 August 2012